ALL MY GOODBYES

Also by Jan Cline

ALL MY *Goodbyes*

AMERICAN DREAMS - BOOK 3

JAN CLINE

WordCrafts

Published by WordCrafts Press
Cody, Wyoming 82414
www.wordcrafts.net

For Mom.

April, 2 1941, Kennewick, Washington

 *E*ven though an arid wind blew across her skin, Martha's entire body shivered. She covered her ears with her palms, trying to deafen the grating noise of shouts in the distance. In a dizzying swirl of movement all around her, she reached for something—someone. As hard as she tried, her hands couldn't grasp that thing in the dark.

Someone called her name. "Martha?"

She tried to jump up and run toward the sound, but her uncooperative legs resisted her efforts. Something squished between her wiggling toes. In an unfamiliar time and place, she wanted nothing more than to leave. Even the menacing movement rushing behind her held her.

"Martha, honey?"

Now the voice came into focus. Mama. Where was she, and why was she veiled in shadows? The other noises split through the air—someone hollering and crying, wailing as if wounded.

"Wake up, Martha. It's a dream," she heard Mama say, her words echoing from far off.

Martha reached until her arms ached and finally touched the warmth of someone's skin. The darkness lightened as she pried open her stubborn eyelids. Perspiration clung to her face and chest, the urge to run still squeezing her stomach.

"It's just a dream," Mama repeated.

How could a vision feel so bad, so dark? Mama's face appeared in Martha's view—a low light behind her from the dew streaked window lit the room. *Her* room—in the cottage. The golden sunrise glowed through her lace curtains. Except for Mama's breathing, there was silence. No hot wind, no screaming voices. Only Mama's frowning face. Why was she sitting on the edge of Martha's bed so early?

Chills rippled her arms. She propped herself up on her elbows. "What's wrong, Mama?"

"You were groaning and whimpering. I heard you when I got up to make Ed's coffee." She stood and rested her hands on her hips. Her faded housecoat was dotted with coffee stains and blotches of dried red jam. The buttons were off by one, leaving a gap up by the collar.

"You better get up. You'll be late getting to the hospital." Mama patted the patchwork quilt covering Martha's cold legs before tip-toeing out of the room. Martha smiled. *I'm awake, Mama.*

Martha examined her bed, wondering why she had felt tied down. The sheets were as skewed as Mama's housecoat. It must have been the same wild dream that had plagued her off and on for a few months. Even though she couldn't recall the details, the sounds gripped her when she awakened. Her heart still pounded in her ears, her hands shaking as she ran them through her tangled wavy hair.

She squinted to see outside her window. Another warm sunny day to wake the grape vines and apple trees from their winter slumber. This morning Martha felt as though she had slept through the season with them. She sat up and swung her legs off the edge of her lumpy mattress. The bedside clock read 5:30 a.m. No time for breakfast. Just bathe, dress, and run. Her first surgery of the day would be her most challenging. Dr. Turner would have her head if she were late.

Mama reappeared in the doorway. "Coffee's ready."

Martha could sense her mother's hesitation as she lingered. "Was it the same dream?" she asked.

Martha shrugged. "I suppose."

The truth was each time she strained to recall the images she saw only in her sleep, her stomach rolled and the shaking started over again. All she could really remember was someone yelling—a man. But at what?

Or who?

Chapter One

*S*he wracked her brain to remember when she had done anything so stupid. She had kept her temper in check until now, but today she had let someone get to that place deep inside where she had buried her short fuse. The last five minutes had ticked by so slowly, so effortlessly. Like falling into a deep hole in slow motion. Climbing back out would mean facing something in herself she didn't understand. Something that compromised her careful control.

The swinging operating room doors whooshed air on Martha's bare legs as she burst through them. Dr. Turner's shouts were muffled, but still resonated in her mind. She couldn't take back her actions, and she couldn't explain why something smoldering inside made her tremble at the most inopportune times.

Her surgical mask caught a strand of her hair as she pulled it off. She threw the mask and her cap in the scrubs bin in the empty white hallway. Her heartbeat pounded as she pushed through another set of heavy doors and away from the bright lights of the cold O.R. Each step echoed the squeak of her shoes against the waxed linoleum floor. There would be no sneaking away from the lion's den.

She had really done it this time, and her gut crunched under the weight of the result. Walking out on a surgical procedure was taboo and unprofessional. Sister Clatilda would never forgive her, a paralyzing thought. She had probably piled the last straw on her aging mentor's patience.

If anything went wrong with that patient it would be her fault. That she knew, and it could cost more than her sinking self-respect. Just as in this morning's mysterious dream, something in the operating room had opened a wound long since scabbed over. She rubbed her sweaty palms on her uniform skirt and held out her hands.

Still trembling. She balled them into a fist. This is what caused all the ruckus. Shaking hands—unable to be still at a crucial time.

Martha stopped to lean against a cold wall—she needed a cooling off. Some slow breaths might help. Mama taught her that as a child, a practice Martha had used many times in her adult life. Especially lately.

Right now she would give anything to go back and do the morning over. The worst was yet to come—telling Sister, and then her folks. Clarissa would have to hear it too. The trouble with living next door to a close friend was that hiding anything was impossible. She might be the support Martha needed—or the friendly voice of reason she had come to depend on.

Even Clarissa couldn't save her from whatever haunted her at night—rattling her through the day. She needed words of hope to save her crumbling confidence and recover her ability to do her job, her passion.

She closed her eyes and tried to imagine what Pop and Mama would say. She had a lot of experience trying to explain her temper to them. If she had to guess their reaction it would be Pop shaking his head and mumbling something about impulsiveness, his hands in his overall pockets. Mama would sit in silence, with her fingers to her lips and shock in her gray eyes. Mama never quit being surprised at Martha's antics, the perpetually hopeful mother.

Martha chased away the imaginary images and took a few more steps to reach the set of padded chairs under the hallway window. She plopped down with a sigh and rested her head in her hands. The sunshine through the window glass warmed her neck and shoulders, but couldn't warm the chill racing through her bones like ice water. From hot to cold and back to hot again. So were her emotions—running loose inside her.

"You must be crazy. You might have caused something bad to happen."

The self-rebuke wasn't enough. Despite having inched the rules to the edge before, she had never disregarded her nurse's instinct to care for her patient, but she had been pushed too hard. By Dr. Turner. The other nurses in the room understood and would surely back her up. Wouldn't they?

Martha groaned. She had stewed long enough, shifting from righteous anger to guilt. The right thing to do was swallow her pride and march over to Sister Clatilda's office to confess. She would explain how poorly she had been treated, but leave out the part about her shaking hands.

She stood and straightened her skirt, hoping to present a good front.

"Sister will understand."

"Understand what, Martha?"

Sister's voice jabbed through the silence. The hair on the back of Martha's neck bristled. She turned and stuffed her hands in her uniform pockets.

"Hello, Sister."

Memories of her escapades as a child on the Nebraska homestead rushed over her. Mama would stand with her hands on her hips, waiting for an explanation. This felt something like the day she clobbered one of the bullies at elementary school with her lunch bucket. When she confessed to Mama with just the right slant of the story, all was forgiven. Martha could always sweet-talk Mama, but Sister was another story.

"Good morning."

Sister's unenthusiastic greeting poured salt on Martha's wound.

The woman took two steps closer. Martha searched her finely aged face, looking for any clue of her demeanor. How could she read Sister's posture when she was covered from head to toe in a heavy habit?

Sister's dark, piercing eyes still reflected that familiar kindness Martha knew so well, but she couldn't tell if it would be enough to spare her job. It would tear her heart in two if she lost her position here. If only she had thought of the consequences before tromping out of the room.

"I hear you've had a rough start this morning. I just finished a short and intense conversation with Doctor Turner. He seemed quite upset and demanded your resignation. Care to tell me about it?"

The words stung hard. Telling her side of the story would only confirm her guilt, no matter how cleverly she told it. Sister had a sixth sense about these things. Defending her mistake might be the wrong tactic. She wished Sister was the kind of nun that you could dislike, the kind who used rulers on the palms of disobedient students. Then it wouldn't hurt so much to disappoint her. A confession laced with blame on the doctor wouldn't soften the offense.

"I messed up." She paused to call up some courage, but felt the insinuation on the tip of her tongue. "But you know how obstinate and derogatory he can be. He's a brilliant surgeon, but the worst doctor in the hospital to work with."

Sister's uncanny ability to be firm and authoritative even in her still silence worked its magic on Martha. She wasn't a child with a lunch pail anymore. She was 25 and a registered nurse.

The balance of employment and unemployment hung in the air like a storm cloud. Martha stood ready for the lightning strike of whatever she deserved.

Sister's voice remained calm, but with a bite to it. "So it's true then? You walked out on an amputation?"

Martha bit her lip. A meager attempt at humility would be futile. Her mind blanked trying to conjure up a more plausible excuse. There was none, and she was about to vex the one person who had never given up on her. This wasn't the time for clever avoidance. Even if she could run back to the operating room and beg forgiveness, the outcome would still be the same.

Martha looked straight into Sister's eyes. "Yes, ma'am. I'm so sorry."

Sister tucked her forearms into her enormous black sleeves— her usual stance just before a reprimand. "It is an offense that requires termination. However, the nursing shortage might just work in your favor. I'm afraid I'll still have to appease the doctor with a strong punishment. I'd like you to come to my office to draw up suspension paperwork. Two weeks should be sufficient. Follow me."

Sister glided across the floor and down the hall to her office. Martha followed, and without conversation or formality, Sister pulled a sheet of paper from her desk and filled in the area for sentence pronouncement. Martha peered over her shoulder to see it. *Two weeks without pay and... what?* A mandatory weekend assignment as staff on county army enlistment physical duty.

Martha pursed her lips to keep protests from rolling through them. When Sister was this quiet, she knew better than to offer any objections, but condemning her to enlistment physical duty felt like an extra harsh blow. She hesitated when Sister slid the paper over to be signed.

Without looking at Martha, Sister spoke. "If you prefer, I

can assign you to an additional week of duty in the hospital laundry instead of—"

Martha could see herself in the hot steamy basement laundry facility, suffocating with only a few tiny windows for natural light. The women down there were grumpy and quite fussy about how things were done. Not much of an alternative. Besides, it was time to prove to Sister, and herself, that this thing living in her dreams, whatever it was, wouldn't stop her from being the nurse she wanted to be.

"Oh. No, Sister. I'll do the physical duty."

Martha blinked back tears as she took her carbon copy of the document and slipped it into her skirt pocket. After several more wise words and advice from Sister, Martha ambled out the office door and down the hall to the empty locker room. Lucky break. No other nurses to see her red eyes or ask a lot of humiliating questions. She grabbed her purse and sweater and hurried toward the front door.

All the way down the concrete steps, driving onto the highway, and steering her Studebaker up the driveway of the vineyard, she cried like a baby. The high ground of the farm couldn't rescue her from the flood of accusations she hurled at herself. No matter how much she wanted to be a caring nurse, she would have to control her impetuous nature, and her dreams, or spend the rest of her career on the brink of dismissal. This time she had gotten off easy, but had to come to grips with the fact she had not been there for her patient. This would haunt her for a long time, joining the other anonymous ghost of regret that hovered on occasion.

She wished she were like the winding river far below. It meandered as it wanted to, sliding over or diverting around the bigger rocks in its path. Today she had run up against a rock dam of her own making. If only, like the river water, she could glide over her obstacles and flow swiftly downstream.

Right now, her rocks seemed more like boulders, daring her to try and get around them.

By the time she pulled onto the graveled space by the cottage her arms ached from gripping the wheel, trying to still her trembling hands. The dream had never affected her so harshly before. Now it had interfered with her ability to be efficient. More than anything, her humiliation stemmed from Dr. Turner witnessing her weakness.

She took a few minutes to rehearse a monologue for her defense that would satisfy her folks. Grown-up mistakes had more consequences than those of her impetuous childhood stunts. Mama might be sympathetic, but Pop would stand firm on his convictions. What could she say to him?

"Um, Pop, I know you would have done the same? No. How about… Pop, you raised me to stand up for—no. That won't work."

The right opening for her speech wouldn't come. She opened her eyes, weary of the whole struggle. She could still hear Dr. Turner swearing. Her blood boiled to think of it, more upset with herself than him now, frightened at why she would be so riled.

She jumped at the tapping on the window. "Martha? Are you all right?"

Clarissa peered into the car, with smiling Hope clinging to her mother's leg. At least it wasn't Mama. Martha needed a sounding board and one had just found her. Clarissa knew her as well as anyone else in her life, like a big sister. Their bond had grown from nurse and patient to a deep friendship. Living next door for four years had made the Wildings feel like family. Even though Pop was nearing the age when he shouldn't be working so hard, Frank Wilding let him do odd jobs and help in the vineyard and orchard.

She opened the car door and leaned down to pinch Hope's

nose. The child's arms wrapped around Martha's neck. Her rosy cheeks graced porcelain skin, like a china doll.

"Marty's home." Hope's mud-caked hand patted Martha's face. Clarissa pulled her away. "Hope!"

Martha laughed. "It's okay. I'll get her back the next time I make mud cakes."

Clarissa shook her head and gently shoved Hope in the direction of the house. "You get back inside the fence, little girl. I gave you a wash pail. I think you'd better use it."

Hope sighed, the sparkle in her eye an unmistakable hint of only partial compliance. "I will, I will."

Clarissa rested her hands on her hips and watched her daughter march to the gate and shut it behind her. "What am I going to do with that child? She's a four-year-old pill."

Martha wiped the flecks of dirt from her face and followed Clarissa's gaze to watch Hope resume a mud pie baking session. "A special gift, that one. A precocious kid like Hope could almost make a person forget their troubles."

Clarissa shaded her eyes to search Martha's face. "Why are you home so early?"

Martha slammed the car door and smiled. "Well, that's a bit of a story." She looked around the yard. "Where is everyone?"

"In the orchard, and don't change the subject. I can see on your mud-streaked face that something isn't right. What did you do…get fired?"

Martha huffed and spit on a tissue to rub on her cheek. "Of course not. Why would you think that?"

Clarissa squinted. "Maybe because the last time you came home early with that look, you had broken some rule at work and been reprimanded."

"Okay, okay. Can we sit on your porch and talk about it? I need to figure out how to tell Mama and Pop I got suspended for a while."

Clarissa put her hands to her face. "Oh no."

Martha's mind whirled with ways to explain to her friend. It would be good practice for telling her folks. She took Clarissa by the hand and pulled her through the gate and past Hope's mud party of one.

Hope held up a palm-full of slimy brown earth. "I'll make you both a biscuit."

"Sounds good." Martha let go of Clarissa and stopped to pat the child's head. "Sounds good to me. See you later." Making her way up the porch steps, she admired the pots of tender young geraniums and sunflowers. She smiled to think how Clarissa's magic touch with seeds and cuttings made Mama jealous. Martha nudged Clarissa toward a wicker chair. "Sit and I'll explain."

Martha's face flushed. She had to come clean with no excuses. Clarissa always knew when Martha skirted an issue.

Clarissa sat in the closest wicker chair. "This is going to be good. I can practically hear your heart thumping." She patted the seat next to her. "C'mon. Take a breath."

Martha sat and kicked off her shoes. After a good toe wiggle she leaned back and groaned. She could choose not to confess, but it would all come out soon. It would be obvious she wasn't going in town to work for the next two weeks.

She felt the fluttering of shame in her stomach and leaned forward. "Why am I so stubborn? I messed up today—lost my temper. Almost lost my job." She'd left out the part where her hands had betrayed her, waiting to see Clarissa's reaction to the news.

Clarissa turned to look behind her and then tapped Martha's knee with a grin. "Just tell me what happened. Everyone will be back soon so hurry up."

Martha wanted to giggle along with Clarissa, but tears brimmed instead. She blinked them back. If she cried now, they would be tears of anger at herself. Clarissa didn't realize the seriousness of her predicament. Yet. She gulped in some air to get all the words out.

"I have probably just earned the demeaning distinction of being the first nurse in the history of Our Lady of Lourdes hospital to walk out on an amputation procedure. Or at least the first nurse to let go of a mostly severed leg before the doctor had finished his handiwork."

Clarissa smiled and let out a half-chuckle. After a moment, her face froze. "You're not kidding, are you?"

"Nope."

"This isn't a joke?"

"Afraid not."

Clarissa fell back into the chair. "Martha Watkins. You didn't."

"Yes, I did." She too slid back, staring at the porch ceiling. "The doctor kept swearing at me and yelling at everyone. The other nurses were near tears. I couldn't take it anymore and set the leg I was holding onto the table and walked out."

Should I tell her what a mess I was… all because of some stupid dream?

Clarissa rubbed her temples "I wish I could say I can't believe it. I bet Sister Clatilda was fit to be tied. Even a kind and gracious nun has her limits. Especially since you're a Methodist." She pressed her fingers to her lips.

Martha scowled. "Oh, that's funny. I don't doubt that I've tested those limits this time, but yes, she was quietly mad. She said I should be used to doctors with brash words, abrupt responses, and overbearing attitudes. She also said if I were Catholic she would make me go to confession. Instead she assigned me to work the army enlistment physicals for the weekend. It was either that or add another week to the suspension."

Her friend laughed for real this time. "That doesn't sound

so bad. A room full of enlistees? Maybe you'll meet some nice young man."

Martha huffed. "That's what Sister said, but I reassured her I would never be interested in anyone enlisting to go to war." *Or anyone else at the moment.*

Why did everyone think she needed to find a man? She had plenty of beaus to nab for a date when she wanted, and she had plenty of time to find a husband. No matter who it was, she would insist on a long engagement—less risk that way.

"Martha, it might be that Sister thinks you're old enough to settle down."

"Not with some soldier, I won't. And Sister says we might get into the war soon. The leaders at her church hear all kinds of things. They think President Roosevelt will have to join in sooner or later."

Clarissa paled, her eyes moist. "I don't want to hear that. James will be of age soon and he's *not* going to be a soldier. Knowing him, he would join up just to fly a plane. What would I do then?"

Europe's troubles were far away and not Martha's concern. Clarissa shouldn't be worried about James. It would probably never happen. The last war had taken enough American men. As she watched Clarissa try to shake off her gloom, she considered how being around a bunch of half-naked young men for the weekend might not be so terrible. Maybe she could get a date to the dance out of the whole ordeal.

"Anyway, I'm worried about telling my folks. This will mean a short paycheck, and Pop wanted to quit barbering. He loves helping out here."

"It'll be fine. They're proud of you."

Proud? Yes. And they would be on her side in the final assessment, but this time their top-of-her-class daughter just might have gone too far. Martha felt sick to her stomach.

Clarissa pushed back a strand of hair from her face. "You know, there are lots of turning points in everyone's life, my friend. This could be one for you. You might just be feeling God nudge you to move forward and trust Him. It's happened to me many times. You've seen that first hand."

Martha groaned. "Why doesn't He just pick me up and put me back down where He wants me? It would be easier."

Clarissa laughed and then twisted toward a noise from behind them. Martha thought it might be the call of a hawk, then it cried again.

Martha turned and whispered. "What was that? Or who was that?"

Clarissa stood and edged to the porch rail, Martha behind her. Coming up the middle row of vines were Mama and Pop. Mama stumbled as Pop tried to hold her up. She winced and stopped every two steps to secure her footing. The pathetic scene stabbed at Martha's heart.

"Clarissa! I need help." Pop's voice shook. They both looked so small and frail. How could they have aged without her noticing?

It didn't take much to guess what had happened. Martha wiped a tear and poked her head around the end of the porch. "Bee sting?"

Pop nodded, huffing and puffing as he half-dragged Mama.

Martha pushed away from the porch rail and tumbled down the steps, her bare feet catching a splinter from the wood. The pebbles beneath her pressed into her skin. She had to get to Mama before Pop dropped his support. Mama's bee allergy had taken a serious turn. Her ashen face paralyzed Martha for a moment. She had to shake it off.

"I'm coming, Pop!"

Waking early, Martha had answered the call of the sunrise

and dressed for a walk through the dew-kissed orchard. Birds were already building their nests in the crooks of the tall branches, adding another chore for Frank and Pop. Birds and apple trees weren't a good combination.

Like the bird nests, her evasion over explaining her suspension would have to be dealt with. Yesterday, Mama's incident had created the excuse she needed. It wasn't really a lie—she would have taken a day off for Mama's sake even if she hadn't been suspended. Pop seemed relieved to have her home, and didn't ask her why she had come home so early the day before. The fact that she hadn't told either of them her news was a good thing considering how worried he was about Mama. It wouldn't be fair to burden them with upsetting news now.

With Mama's hives receding and Pop making her rest, calm had returned to the cottage. Even the rolling thunderstorm from last night had cleared, leaving a heady, fresh-washed leaf fragrance in the air. The rumbling had pressed in on her in the heavy darkness of her room, but before dawn, the gales had ceased and the new sun split the clouds. As she meandered back to the cottage, she prayed for a fresh start today.

She picked up the hoe leaning against the shed and surveyed the small garden behind the cottage. She pulled on gloves and repeated her transgression in her mind while she dragged the tool between rows of wet, dark, mounded earth. The heat of the mid-morning sun settled on her shoulders as she guided her tool between sprouts of cabbage, peas, and beans poking through the dirt, a foreshadow of the dreaded blooms that would soon attract more bees to taunt Mama. She wouldn't be able to keep her stubborn mother from gardening. Pop would have to be firm with her once the little flowers appeared.

Martha had already given instructions for Mama to rest while Martha was busy for the next few days. Her uniform was pressed and ready to meet the lines of young men dreaming of the glory of war, unwilling to wait until their number was called for duty.

Martha leaned on the hoe to gaze over the vineyard. If they had to move from this place, she would miss it terribly. Not just the painter's palate of colors, or the smells of fruit and earth, but the people. There were so many wonderful memories with Clarissa and the boys, and Hope. Watching Frank turn the place around after his brother William's death in the barn fire had been an inspiration. She thought back on seeing William suffer as he lay dying. That day made something click in her head. Tending his and Elijah's burns had taught her enough to want to specialize in burn care someday.

Any life she could save would suit her purpose—no more deaths on her watch. There was no burn unit at the local hospital, so she would have to eventually move somewhere else. What would the folks do without her?

"What are you daydreaming about?"

James's voice broke through her thoughts. She turned to see the young man standing behind her, hands stuffed in his jeans pockets. His shoulders had broadened over the last year, and his sandy-colored hair had darkened to a rich brown. A good looking boy for sure, but you could see William in his smile and wide eyes. Martha wondered what Clarissa thought about that.

She forced a convincing scowl. "Why didn't you go to school this morning?"

He smiled. "It's the Friday before semi-finals. Seniors get the day off to study. Which I won't be doing. I'm going fishing with dad."

Martha pulled off the gardening gloves strangling her fingers. "Oh. I didn't realize you were so smart that you didn't need to study for some of the most important tests of your young life."

James shrugged off a smirk. "I'll study tomorrow. Geometry and English are the only classes I'm worried about, but Mom promised to help me. I guess she was pretty good at words and figures when she was in school. Besides, there's still one last final in each class later. Graduation's not till June."

He squatted and picked up a handful of dirt. He sniffed it and let it sift through his fingers just like she had seen their friend Elijah do.

"You want to be a farmer like your dad? He and Elijah taught you enough to give you a start."

He stood and brushed off his hands, slapping them together. "Good ol' Elijah. Wonder where he is now?"

"You miss him don't you?"

He nodded and looked into the distance. His gaze followed the rows of vines to the hills across the river and then up to the sky. She couldn't guess what he was thinking. He had changed, as all young boys do when they're trying to find their own way.

"Yeah. I miss him."

"Your mom does too. She loved that old guy. Too bad he felt he had to move on. He was the kind of person that everyone could love. I sort of got attached to him myself."

James's Adam's apple bobbed. She had touched an emotion—a rare sighting in James. His tough exterior never cracked much, except when he talked about Elijah, or flying. Planes and aviation always produced exuberance in his speech.

"He understood about me wanting to fly. Mom and Dad don't. They want me to stay on the ground where it's safe." He shook his head. "You would think they would have learned there isn't anywhere safe if it's your time to go. Wouldn't they be surprised if I just up and joined the Air Corps and—"

He stopped short and flashed a look at Martha. His face flushed. He cleared his throat and toed the ground, bringing up wet clumps of dirt over his shoe. Martha took the few steps to the old tree stump at the edge of the garden and sat on it. She let the hoe drop next to her. James wasn't the same kid she grew so fond of over four years ago. He wasn't the blooming young man of even a few months ago. Lately a kind of restless anxiety consumed his countenance.

"You wouldn't hurt your mother that way, James. You don't join the armed forces just so you can fly. There are other ways, and you have lots of time to decide about that." She threw the gloves on the ground. "Don't rush off like so many young men are doing these days. I guess I agree with your folks. I'd rather you stay safe and sound on the ground too—doing something solid like farming. Your dad would love that."

Her speech rolled off her tongue, surprising even her. Like James, she had been a rebel. She never let anyone dictate her direction in life—not even her folks. A fine one she was to try and sway James into a more traditional attitude. Yet even though she wasn't a mother, she could understand how Clarissa must feel.

James huffed and scrunched his face. "Well, if you heard Mom and Dad talking about…"

The door slammed at the back porch of the big house. Frank appeared, fishing poles wagging in his hand as if already teasing an unsuspecting fish. He searched the friendly sky and leaned the gear against the steps before retreating into the house.

James walked backwards, his eyes locked on Martha's. "Guess I'd better get my stuff together. Dad's ready to get going. See ya."

"Catch enough for dinner. Pop loves catfish, you know."

She wondered about his unfinished words. James seemed serious about something more than flying. He wanted to tell her, she saw it in his troubled eyes, and she wished they had a few more minutes to discuss whatever he had heard from his parents.

He waved and ran toward the back door. Frank and Clarissa stepped onto the porch. With Morgan in school and the men gone, she and Clarissa could have a few hours to chat—if Hope took a good nap, and Mom and Pop didn't need her.

She pulled on one glove and then yanked it off again. She'd rather feel the earth between her fingers, even though it would pack under her nails. At least she knew how to scrub them—many hours of practice before surgeries. Surgeries she wouldn't be part of for a while.

She picked up the hoe and took a step forward. She tried to catch Clarissa's eye as she mumbled, "You almost forfeited your scrubbing days permanently. When are you going to tell Mama?"

As Frank and James jumped into the cab of the truck, Clarissa finally turned in Martha's direction. "Come over later?"

Martha smiled and nodded, returning to her self-talk.

"As soon as you finish weeding, you need to tell them."

She felt eyes on her and looked up to see Pop standing on the top back step.

His bushy brows raised, scrunching the wrinkles on his forehead. "Tell us what?"

Martha's throat closed. Time had run out for her secret. She looked down at her dirt-covered oxfords. "Hmm. Well, how about I tell you both at the same time? Is she up?"

Pop spit a mouthful of tobacco in the bushes to his left. "Yep."

She hated that habit. Mama did too, but he had chewed for years. No stopping him now.

"Okay. I'll be right in."

Pop wiped his mouth with his brown-stained white hankie and disappeared through the screen door.

Martha released a foreboding sigh. She could hear the radio playing "The Breakfast Club." Mama always got a kick out the salty antics of the actors. If only Pop would break down and buy Mama a television set, but his aversion to new inventions kept him behind the times.

She brushed off her trousers and left her shoes outside the door. Biting her lip, she sauntered into the kitchen, wearing her best everything-is-fine smile. Mama sat at the table, sipping a cup of tea, her lower lip still showing some swelling.

Pop jumped right in. "Martha has something she wants to talk about, Mama." He watched Martha, straight-faced.

Want wasn't the right word for what she felt, and it was almost as if he knew what she was about to say.

Martha slid onto a kitchen chair. Pop poured more tea into Mama's half-empty cup. They seemed content to wait for her to speak. Her tongue stuck to the roof of her mouth, even her teeth were dry. She could stall by drinking a glass of water, but the only thing to do was to blurt it out.

"I made a mistake at work and got suspended."

She tried to read the faces of the two people she loved so much. Pop didn't flinch. He paused and then returned the tea pot to the stove. Mama's reaction was more than what Martha expected.

"You what?" Her uncharacteristic scowl and sharp tone sliced through Martha's heart like an arrow.

"It's only for a couple weeks, but I won't get paid while I'm off." She looked into her father's eyes. "I'm sorry, Pop."

Mama stood and stared out the window, her chubby arms folded across her chest.

"What did you do?"

Martha picked up the salt shaker and twirled it. How much should she tell? Another look at Pop's face told her the answer.

"Well, I was assisting on a leg amputation with Dr. Turner, and my hands were still shaking from that silly dream. He kept shouting at me to hold still and swearing at me because I wasn't holding the leg still enough." She let go of the salt shaker and straightened her posture. "I got angry and set the leg down before he made the last incision. Then I walked out."

Mama didn't move from the window or look at Martha, but her shoulders tensed at Martha's last words. Pop let out a long sigh and shook his head, then sat in the chair next to Mama's.

Pop avoided Martha's eyes. "I'm surprised at you, Martha. That sounds like a serious mistake."

He stared at the top of the table, then wiped his hand over the salt scattered by her fidgeting. He swept the salt into his other hand and closed it into a fist.

Martha blinked back tears and pressed her hands to her churning stomach. Why didn't Mama look at her? She had hurt them, or at the very least, made them mad.

Mama remained staring out the glass, but seemed to be mulling something over. "Seems like your nightmares are causing problems. Did you happen to mention them to Sister?"

"No. Why complicate things even more? Sister was gracious not to fire me. The nursing shortage probably saved my job." She swallowed down the thickness in her throat. "I'm sorry to have disappointed you both. I don't know how to make it up to you. I'm very angry with myself, so I can imagine how you feel. It won't happen again."

Mama finally turned around to face her. That familiar look of knowing mixed with sadness showing in her eyes. "You have a bit of a temper, Martha, but this is unlike you. We can't afford for you to get fired. And it's not good for your record as a nurse."

Pop stood and tossed the salt from his fist into the sink. "Oh, Mama. I think we'll get along fine without her paycheck for a while. I'll just put in an extra day or two a week at the barber shop to make up for it. Martha knows she made a mistake. Life will get back to normal."

His voice was like a calming salve on Martha's bruised ego. Pop's gentle ways made everything seem all right, even though Martha knew he counted her offense as serious. He would take his concerns out to the vineyard and stew over them in his quiet way.

Martha stood and gave him a rare hug. He and Mama weren't the hugging type, but Pop didn't resist her. He patted her back and grunted.

Mama set her tea cup on the counter. "Well, maybe you should refuse to work with that doctor again."

Martha stifled a laugh. Leave it to Mama to hope for the impossible. It would be more likely that the mad doctor would ban her from the operating room. She wouldn't mind.

Pop rubbed his stubble-covered chin. "I think I'll shave and go into the shop for a few hours."

Martha felt a check in her chest. He was already working to compensate for her mistake. She would find a way to make it up to them. Figuring out how would take a while. There must be a way to earn some cash over the next few weeks. She just had to get through the enlistment physicals with no more dark marks on her record. Perhaps one of the other nurses knew of a temporary job.

She headed back to the garden. "Just stay out of trouble tomorrow." It should be easy to do. How could anything go wrong with exams for the army?

$\mathcal{T}$he morning had been a whirl of moving from station to station, keeping obnoxious young men from dawdling. Martha finally had a moment to flop in a folding chair at her exam station in the Pasco High School gym. Fatigue had taken over any good attitude she had to start with. Her enthusiasm for the opportunity to prove herself to Sister had given way to impatience and boredom.

After Mama's bee sting incident, she thought about asking Sister Clatilda to let her out of exam duty, but this morning had brought diminished symptoms for Mama. So the enlistment stint was inescapable, a stop sign on her road to redemption. Although it was a chance to serve her country in some offbeat way, this duty hadn't been anything glamorous for certain. At least not yet. After tomorrow she would be done with it. Then what?

She adjusted her nurse's cap and added a re-coat of lipstick. She held her hankie to her nose. The persistent acrid tang of body odor permeating the room reminded her of all the rival basketball games she attended here. Pasco High versus her alma mater Kennewick High were the best games ever.

The gym wouldn't be used for ball today. Instead of basketball shoes squeaking against the wood floor, bare heels thumped back and forth. Instead of shouts from fans in the stands, only quiet exchanges could be heard between young men preparing for another kind of game. A serious game that no one could win. Bleachers and chairs had been replaced with a long line of cloth-clad tables. No cheerleaders—only nurses in crisp white uniforms procured blood pressures, temperatures, and then drew vials of blood. How things had changed for nurses and soldiers alike from childhoods void of the cares and woes of war.

All around the gym, young men flirted with pretty nurses, and the nurses flirted right back. Martha did too. She didn't hesitate, considering what these men might face in the future. No point in denying a simple pleasure to a soon-to-be soldier.

Martha studied the faces of dozens of them jockeying for a place at the end of the lines, hoping to delay their turn to submit to the doctor's pokes and prods. The most personal exam would be second to last—behind the curtain in the far corner of the gym. A nurse stood outside the draped cubbyhole, urging the stallers to get the whole thing over with. One by one they entered, white-faced and slouched. Then one by one they exited, flushed and smirking, having conquered a new manhood rite of passage.

Most of their faces had baby-smooth skin, just boys who should be dribbling in the next season game of hoops, not joining the army. Here in this place, they handed over their lives, whatever their age.

"Why do they do it? Why don't they just stay home until their number is called?" Martha mumbled to herself as she poured more rubbing alcohol into the thermometer jar.

Nurse Joanna trudged past her, balancing a stack of files and clipboards. "Are you as exhausted as I am, Miss Martha?"

Martha laughed. "From the looks of the bags under your eyes, I don't think so."

"Thanks a bunch. I was hoping to look nice for all these gorgeous men." She hurried to the end of the gym and handed her stack to another nurse.

Men? Hardly. At least not yet.

The charge nurse waved from down the line of tables. "Gonna need you over at the shot station in about 15 minutes, Nurse Watkins."

Martha returned the wave. Just enough time to lean her head against the wall and close her eyes. Waking at 5:00 a.m. to leave the vineyard in time for duty here left her groggy. The drone of voices and the tinkle of instruments in steel basins threatened to lull her to sleep.

Someone touched Martha's arm and she jumped out of her pleasant drifting and dozing. Had it been 15 minutes already? "They want you at the shot station now." Nurse Susan smiled and walked backwards as she gave one last order. "Don't forget, we're all going out for bingo tonight."

Bingo. This is what her social life had been reduced to, but even a boring night of bingo would be a welcome relief from the chore of preparing doomed soldiers for the armed forces.

Martha saluted. "Yes, ma'am. I'll be ready."

She straightened her cap and scurried to her new assignment. Working independently suited her, especially since there were no strict Sisters or cranky old surgeons to deal with here. Only first-year residents, eagerly fulfilling their training hours. Martha tapped Nancy, the shot nurse on the shoulder.

Nancy squinted up at her. "Oh, good. I need a break." She swiped her forehead with the back of her arm, and threw her handful of cotton swabs back in the decanter before leaning hard on the table. Martha rolled her eyes. Nancy had been given to dramatic gestures all through training, sometimes fooling the Sisters with her feigned frailty.

Martha ignored her, moving into her position at the head of the line of young men, ready to administer the first round of immunizations. She nodded to Nancy. "I'm glad to—"

The bare backside of one young man met her mid-sentence as she turned away from Nancy. He was slightly bent over, holding his white knit briefs below his left cheek. Martha swallowed a gasp. She had expected to at least greet the soldier before grabbing his derrière.

Nancy side-stepped to stand next to her. She leaned in to whisper to Martha, "Steady. How did you think you would give these shots? In their arms?" Martha turned her hot face to see Nancy wink. "Enjoy."

Nancy playfully pulled off her cap and sauntered away, spinning it on her finger.

Some of the men in line smirked, some blushed, but most eyes followed Nancy's swinging hips. Not at all an unusual occurrence for the well-rounded redhead.

Martha's face now heated all the way back to her ears. She had attended many naked patients in her short career, but none quite so—healthy—and handsome.

The young man in front of her craned his neck to look back. "We gonna do this, or are you just taking a long look?" The next three men in line burst into laughter.

Martha bristled. She stiffened her posture and reached for a prepared syringe. Within seconds she took aim and administered the injection with enough force to puncture a turtle shell. Her precocious patient jumped.

"Hey!" He bolted up and glared at her.

"Next." Martha waved him on.

The line stilled. Smirks and chuckles ceased as each one complied, receiving their medically necessary pinch of protective serum…until the last man. Martha paid little attention to him as she gathered up the last syringe. She plucked a cotton swab from the canister and dabbed it into the alcohol. She swung around to meet the rump of her next target. Instead, her eyes beheld the best-looking man she had seen in a long time, older than the others. His piercing blue eyes were fixed straight ahead. He was at least a foot taller than her.

"Ma'am. I hate needles," was all he said. His rich, deep voice shook ever so slightly. His face whitened as he tipped his head to stare at the syringe in her hand.

Martha let out the breath she held tight since the first sight of him. "It won't hurt a bit, soldier." *Don't lie to him.* She held his pleading eyes in her vision, maintaining a professional air.

"No disrespect, ma'am, but I know it hurts. I don't mind the pain, it's just the needle I hate. Isn't there something I can drink instead?"

He wavered, his weight switching from one leg to the other. Still no color graced his perfect features.

Martha choked back a giggle. "A drink?" She looked around him to see no one close enough to hear their banter. There was every chance that his buddies had put him up to this prank.

"Soldier, are you joking with me?"

"No, ma'am."

Her heart sank to realize his genuine fear. *What are you going to do now?*

"How about I do it really fast?"

"It's still a needle. I refuse to accept there isn't another way."

She slid the syringe behind her back in slow motion, keeping eye contact with him.

Time to use her soothing nurse voice. "What's your name, soldier?"

"Clark Jensen."

With her other hand she touched his left arm, turning him slightly while she spoke in low tones. "Where are you from?"

"Around here, ma'am. I live—"

"Well, so am I. I wonder if we've met before. You look sort of familiar."

His tight muscles relaxed slightly as she named some of the places she frequented in town. She gently guided him into position, but it was obvious she would have to wrestle him for a chance at his backside. There was only one way he was going to get this shot. She had to do it. In his arm. Now.

"Ah!"

A startled Clark Jensen jerked his head toward her and opened his mouth wide. Without a word, he sank onto one knee. Martha caught him with her free hand and pulled him up as fast as he had fallen.

"No fainting on my watch, mister."

Color returned to his face—shades of crimson and pink. The grip he had kept on the waist of his shorts loosened. Martha tossed the used syringe into the metal basin. "You're finished here, Mr. Jensen. I'm sorry I had to surprise you like that. You might feel some effects since I had to shoot you in the arm instead of your backside. Nothing more than some pain, swelling, tingling, and hot flashes." She hadn't meant to be so facetious, but he should have been more cooperative.

His neck reddened. "I'm feeling the hot flashes now, ma'am." He studied Martha as she spread a small Band-Aid on his arm. "What if I have more symptoms and need tending to? Where can I reach you?" He mustered a crooked smile.

Was his speech slurred? Martha stepped back and scowled, noticing his eyes had glazed. "Reach me?"

His smile straightened. "Yes, ma'am. You're the one who tricked me. You should cake tare of me if it fire-backs, you don't think?"

Martha's heartbeat ramped up. He wasn't making sense. Cake tare? *Not a good sign.* "You're the one who wouldn't drop his drawers."

Clark scratched his head with one hand and leaned on the table with the other. The redness drained from his neck and his face. His eyes blinked over and over.

Martha reached a hand toward him. "Soldier, why don't you go sit down for a few minutes before your next exam station?"

She would get rid of this guy one way or another, even if he *was* cute.

Clark nodded. He swaggered three steps before hitting the gym floor like a dropped bomb, face first.

"Clark!"

Martha knelt beside him. She pressed her fingers on his neck. *Not dead.* Her thoughts were of the shot in his arm. She had broken protocol, but not any hard and steadfast rules of procedure. Still, what if she caused... she could hear Sister Clatilda whisper in her head. *You're in trouble again, Martha?*

Nancy appeared out of nowhere and stood next to her, along with one of the older interns.

"He fainted after I gave him a shot," Martha confessed. "In the arm."

The intern threw her a sharp glare. "Why not the buttocks, nurse? That's usually where these shots are administered."

Clark moaned. The intern pulled a capsule of smelling salts from his pocket and snapped it open. Martha explained the scenario as he waved the pungent odor under Clark's nose.

"He wasn't cooperating, Doctor—refused to have the shot. I did what I had to do."

Nancy crouched next to the intern and batted long lashes. "I guess I should have stayed at the post, but I was worn to a frazzle, Doctor. Perhaps I could have persuaded him to cooperate. Poor Martha's not to blame."

Martha's heart raced. *Brown-noser.* What Nancy needed was a good sock in the jaw.

"I'm sure Miss Watkins did her best. He's coming around now." He nodded to Martha. "No harm done."

Nancy's face reddened, matching her fiery hair color. She stood and joined the small crowd of whispering on-lookers.

Clark fluttered his eyes open and surveyed the group. His crimson face pricked at Martha's heart, knowing he must be mortified. She was familiar with the feeling, the humiliation.

He looked straight at Martha. "What happened?"

Despite her pity, she wouldn't let him off the hook for being so stubborn. "You tripped over your big feet and fell flat on your face. That's what you get for ignoring my instructions."

The doctor smirked and felt for Clark's pulse. "You're fine. If I were you, soldier, I'd obey the next nurse." He left Clark and Martha, and dispersed the remainder of the crowd.

Clark propped himself up on his elbows, and then jumped to his feet. He wobbled to one side and grabbed Martha's arm to steady himself. She stood her ground, but glared at him.

"If you're finished causing a scene, I need to get back to work." She removed his hand and stepped back. Then pity kicked in. "Well, you should go sit for a while before getting dressed. There are juice and cookies at that table over there." She pointed to the side of the gym. "I'd have some sugar if I were you. You'll feel better soon."

"Thanks, nurse." He didn't turn in her direction again. She kind of wished he had. For the second time this week she had goofed with patient care. Her stomach panged.

Martha checked her watch. Two more hours and it was back to the vineyard to have a quick dinner with Mama and Pop, then to bingo. One more day of this duty and then no more gang enlistment exams for her.

She'd rather not see an enlistee again for a long time.

He didn't know whether he liked her or resented her. He'd never met such an impertinent young lady, especially a nurse. Clark's mind replayed the incident as he dressed in the cold locker room. Locker doors clanged as men finished dressing and exited the gym. A few of the unfamiliar faces next to him stared and some of the men chuckled.

A short stocky young man stooped in front of him. He threw his hand to his forehead and acted out a fainting spell in front of Clark while two others stood by. They left the area roaring with laughter while Clark's jaw clenched.

Yep, he resented her. She had no right to embarrass him that way. Miss smarty-pants should be fired for putting him through such an ordeal. She must have broken some sort of rules. Seems like no one these days knew how to be efficient and professional—his pet peeve. Still, she was pretty. He stood and slipped on his jacket.

"Going back for more, Jensen?" Some baby-faced kid hollered as he jogged passed Clark.

A few others slapped him on the back as they filed out the exit. It was clear the entire gym had become an audience to this escapade. The clock above the lockers said 5:00. She might still be there. He needed to set her straight for the good of her career, and to let steam off his indignation. The image of her nametag flashed in his mind, but only her first initial and last name had been printed on the badge. M. Watkins. Should he try and guess? And risk being embarrassed again at calling her Mary when her name could be anything from Margaret to Matilda? Not a chance.

He slipped his bloodied handkerchief in his pants pocket. His nose had oozed red the rest of the afternoon from his fall. Once in the locker room, he stopped the flow. She owed him a nice new handkerchief. It was the least she could do. He would play it safe and call her Miss Watkins.

The other men had gone. Clark wound his way through the maze of lockers until he emerged inside the gym. Nurses and doctors busied themselves putting away instruments, gathering clipboards, and covering tables with white sheets. He searched the group to see if the nurse in question was among the white-suited crowd. He had a few words to say and they bounced around in his head as he took a few steps into the space, keeping an eye out for a nurse with curly black hair.

"You lost, soldier?" An older man in a white coat approached Clark. "You're too late for a physical, if that's what you're thinking."

Clark glanced his way. "Oh, no, sir. I've had mine, thank you. I'm looking for the nurse who gave me a shot today."

"Well, most of them are still here. Why don't you wait outside at the front of the gym? They'll all be going out soon."

Clark read his watch. He would need to be back to work at the gas station in an hour. "Sure. I'll go out the locker room door and wait around front. Thanks."

Running was out of the question. His muscles were still stiff from the infamous meeting with the floor. His red face and sore nose wouldn't be his best presentation, but he strolled as fast as he could between the tennis court and the brick gymnasium until he reached the front steps. A redhead stood halfway down, unpinning her nurse's cap. When she spied Clark, she smiled.

"How are you feeling? That was some fall you had." She hurried down the steps and stopped at the bottom near him. "Martha should have been more careful with you." She batted her eyelashes at him. He moved back—away from her intrusion in his space.

Martha. That would be the M. on her badge. He smiled and twisted to look around the girl. "Martha, huh?"

The redhead's flirty face turned sour. "You better see about that shiner forming on your right eye."

He frowned and reached up to touch his cheek. He winced— another reason to hate Miss Martha Watkins.

"I'm fine." He wasn't fine. Now he was embarrassed all over again. "Is she still in there? Martha, I mean."

The girl scowled. "Yes. Out any minute. Bye." She stormed down the last steps and down the walkway toward the parking lot. Without turning around she hollered. "You could do better, soldier."

Do better? Whatever she thought his intentions were, she had guessed wrong. If she hung around, she would see how he just wanted to...

"See you tomorrow," were the first words out of her mouth. The doctor next to her turned and walked down the side steps as he answered.

"Another fun day. Have a nice evening, Martha."

She pulled off her cap and stuffed it in her wide skirt pocket, then tucked her hair behind her ears. That's when their eyes met. His angst mysteriously dispelled, even though she squinted at him. He leaned on a concrete pillar to watch her descend.

"Did you forget something, Mr. Jensen?"

She knew his name. Yes, she was pretty, this Martha person. This nurse who treated him so carelessly. Why did she have to be so smart? With each step closer, his fiery monologue faded. When she stopped three steps above him, all he could do was stare.

"Are you feeling better?"

Now was his chance. "No. I mean, yes. Well, now my eye hurts where I hit the floor."

She leaned forward. "Oh, dear. It's going to be blue soon."

And it would be all her fault. She didn't care.

"You know, Nurse Martha—"

"Mr. Jensen. I'm so sorry for what happened. I didn't expect such a strong reaction. Technically it's acceptable to give that shot in the arm. I hope you don't have any more lasting effects, but I did what I thought was the only way to get you inoculated. If you pass your physical, you'll have to get more, you know." Her eyes met his again for a moment. "And you signed off on getting these preliminary shots today, remember?"

"Oh. No, I don't. Well, it's all right. I'll survive."

"That's good. Gotta go."

She hopped down the last few stairs and headed to the parking lot. She would be gone and he didn't get to voice his resentment. What resentment? His feelings were a jumbled mess now. She had charmed him to distraction and now he had to be firm.

"Miss Watkins." He found enough strength to run, and caught up with her as she reached her car. She fumbled in her purse, but looked up at him.

"You're mad, aren't you?" She leaned against the car.

What now? He had a captive audience for his lecture on professionalism and bedside manner, but the words got stuck.

"Maybe." He tipped his head. "Do you like being a nurse?"

She paused, looking around the parking lot. "Yes. Very much. Why do you ask?"

He couldn't say why. He didn't know. All he did know for sure was that he wanted to find out more about Martha Watkins. He hoped she would let him try.

"Just curious." *Be honest.* "Look, I was going to yell at you for surprising me with that shot. It was humiliating to faint like that, and I admit I was angry."

"Was?"

"Well, yes." He crossed his arms over his chest. "I've decided to give you a chance to make up for it. How about dinner tomorrow?"

"You want me to buy you dinner to make up for it?"

"No, no. I'm buying!"

She scrunched her face. "Can't."

His squirmy stomach clenched. "Can't or won't?"

She resumed rummaging through her purse. "Can't." Without looking up, she continued. "But if you grab some sandwiches and sodas we could have lunch out here tomorrow on the lawn on my break from physicals."

His heart thumped against his chest. Progress being made when he hadn't dreamed he would head this direction with Miss Watkins.

"I can do that. What time?"

She pulled out her keys and jingled them in the air. "Thought I'd lost them. How about 12:30?" She walked around her car and swung open the driver's door. He jumped back to miss being hit by it. She slammed the door shut and rolled down the window. "Don't be late."

Before he could respond, she started the motor and backed up the car. He gave a slight wave as she pulled away, the back of the car pulling onto the street. His stomach still jumped as if something important had just happened.

He couldn't reason why he now had a date with this nurse he knew nothing about, except that she was impetuous and pretty. This had gone all wrong. He should have reprimanded her, but instead he would be making bologna sandwiches for lunch tomorrow. Everything was out of order and out of the ordinary.

But he didn't mind at all.

Bingo turned out to be even more tedious than she expected, and she had disappointed the girls by leaving early. Tossing and turning most of the night, she fretted over the talk she heard during the enlistment exams yesterday. The world was obviously not in the peaceful state she had believed. Her small world of country air, aging parents, and white uniforms seemed too simple, too sheltered. Why couldn't countries get along instead of fighting and ruining a peaceful existence for innocent people? She thought her life would remain untouched forever. Yet listening to the young men talk of possible war and all their buddies who had already signed up, she felt an urgency for her own future.

In a perfect world, she would meet the perfect guy, live in a perfect house, and be the perfect nurse. But if Sister Clatilda and the headlines were right, all the eligible men would enlist and leave young ladies to only dream of finding true love. Her only hope would be if the rumors of war never came true, or that some handsome intern would win her heart—one with bad feet.

Her worries had faded a bit this morning, but she still had to deal with the clumsy Mr. Jensen. Martha grabbed Clarissa's hand as they stood in the yard admiring the dew on the grape leaves. Their morning walks had been a lifesaver for Martha, and her friend just had to give her some advice today. Why she had agreed to have lunch with a needle-shy man she didn't know? Clarissa had to help her think of a way to get rid of the young man.

She looked at her watch. Only a few minutes before she had to leave for town. Clarissa had to advise her.

"Tell me how to deter this guy."

Clarissa laughed. "You're the one with dating experience, not me. Just tell him you have to work through lunch."

"I don't know how to get in touch with him." Martha groaned. "I'm doomed for today. I'll just be cold and aloof so he won't want to see me again."

Clarissa put her hands on her hips. "Oh yes. That's you all right. Cold and aloof."

Morgan stuck his head out the back door of the big house. "Mom, dad is having trouble getting Hope ready for church." Morgan had become the quintessential whistleblower of the family. Clarissa never scolded him about it. Martha figured her friend thought the boy deserved some slack due to his health issues. Although he had seemed to be a more normal 12-year-old these days.

Clarissa shook her head. "That child. I'd better go rescue

Frank." She turned to walk away but spoke over her shoulder. "You know, maybe you should give this guy a chance. He might be all right." Her stride quickened before Martha could protest.

"He's not my type," Martha hollered after her.

She rubbed her arms below her uniform sleeves. She would need her sweater at least for the rest of the morning. With any luck this cool breeze would blow in enough rain to call off her lunch date.

Clarissa opened the porch door as Martha passed. "Will you be home for dinner tonight?"

Martha nodded. "Yes. Why?"

"Frank and I would like to talk to you and your folks if you're not busy." Hope tugged at her mother's skirt. "See you later then?"

"Sure."

Martha wondered about Clarissa's tone. If there was something to talk about, it had to be farm business. But why would she be included? Martha stopped at the bottom of the cottage porch steps and gazed at the big house. The sun had cleared the foggy haze over the brown hills beyond. If things hadn't worked out for Mama and Pop to be a part of the operations here, Frank might be planning to find someone else. Leaving would devastate them. Pop would have to keep barbering full time, but at least Mama wouldn't risk any more bee stings. Where would they live?

"Don't be ridiculous. It could be a thousand things they want to talk about. Maybe there's a bonus coming, or maybe Frank is taking Clarissa on a well-deserved vacation. Don't blow this out of proportion." Overthinking seemed to be her dominant trait lately.

She pushed the door open, nearly hitting Mama, who had her hand on the door knob.

"I heard voices. Who were you talking to?"

Martha laughed. "Myself."

"Hmm." Ruth shuffled to the kitchen.

"Clarissa said she and Frank want to visit with us tonight. We can go over after dinner if that's okay."

"Well, yes. What's that all about?"

No sense in worrying her mother with speculation. A shrug seemed to satisfy.

Ruth held out a brown paper bag. "Here's your lunch. Better get going."

Lunch. Back to that again, with no ideas about how to persuade Clark Jensen he needed to find another conquest. She would have to endure lunch and wing it for the rest.

"Save it for me. I have a date for lunch." She shook her head at Ruth's gentle smile and it quickly disappeared. "Don't ask, Mama. Don't ask."

As she took a step toward the door, she changed her mind. She reached back for the bag. "On second thought, I'll take this just in case."

She bounded out the front door. For all she knew of this young man, he could stand her up. She only agreed to lunch because she felt sorry for him, and guilty for making him faint.

She really should have let one of the other nurses, or better yet, a doctor persuade Clark Jensen about the shot. If she had, she wouldn't be guessing if she'd have to share a bench with this suitor.

"Hana."

It was a brilliant idea. She would call Hana from the gym and tell her to meet her for lunch. A dirty trick on a nice guy, but it would work to show him she wasn't interested.

A heavy weight lifted from her attitude. Now if only Hana would go along with the charade.

Chapter Three

*C*lark unfolded a napkin and placed it on the rich green grass in front of the gym. He wiped his sweaty palms on his pant leg and searched the park-like area. His heart thumped. He'd sure like to figure out what it was about Martha that set him on edge. Her casual manner should put him at ease, but as he waited for their lunch date under the biggest oak tree he had ever seen, his heart pounded. No other girl had made him feel this way, and even though he barely knew Martha, he looked forward to seeing her again so much, it rattled him.

He closed his eyes and huffed. No one was going to wrap him up in a vice.

"I've got bigger fish to fry."

"Is that what you're having for lunch—fish?"

He opened his eyes to see Martha, her arms crossed and brows scrunched. Before he could stand all the way up someone sauntered up next to his date. As he straightened, he could see a lovely, petite Japanese girl with a smile that rivaled any he'd seen before. A large tote hung from her shoulder over her white nurse's uniform.

Martha laughed and put her hands on her hips. "I don't like fish. I hope that's not what you brought me for lunch."

Clark tried to speak, but as he watched the two women throw down a blanket and sit, he could only squeak out a sloppy hello.

Martha pointed to Hana. "This is my best friend, Hana Kato.

Hana, meet Clark Jensen." Martha made the introductions while she helped Hana pull items from the tote. "I talked her into helping with the physicals today."

Clark managed a small wave. "Nice to meet you, Hana. Are…you staying for lunch?"

Martha and Hana exchanged half smiles. "I didn't think you'd mind."

Martha's high tone riled him. Mind? After thinking of nothing but having time alone with Martha for the last twenty-four hours? She was toying with him, and he didn't like being on the other side of a joke—again. He brushed the grass and sat.

"Why would I mind? *Two* beautiful women to share lunch with is a bonus."

Hana winked at Martha, who coyly avoided Clark's stare. A good thing, lest she see the aggravation behind his smile. He could play this game if she could, and enjoy it. Or at least pretend to.

"So, what do you do, Clark?" Hana pulled half a sandwich and an apple from her sack.

"Me? Oh, I'm just a grease monkey. Dad owns an auto repair shop and I help out since I finished last college semester. I like getting my hands dirty—working on motors and making them sing." It was true, except that he longed to hear plane engines more. As soon as he heard the results of his physical, he would be able to share his pilot ambitions. No point risking a jinx, even though he knew his future was God's business.

He reached in his own sack and handed Martha his lunch offering. "Hope you don't mind balogna."

"Love it." Martha took the wrapped sandwich from him.

"Oh, here's a soda." He flipped the top from the bottle and held it out to her. "Dr. Pepper okay?"

"Fine."

Hana swallowed a bite of sandwich. "Your job sounds

interesting. My brother, Martin, likes tinkering with motors. When he's not too busy being a bratty 14-year-old."

Clark itched to say something to Martha, but instead soaked in her silence, determined to win this game of—whatever she wanted to call it. He watched her through his peripheral vision, catching a glimpse of her shiny black curls as they swirled around the base of her nurse's cap. No make-up—she didn't need any.

Clark turned to Hana. "Do you mind if I ask where you're from? I see you have a different heritage, like I do." Clark bit into a chunk of cucumber.

"My family lives in the Seattle area. I came here to finish nursing school so I could help my aunt. After graduation I decided to stay for a while." She nudged Martha. "Martha couldn't get along without me anyway."

Martha frowned and finally spoke. "Oh, right. It's the other way around I think."

Her contagious laugh made him smile. He feared she would win whatever game they played from now on. And if Hana would just leave, he would tell her so. While Hana and Martha bantered, he leaned back on his elbows, drinking in the exuberance of their friendship.

After a few moments, Martha's laughter stopped when she met his gaze.

"I'm sorry. We seem to have forgotten about you." She shifted her position on the blanket to face him. Hana returned to her sandwich after covering her mouth, failing to disguise a giggle.

He had to play this right. *Be nonchalant, slightly aloof.*

"I've been duly entertained. You probably need a break from the pressures of enlistment physicals. Any uncooperative soldiers on your shift today? Any fainting fighting men?"

Martha scrunched her nose. "All cooperative, and no fainters, thank goodness." She took a bite from her apple and held out her palm. "Have you forgiven me for yesterday?"

Hana stared at Clark, wide-eyed. He stole a look at both of them. He would make her wait a bit for his answer—make her squirm. Although Martha didn't seem the pins-and-needles type, so he had to choose his words.

"Forgiven you? Oh sure, Besides, I'm happy to facilitate a valuable lesson for a beautiful, young nurse."

Martha stopped in mid-chew. If her mouth hadn't been full, he was sure her jaw would have dropped. He stifled a chuckle, but locked onto her glare. He must have hit the target, although he wasn't sure what he was aiming at. Any spot in her heart would do. This feisty woman would be hard to win over, but he'd try, even if it cost him some embarrassing moments. She had a way of getting the upper hand. Something he planned to remedy. He only had get organized and confident.

"Well, I think I'll go freshen up before we go back." Hana stood and brushed crumbs from her white skirt. "Nice to have met you, Clark."

Clark jumped up from his lounging position and reached out his hand. "You too, Hana. I hope we'll meet again."

She smiled up at him, her oriental eyes glistened approval. "Oh, we just might."

When she hurried away, Clark caught a glimpse of Martha's frown. Another target hit, but not by him. He reclaimed his spot on the grass and sat cross-legged to face her. She busied herself picking up apple cores and napkins from the grass.

Clouds had covered the sun, but the warmth of the afternoon felt good on his face. He only had a few more minutes to make an impression. He fished out a pickle wrapped in waxed paper from his lunch sack. "Nice girl. You two have been friends for a while, I take it."

"We have. She's a peach, and a fine nurse. I wish I had her…" She looked up, her eyes wide.

"Had her what?"

Martha blushed, blending in her freckled complexion. "Never mind."

"No. Tell me. What is it about Hana you wish you were more like? I'm interested."

Martha leaned back. "And why are you interested?"

He shrugged. "Okay, maybe I'm just curious." No sense giving away his growing attraction.

She turned away for a moment, picking a fallen leaf from the blanket and twirling the stem between her fingers. He waited for her to make up her mind about revealing more of herself. If not, he wouldn't pry. Something about her hesitancy was telling.

"Well, it's just that she's so calm all the time. She doesn't let anything or anyone get to her. I'm too—reactive. Just one of my many faults."

Clark subdued a grin. She was honest. He liked that. There was still something just underneath her confession that she held inside. Some secret he would spend more lunches under this tree trying to discover. For now, he knew he had to seem less interested, or at least let her think he wasn't.

"Well, I know you have to get back. We'll have to do this again sometime."

He sat up to kneel and gather his things. He could see her frown out of the corner of his eye. He stood and reached over to help her up, but she looked away.

"Yes, well, I do need to finish this duty. Thanks for lunch." She pushed herself up and stuffed her wrappings in his bag.

He grabbed the cream-colored blanket from the ground and began folding. He noticed the stamp on the edge. *U.S. Army.*

He couldn't resist. "Are you joining up?"

She froze and smirked in his direction. "Not on your life. The army doesn't need me."

She took the blanket from him, her cheeks flushed.

Clark reached out his hand. "Thanks for having lunch with me."

Her grip was strong—enough to let him know she felt something. He would find out what, eventually.

The beautiful, big farmhouse seemed to shake with Frank's words. Martha wondered how she couldn't have known this was coming. She thought she and Clarissa could read each other's minds. Her friend had kept the secret very well, and now she knew what James was trying to tell her the other day by the garden.

Frank sat with his hands clasped in front of him, leaning forward in his chair opposite Martha, Pop, and Mama. "I know it must be a shock to you all. I'm sorry."

The fancy overstuffed sofa felt as though it would suck Martha down into its softness. Clarissa came from the kitchen and handed Pop a mug of coffee. "We've been praying about it for a long time and feel it's what we want to do—what we need. I hope you understand." She studied Martha for just a moment.

Martha's lungs seemed void of air. Frank's announcement stung as if it were a real prod poking her in the heart. Her clogged throat caught the question she wanted to ask. Why? Why in heaven's name would they move back to a homestead covered in sand and dust? They just couldn't mean it.

"I know what you're all thinking," Frank continued. "It doesn't sound reasonable or logical to give up this wonderful vineyard to go back and start over with a broken-down dirt farm, but we must do what we feel is right. God will take care of the rest."

Martha shot a look to James. His twitching jaw and red neck told her how he felt. He wasn't like Frank, and this was eating him. She choked down tears for him, and for herself.

She could feel Clarissa's gaze on her, but couldn't bring herself to meet it. Her chest hurt to think of how much distance this would create between her and the woman she loved as a sister.

Pop was the first to answer. "We'll miss you. What will become of this farm?"

Martha listened to Pop's shaking voice. This could change everything for them as well as her. Maybe even more so. And James. What about James? He would graduate in a month. This was insane.

"I'm not sure yet, Ed, but I've spoken with George. You know we're pretty close to owning the place outright and I don't think he's too happy about having to find another buyer. He may just end up leasing it out. I don't know how you feel about staying on to help more, but I would be happy to mention it to him. He likes you."

Pop nodded. Mama wiped her cheek with a tissue, then stuffed it back in her apron pocket. Martha's question still stuck in her throat. She swallowed hard to push it down, but instead, it burst out.

"What are you thinking? You really want to go back to that misery?"

She winced the minute the words were out in the open. They sounded cruel and selfish. Clarissa came to sit by her, slipping her hand into Martha's.

"It's better there now, and people are starting to return. We feel like we need to go back to our roots. Finish what we started. It breaks my heart to think of my little homestead out there disintegrating. I want to reclaim it, even though it means leaving loved ones and happy times."

Martha searched Clarissa's eyes. The soft wisdom she had come to depend on lit her porcelain face with a joy that Martha hadn't seen there before. It suddenly struck Martha that Clarissa hadn't just left a house behind. Her two infant children were buried there. She couldn't imagine what it would be like to lose a child, much less leave them behind, alone on a barren farm with no one to look after their graves. They called to her, and always would until she returned. Her selfish need to keep Clarissa close seemed petty.

She hugged Clarissa tight, feeling the warmth of her friend's arms returning the embrace. "You go where you need to go. I'll miss you, but I understand. You and Frank can do anything you put your mind to." She glanced at Frank, who smiled. James only stared at the floor, tapping his foot like a nervous groom.

Frank stood. "Think over what I've said about staying on, Ed. Let me know if you have any questions. We'll stay till after James's graduation."

Pop shook Frank's hand. "I'll consider it."

Out of the corner of her eye Martha watched James flinch as though he would explode. His fists clenched as he jumped to his feet. His desperate stare was almost audible. He didn't need to voice his opinion. It permeated the room.

Clarissa let go of Martha's hand. "James?"

He didn't answer, but bolted from the room. Frank rubbed his forehead and huffed.

"I'm sorry. He's not as excited about this move as we are, obviously."

Clarissa rose from the sofa. "Frank, go talk to him."

Martha's head throbbed, but she couldn't let him go that way. "Let me go. He might open up with me."

Frank exchanged looks with Clarissa, then nodded to Martha. "If you think you can get through to him."

Martha headed for the door. Get through to him? If that's what Frank wanted, he would likely be disappointed. What James needed was someone to listen. Someone to encourage him to think things through and come to his own decisions.

He would be 18 soon, and like it or not, his parents would have to start letting go.

James had found a spot to sit under the old red-leaf maple tree in the yard. He sat facing the barn. She came up from behind him and cleared her throat. He twirled a gold coin in his hand, his knees bent, his back leaning on the tree trunk, like the boy she met so long ago. He didn't look up when she stood next to him, but stared at the barn as if he wanted it to speak. She imagined he would give anything to see Elijah walk through the barn door.

Martha sat on the ground next to him. Pebbles poked her backside through her jeans. James could have found a more comfortable place to brood, but she could work with this. "Feeling better?"

His smile surprised her. He twirled the gold coin for a moment longer, then held it up, inspecting it like a treasure.

"Remember this coin? It belonged to William, my real father. He gave it to me to try and bribe me to go away with him. I gave it to Dad, but he gave it back to me after the fire." He paused. Martha held her tongue. "Maybe if I had run away with William, he wouldn't be dead and I wouldn't be heading back to Kansas."

Martha let out her breath through a soft whistle. "That's a big maybe. Waste of time wondering about what if this or that. So you don't want to go back to Kansas—that's pretty clear to everyone."

"Guess I shouldn't have stormed out like that, but I don't understand why they want to do this. It's crazy. I want to join the Army Air Corps and fly. Instead I'll be helping unearth a house covered in sand and digging a new well for water."

Martha rested her elbows on her drawn knees. "I see how that wouldn't appeal to you. Everyone should be able to do their dream. It's just… sometimes you have to wait for the right time. You owe it to your parents to listen to them and wait for your time."

James slid the coin into his pocket and pushed himself up from the ground. "Don't have much choice right now. I'll think about it. I know Mom and Dad need me."

Did he really know how desperate his mother was to keep him close? It was one thing Martha was sure about where Clarissa was concerned. She would feel the same with any loved one who wanted to be reckless with their choices.

He held out his hand to help Martha up. She felt his callouses against her palm. He had put in many hours on the farm already. No longer skinny and lanky, he was strong and ready to do any job. Persuading him not to fly would be a large task. Poor Clarissa.

"Sorry for making a scene."

Martha gave him a gentle sock in the arm. "You can't outdo me. Your scene was kindergarten stuff compared to mine."

His puzzled scowl tempted her to tell him, but he didn't need to know her transgression. She had the feeling he had her on a short pedestal, and she didn't want to fall off just yet.

"Never mind. Let's join the group of criers in there. You're not the only one hurting over this, you know. I'm losing a dear friend, and maybe a place to live."

"Sorry."

"It's okay. We all have to move on sometime. I just want your mom to be happy. I'll be blubbering when she drives away."

James socked her back. "You're funny."

Funny. She felt anything but humorous. Thinking of what this all could mean for everyone wasn't a laughing matter. Neither was the thought of James joining the army to fly planes. She wondered what all the mothers in America were going through in these troubled days with whispers of war. Lots of young men like the ones at the enlistment physicals would break the hearts of their parents. Men like Clark Jensen.

James walked ahead of her. She lingered, recalling the image of Clark diving face first to the gym floor. She wanted to laugh, but couldn't. He was like James—on the road to breaking hearts, but not hers. The note on her car when she was done at the gym should have set her off. But like James's persuasive charm, Clark had *told* her—not *asked*—that he would see her later. She would have this one last date with him, then he would be out of her life—off to join a stupid war. James wouldn't do something that rash. Or would he?

She looked up to see James holding the door open for her. "Such a gentleman." She socked him in the arm as she whizzed past him.

"Gotcha last."

He froze. "Not if I catch up with you."

She felt him close behind her. If they joined the others now, it would be a puzzlement to them how James could change his demeanor so quickly. The sinking feeling came over her that he could change back just as fast.

He likely would.

Clark waltzed through the kitchen door and dropped his opened letter on the table. The quiet house meant his parents weren't home from the farmer's market on Greene Street. Their usual routine on Saturdays hadn't changed in years. His mother would bake a pie tomorrow from the sweet potatoes she bought today, and his father would file through used *Life* magazines he picked up from the second-hand vendor.

Clark would spend the evening reading the material the enlistment officer had given him, if he could find the dresser drawer where he had buried it. When his parents returned, he'd have to find the courage to tell them he had passed his physical and completed his army enlistment. He dreaded the looks of shock on their faces.

He slung his jacket over the back of the chair and sank into the seat. His mind flashed back to the posters hanging in the window of the Davis's Drugstore window. Uncle Sam pointing—"America needs you," it said; accompanied by a picture of armed uniformed soldiers lining a foxhole. Would he be up to this job? Yes, he knew it deep inside. But not on the ground in some foxhole, shooting at men one by one. His offensive position would be in the air. His dream to fly was about to come true, or at least one hurdle accomplished. He would be drafted soon anyway. Why not serve doing something he loved?

Now the bigger question remained. What would his folks say? The sound of footsteps on the porch pulled him back to earth, into a battle of wills. He gathered up the letter and rested it on his lap just as the screen door creaked. His heart beat too fast to catch a deep breath.

Clark turned his head. "Hey, you two. Where've you been?" A nervous question, considering he already knew. If he wasn't careful, they would see right through him.

Mr. Jensen set two large, brown paper bags of produce on the counter and frowned. "I think that's obvious. Go help your mother with the rest while I unload these."

When Clark stood, the letter fell to the floor. His father stooped to pick it up before Clark could snatch it.

"It's just some information. Uh, I need to talk to you and Mother about it tonight."

Mr. Jensen stared at the envelope with a government return address in his shaking hand. He pushed his dusty brown fedora hat back past his hair line. After what seemed to Clark several minutes, his father looked up at him with tears brimming.

"You're going to join the army, aren't you, even before they call you?" His voice shook just enough to let Clark know this would be a difficult discussion.

"I—"

The creaky door sounded again. "Don't suppose I could get some help here." His mother let the kitchen door slam as she struggled to hoist bags on the table. She slipped off her cardigan sweater and draped it over her arm. "There are a couple more if—" She looked first at her husband then at Clark. "What's wrong? Did I forget something at the market?"

Clark grabbed one of the bags about to topple. "No, Mother. I'll get the rest of the bags out of the car. Just sit here till I get back." He studied his dad's face, who had pulled the letter out and scanned it.

"Leave them, son. Let's talk about this now. Mother, Clark is going to join the Armed Forces." He threw the letter on the table in front of her. "See for yourself. He already passed a physical."

Clark sat at the opposite end of the table as Mrs. Jensen refused the paper handed her. Her face paled for a moment, then she looked into Clark's eyes.

"Is this true?"

"Yes, Mother, but you need to let me explain. Dad didn't give me a chance." Clark kept his tone respectful, but inside his stomach fluttered. If he could just make them understand.

His mother leaned against the kitchen counter and pulled a hankie out of her housedress pocket. He knew she would cry. He wanted to put his arm around her small frame and comfort her.

"Since the age of nine I knew I was meant for the air. That was the year you took me to the air show at the Benton County Fair, remember Dad?" Mr. Jensen nodded and looked away. "Watching the surplus World War I Jenny planes flying their daring patterns above the crowds sent shivers up my spine. I'll never forget it."

"You came home and exclaimed that you were going to be a pilot." His mother smiled, but her eyes sparked with moisture.

Even now, just like that day, the thought of soaring through the clouds excited him. His parents raised him to be adventurous and confident. They would have to realize he had made up his mind. He knew they worried about a war, but he would have had to serve at least one year anyway, sooner or later.

"Maybe the Army Air Corps will be my way to reach for the sky, Mother."

She took his arm and patted it, then wiped a tear away with her finger. She had never been an overprotective mother, and Clark hoped she wouldn't start now. He didn't like the sadness in her eyes or the stoop in her posture. When had her hair turned salt and pepper? Wrapped up in his own life, he hadn't really looked at her closely for a while.

Mr. Jensen sat next to his wife. "I don't want you to go, Clark. There is likely to be a war, and I don't want you in it. You don't need to fight someone else's battle."

"Dad, I'll have to sign up eventually, and if there is a war, do you think they will let me off the hook? I hope we do get in it. Oma and Opa have been there all this time. Someone has to step in and stop the madness over there, for them and all Europeans. Just the fact that we haven't had word of them for a year…" Clark grasped the back of a chair and waited before pressing further. Mrs. Jensen sniffled. His father turned away from him.

Perhaps his parents didn't know the seriousness of the world situation. Perhaps it was best not to speak of it until they had a chance to accept his decision.

Mr. Jensen rubbed his face. "I'm worried about what's going on over there too, son, but there isn't anything more we can do." He tapped a folded newspaper on the table. "This reporter says that there are stories of how families are scattered all over Europe to escape persecution, or even imprisonment. At the very least they are losing their German citizenship. Don't you think I want to find them and get them out of there? We have no choice but to wait. You joining up now won't make any difference."

"It will to me, Dad."

Mrs. Jensen rose to stand next to her husband. "You know, Clark, we need you here with us. Who knows what might happen around here to folks of German descent if things get worse."

Mr. Jensen took off his hat and turned his somber face to Clark. His eyes had gone from bright to dull. "You're of age. You'll do what you wish, I suppose."

"I'll be all right, Dad. Don't worry about me. I need to do this. Who else better to avenge our family than me?" His words soured as they left his mouth.

Mr. Jensen shook his head and shuffled out the door, mumbling as he trudged down the steps. Clark watched him through the screen door, wishing contention hadn't ruled the day.

Clark felt his mother's hand on his shoulder. "He will have a hard time with this. Give him time."

"I will. I just wish he understood the way you do." Clark eased out of his chair and wrapped his arms around his mother.

She shook her head and turned her gaze to the window. "I *don't* understand. I only trust you to do what you must, that's all. No mother wants her son to go to war." She patted his cheek and turned to follow her husband out into the yard. They didn't bother with the rest of the groceries. Instead, they strolled into the yard together and inspected the tulip and daffodil bulbs. It had always been their way to deal with pain… play in the garden.

The pendulum clock above the kitchen sink window ticked away minutes. He had to give his dad time, but there were only weeks left before he had to leave. His jaw clenched as he picked up the envelope from the table. Even though his father opposed him, nothing had changed in Clark's determined mind. If anything, his conviction had strengthened.

As he stood at the screen door watching the sun hug the horizon, he thought of Martha. The note on her windshield had done the trick. When he called, she had said yes to going out again.

What if she wouldn't see him after finding out he had officially enlisted? He hardly knew her, but one thing was for sure—he cared about what she thought.

He would have the chance to find out. Tonight at the dance.

Chapter Four

Clark searched the outside of the little, white house Martha called *the cottage*. She had described it adequately. The porch did sag, the roof needed replacing, and it was still cute as could be. Even in the twilight, the velvety vines in the distance commanded his attention. A lovely forefront for the majestic landscape beyond. His dad would love to own a place like this.

Martha peeked out the living room window, then disappeared. As much as he wanted to wave, he wouldn't let her know he saw her watching.

He hadn't attended a dance for so long and wondered if she could jitterbug. Somehow she didn't seem the type to fly around the dance floor to the pure swing sound of Benny Goodman. Then again, she had shown him her playful side. Her teasing and lighthearted comebacks were indications to him she might be a fun-loving date.

He stepped out of the Ford Tudor sedan, checked his tweed trousers and buttoned the top button on his new white short sleeved shirt. His stomach fluttered as he took the creaky porch steps two at a time. Pop was on the other side of the screen door and invited him inside.

"Hello, Mr. Watkins. I'm Clark Jensen."

"Thought so. Hello." They shook hands and Mr. Watkins pointed to the woman at the sink. "Martha's mother, Ruth."

Clark waved at the woman who smiled sweetly and nodded.

"Martha. Clark is here," Pop called to the hallway.

"Coming." He heard her footsteps getting closer.

This was the moment he had waited for all day. He looked up just as Martha reached the kitchen. Her red and white dress cinched with a red belt accentuated her figure. The square-heeled strapped sandals made her look ready for dancing. Impressive. His eyes scanned her from head to toe. He puckered his lips to whistle, but then parted them into a smile.

Pop eased into the big overstuffed chair. "I hear you're enlisting."

Clark inched around Mr. Watkins as he talked, moving toward Martha. She met him half way, grabbing her pocket book from the table by the sofa.

"Ready to go?" Martha strolled over to Pop and patted him on the shoulder. She hooked Clark's arm and pulled him out the front door. She let go of his hand and sauntered toward the car. The quick exit had been awkward. Clark turned and saw Mrs. Watkins standing at the screen door.

"Good night, ma'am."

She smiled. "Have a good time."

"Night, Mama."

Clark opened the passenger door of the car. Martha took a step back and whistled.

He stroked the trim on the door. "My cousin's. He lets me borrow it while he's away at college." The hours he had spent polishing up the rig had paid off. Until he could be on his own, this would be the best he could do for a vehicle. Besides, he wouldn't need a car for all the months of military training.

"Hmm. Snazzy." She stepped in and he pushed the door shut. Once in the driver's seat he started the engine. It backfired once, twice. Martha put her hands to her ears. "Are you sure this will get us to the dance? People are going to think we're shooting out the window at them."

Clark laughed while cringing on the inside. Great first

impression he had just made. "I can take a little noise. It reassures me that the engine is still running, and it sounds like an airplane. Are you still game?"

Martha nodded and dropped her hands to her lap. "Let's go. The swing band awaits."

As they bumped down the road he wondered if he would have to start the conversation. Just as he opened his mouth to break the silence, she chimed a question.

"So what do you want to be when you grow up?"

"When I grow up?" He frowned as he dodged another pot hole.

"Yes, when you grow up. You know what I mean." She tilted her head and stared at him.

"Not sure yet. Maybe a professional dancer after tonight."

Her face lit up. "Now that would be something to see. You don't seem the musical type, though. What classes did you take in your short college career?"

The comment hit a nerve. "Short? How do you know I'm not going back?"

She leaned down and loosened the strap on her left shoe. "Hey, do you suppose there will be a contest at the dance? I could use some prize money."

He didn't mind the change in conversation. He would find a way later to explain why he wouldn't be in college for a while. "Don't know, but we'll find out soon. Don't count on me for a winning partner. I confess. I'm not the best dancer in town."

Her smile warmed up the car. As they pulled into the edge of town he rolled down the window and hung his arm out. The cool breeze settled his nerves.

"Hope you're ready for a crowd. Kennewick is bustling with activity tonight." He pointed to the cars lining the downtown streets.

The lamp posts flickered like fireflies, waiting for darkness before illuminating the sidewalk. Band music soared through the air, flowing from the Mason's Hall. Young couples dashed hand in hand toward the building, laughing and whooping.

Businessmen hurried to close their doors for the day, flipping over the open signs in the windows. Clark waved out the window to Mr. Montgomery, the pharmacist, as they drove by the drug store. Someone pulled out of a parking spot just ahead and Clark sped up to pull in. "Perfect spot."

Martha slid off the seat when he opened the car door. As she brushed by him, he could smell her hair. Gardenias. He imagined nestling his nose in her black curls as they danced. She would easily be one of the best looking girls in the place.

"Looks like it's crowded. We better get in there." Martha pulled at his arm.

They dodged honking cars to cross the street and hurried to the line in front of the dance hall. Two young men monitored the doorway, dressed in blue jackets with an insignia on the pocket. They snatched tickets from couples entering the building, laughing loud and sizing up the girls as they passed. Clark recognized the logo for Future Farmers of America. This was their annual fundraiser dance, one he had never attended.

The younger one, a customer at his father's gas station, had often been rude and made cutting remarks about Germans. These particular rich boys had turned the local FFA chapter into an exclusive club for bullies, all self-proclaimed as superior.

Martha pulled him into place at the end of the fast moving line of squirming eager dancers. "We'll be in soon at this pace." She smiled, but nothing could stop his shuddering nerves from spiking to high alert.

Clark's stomach tensed trying to judge the demeanor of the obnoxious doorkeepers. As the line moved forward he kept his eye on them until they reached the entrance. They looked him up and down, smirks plastered on their faces. Perspiration formed on Clark's upper lip. Time to stand firm. They weren't the customers tonight. He and Martha were.

"Well, Steve. Should we let him in?" The taller, lankier of the two men spoke when Clark held out his four dollars. Then came the familiar sinking sensation signaling something was about to go wrong. Steve inched in front of the doorway.

"Gosh, I don't know, Randal. Do we have to let a Kraut in here?" The second man raised his voice and responded without looking at Clark or Martha. "What do you think?"

Clark reached behind him and took Martha's hand. He hoped she couldn't feel him trembling. He remained in place with one arm outstretched, clenching the bills. "Take the money, boys." His voice was firm and steady, but he felt Martha's arm tense.

The pause from the ticket-takers drew attention, especially Martha's. She wiggled behind him, trying to get free from his grip.

"You have no right to keep me out, gentlemen. This is a public building and my money is as good as anyone's." He tightened his grip on Martha's hand. To his left he could see of a group of young people fall out of line to peer ahead.

"What's the hold up?" One of them hollered from the back of the line.

Martha slid around Clark. She blurted out before he could stop her. "What do you think you're doing? You can't keep us out. Take the money and get out of the way."

Steve's jaw twitched and he flashed a cold-as-steel look at Clark.

Releasing her hand, Clark stepped in front of her, his pulse pounding in his neck. His eyes searched the young men's red faces. The shorter man let out a terse laugh and snatched the money out of Clark's hand. "Guess the little lady has saved the day, Kraut." He held out his arm through the entrance. "Have a nice evening."

Assertively guiding Martha through the door wasn't enough to keep her from stopping in front of Steve. She glared at him and opened her mouth. Before she could speak Clark jerked her arm and bolted into the dance hall. Once inside, he exhaled, relaxing his aching lungs. His hands shook, but he managed to reach in his pocket for his handkerchief. He turned away from Martha to wipe the perspiration from his face. Martha shuffled around to stand in front of him.

"What was that all about? Do you know those goons? I can't believe—"

"Martha, let it go. I'm used to it. It goes along with the heritage, at least in the recent world climate." He managed a smile. Nothing pretentious about this girl.

"You mean this has happened to you before? However do you tolerate it? I would be busting people in the chops for that kind of behavior. Do you want to leave? I don't mind." Her eyes scanned the steamy room, her red lips pursed.

"Not before we dance, Miss Watkins." He took her hand and led her toward the band blasting a rendition of Benny Goodman's *Sing, Sing, Sing.* Bodies flew past them as some of the young men spun their partners around the floor like tops.

"Looks like jitterbug fever has taken the room hostage!" Clark yelled over the noise and music. "I think we will do well if we keep moving around the outside of the crowd."

Martha nodded hard.

Her hands nearly slipped from his grip a few times, but he held on tight as she leaned back, jiving to the beat. Just at the point where Clark lost his energy, the music gave way to whistles and applause. He could hardly clap with the rest of the crowd. He leaned over with his hands on his quivering knees.

"If I could… catch my breath, I'd… laugh at you!" Martha patted him on the back.

He shook his head and rested one hand on her shoulder. "I thought I was going to drop you on the floor."

Martha laughed. He would be happy now even if they never danced again and time would stop at this moment. All the unpleasantness of ten minutes ago disappeared.

"Hey, Jensen." Clark turned around to see Bobby Marshal standing nearby with a dazzling girl on each arm. The young man waved an unlit cigar. He wore two-toned brogues and a black fedora cocked to one side.

"Hey, Bobby." Clark took Martha's hand and led her to the small group. "Martha, this is Bobby, an old friend of mine."

"Pleased, Martha." He tapped Clark's shoulder. "You're not such a dead hoofer after all, Jensen."

He looked from his right side to his left. "This is Paula and Sheila, my new friends."

Clark squeezed Martha's hand, hoping she would suppress the urge to laugh as he was.

"See you've done well at your dad's movie theater, Bobby. Guess dropping out of college was the best thing you ever did."

Bobby nodded and grinned. "Well, you know. People go to the movies to escape all the bad news." The music started again, cutting off his chatter.

Clark jumped at the chance to get away. "Oh, gotta go dance again. See you around, Bobby."

Martha looked back at the girls and waved as Clark pulled her back onto the dance floor, leaving his fancy friend behind.

Clark shook his head and took Martha by the arms. "Some big-shot, huh? We used to be good friends till he couldn't take the cracks about me being a German. I think he was just too chicken to defend me." He whirled her around for two more songs before exhaustion set into his bones. He was out of shape. Something the army would soon remedy.

"How 'bout we find a place to talk, away from this madhouse?"

He motioned toward the door. Luckily, the troublemakers were gone. Clark had a feeling they would have been on the other end of Martha's wrath on the way out.

Martha fussed with her hair. "Whew. I'm with you. Let's go."

He hoped she didn't notice how relieved he was. He would much rather be alone with her than expend all his energy on a dance floor.

Besides, he wanted to tell her his news.

The bottle cap snapped and then tinkled as it fell to the oil-stained cement floor. Clark tapped the Coke machine. He pulled out another nickel and held it up to Martha. "Want a Coke?"

"Sure, if you can afford one for me too." She strolled over to retrieve her drink and let her eyes follow the walls up to examine the hubcaps and fan belts hanging on hooks. She had swallowed hard when the dank smell of grease and gasoline first reached her nostrils, but was getting used to it now. No worse than adjusting to the bitter, antiseptic smells at the hospital. Although this place could use some scrubbing.

So this was where Clark's family worked. They truly were chasing the American dream, running a family business like this car repair shop. A tall stack of rubber tires filled two corners of the room, and rows of rusty tools lined the long bench that ran the length of the wall. Greasy gloves and rags lay on the floor. She could almost taste the oil dripping slowly from a large can on a stand.

Clark dialed in a tune on a dust covered transistor radio. He picked up some dirty rags from the floor and threw them in a bucket.

"Nice place you have here." Martha held back a smirk. Although it wasn't the first place she would have chosen for a date, she went along with the tour of Clark's domain.

"Well, we're proud of it. It's not much of a business, but it provides a living for my family. It's been a good life, but my father has his eye on a few acres north of here on the river. He'd love to farm the place if it comes up for sale."

She couldn't tell him about the vineyard becoming available until Frank provided more details from George, but sometimes Pop heard of properties coming available. "Maybe Pop could make some inquiries. He knows a few farmers around here."

Martha moved over to an old leather chair by the office door and dusted it off with a rag. She hoped he would come and sit closer to her. It was time to discuss the incident at the dance. She had questions about his German heritage, and wanted to ask while she could.

Clark sat next to her on a wooden box and gulped his Coke. "That would be nice if your dad had any suggestions." He let out a long sigh. "Me? I'd love to work in the outdoors, but not on the ground." His face flushed and he stared at the floor.

Not on the ground? Martha crossed her legs and leaned back into the chair, being careful not to snag her skirt on the tears in the leather. She held her breath for a moment but then gave in to the urge to bring up what could be a sensitive subject.

"Clark, what are people so afraid of? I mean, about Germans? You're as American as I am. Born here, right?"

Clark guzzled the last of his soda and set the bottle on the floor. The radio on the tool bench played Billie Holiday's *These Foolish Things*. Not fitting for a greasy filling station, but perhaps it would do for a slow dance. Yet, she was more interested in finding answers.

"Would you tell me about your heritage?"

Clark laughed.

"I'm serious." It was too late to take back the question.

"Well, this is rather sudden, isn't it?" He pulled up another box and put his feet up. "Not much to explain. My mother and father were born in Germany and came here to America when they were young adults. Then me and my brothers and sister came along. That's it."

"Brothers? Sister?"

"Yep, two brothers and one sister. They're grown and away. One in college. My grandparents are still in Germany, or somewhere in Europe. Things could be very bad for them there. We haven't been able to find them. We're pretty worried that the Nazis might have them imprisoned like so many Germans who don't support him." His eyes sparkled with moisture.

"Support who?"

Clark's eyes fixed on his folded hands. "Hitler."

If she could look deep into Clark's soul at this moment, she guessed she would see fear and anger, and maybe his own brand of hate. A wave of compassion rushed through her. Her problems seemed silly compared to Clark's. She could lose her job, but he could lose grandparents he obviously cared about deeply. And now came the tough question.

"Are they, your Grandparents… Jewish?"

"No. Just Christian people who hate what Hitler is doing to their country."

She knew so little, and felt ashamed. All the rumors and stories in the papers must have some truth to them. To her, all the reports had been like a flag flapping in the wind—just political noise. The man in front of her was living truth she knew little about.

"You must feel helpless knowing they're over there. But what can you do?"

Clark's expression changed, as if he were holding back a secret. He turned away for a moment, and then his eyes locked onto hers.

"Just wait, I guess. It's bad over there, and I might have a chance to help." He paused and she wondered if he were going to explain. What could he do?

"I passed my physical and I'll be heading to basic training soon. I want more than anything to be accepted into the flight program with the Army Air Corps. I hope to finish up my flying lessons as a recruit."

She could barely hear his last few sentences over the ringing in her ears. Heading to basic training? She had forgotten all about how she had met him in the first place, blinding herself to the fact that he indeed wanted to be a soldier. She had come to like this guy—a lot. Now he tells her he's going to fly away to fight in another country. In a war America isn't even in… yet. Clark must think it was going to happen, and her stomach flipped just to think of the ramifications of America at war.

She clenched her fists to keep them still. "I don't know what to say, except I guess now I understand why you would want to go off and get yourself hurt, or worse. It's about more than flying. It's tied in with your heritage."

He didn't seem offended, but she imagined he might be tired of explaining. He shrugged, then stood to turn off the radio and held out his hand.

"Are we leaving?" Martha glanced at her watch. "Oh, I didn't know it was so late. I should be going home." She got up without taking his hand. Clark reached over and touched her shoulder. He turned her around and looked at the back of her dress. She laughed as she craned her neck to see.

"I suppose I have motor oil on my behind. I'm prone to such accidents."

"Clean. No stains." Clark kept his hand resting on her shoulder. He didn't move until she turned and took his hand. She could feel his strong grip and calloused palm. If only it weren't so late, they could go for a long ride up the hill to see the city lights. Not tonight. It was too soon in their relationship anyway. A relationship she would now have to end, considering his confessed ambitions.

"I hate to leave the Taj Mahal, but I really do have to get home. Pop and Mama will wonder where I am." She stepped away, pulling him along. His grip on her hand tightened, but he relinquished his stance. Her feet slogged along as if they would rather stay.

Clark opened the car door and she climbed into the passenger side. Before he came around to the door she slid over. He smiled as he settled into the driver's seat. She didn't want to mislead him, but they had shared a few important moments, and she felt a strange sense of closeness. He started the engine. Bang! Martha jumped and grabbed his arm.

"Sorry. Should have warned you." They laughed together as Clark pulled onto the quiet street. The dance had ended and only a few cars lined the parking slots.

"One of my old boyfriends had a car like this in high school. When he would come to pick me up, the noise would scare Mama."

"An old boyfriend?"

"Nothing serious. We grew up together."

"Hmm. Competition."

The traffic signals started flashing circles of red. It *was* late.

"No. Really. So, I'm wondering about your parent's decision to come to America."

"I'm surprised you're still interested in this story." Clark turned the car on to Valley Country Road that led to the vineyard. "Just looking for a better life I guess. They never talk much about it. No one hardly notices they have an accent, except people like those fine young gentlemen at the door tonight." He nudged her with his shoulder. "I'm sorry that happened, Martha." He grabbed the steering wheel, his knuckles white.

The thought of the incident made her chest ache. Or was it the announcement from Clark about his future? She could feel his arm against hers, the musky smell of his cologne. Was this really the same young man she treated so badly at the gym that day? She might have to try and change his mind about enlisting. After all, he had pursued her. Why would he do that knowing he was going to disappear from her life, maybe for good?

The bumps on the driveway to the cottage brought her back to the moment. She saw the glow from the window on the side of the house.

"Hmm." She ducked her head to look through the windshield. "See, I told you Pop would be waiting up. The light is still on in the kitchen, and I bet he's making hot chocolate. He loves his hot chocolate at night."

She wanted time to slow. It was nice to have a young man to talk to. Clark put her at ease by his casual straightforward manner, but her instinct told her the evening should come to an end. Her pledge to herself about not getting involved with a soldier played with her fondness for Clark. A game she couldn't play, or win.

The car came to rest near the front door. He reached to turn the key, but she stopped him, remembering the backfire.

"You'd better leave it running. I don't want to scare Mama out of a deep sleep with the sound of a cannon." She grabbed her pocketbook from the seat next to her and put it in her lap. "Thank you for a great time tonight. I'm glad we didn't stay at the dance. Those thugs would have probably bothered you again. As I said, you handled the whole thing better than me."

He opened his door. When he reached for her hand to help her out, he leaned close to her and kissed her soft and long on her right cheek. She felt her skin tingle. He pulled away and winked, then helped her slide over the seat and out the door. The engine hummed while he escorted her to the front door. The light from the kitchen extinguished, leaving only a small light in the living room. Martha tipped her head toward the house.

"Once he hears I'm home he sneaks off to bed." She shook her head. "Thanks again." She inhaled his cologne one last time. "Good night." She reached for the screen door.

"Good night. Can I call you tomorrow? No, wait, I have an appointment with the enlistment officer. The day after?"

There it was again. The cold reminder of his impending departure and army life.

"Sure." She shut the screen door. She opened her mouth to change her answer. She wasn't at all sure. In fact, she knew she should never see him again. She'd call him tomorrow and take the day to think of an excuse to cancel the date. "Well, I appreciate you answering my questions about your family. It's all very interesting. Good night."

"Thanks for asking. Night."

She stepped back into the darkness of the room and watched him through the picture window. He slipped into the idling car and backed it down the dark drive. This could be the last look she ever had of him. The thought stung, but her resolve had to rule over her heart. Feelings had to take a back seat.

"Play it safe. Don't get more involved. Tempting as it is, I could never be serious about this guy."

The argument rang in her thoughts as she crawled into bed. By the time she closed her eyes, she had rehearsed her speech three times. The only mystery left was how he would take rejection.

"I think you're making a big mistake, Martha." Clarissa wiped her hands on her apron. "And this newsprint is making my hands black."

"Here." Hana tossed a wet towel to Clarissa. "And I agree with Clarissa. He seemed really nice the day of our picnic."

Martha bobbed her head up to see over the pile of boxes

between her and her two closest friends. Neither of them had ever steered her wrong, but they didn't know what they were talking about. She'd have to break the news to them about their naiveté.

"You're ganging up on me. I'm right about this. I need to cut this thing off before it goes any further."

She sounded more convincing than ever, but her gut told her the others within earshot of her ramblings weren't fooled. These two women knew her too well.

She stood and weaved over to the table where Clarissa had been filling a box of trinkets for an hour, examining them one by one. Each had a story, and Clarissa took time to tell them all until Martha had interrupted with her date report. Hana leaned on the other side of the table, smirking at Martha.

"Don't give me that look, Hana. You really can't say much about it, Miss picky-about-men. Why don't you go out and fall in love with a soon to be soldier?"

Clarissa bowed her head and snorted softly.

"And you, Mrs. Wilding. Your husband is safe on the ground with his tractor and snippers and shears. He's in no danger."

Clarissa's mouth hung open. She glared at Martha. "You can say that after all that went on here about four years ago?"

Oops. "Okay, I'm sorry. Bad analogy. But you have to admit I deserve to be cautious."

Hana turned to face her, arms crossed over her chest.

"Cautious I'll give you. Paranoid is something else. What you deserve is to be happy and follow your destiny. How do you know Clark is not the one for you? Has God sent a letter from heaven telling you to run from love? It's time you settled down." She picked up another glass serving bowl and wrapped it in red checked seersucker fabric from Mama's remnant stash. "I just don't want you to throw away a good guy out of fear."

Fear? It wasn't fear. Just common sense. Didn't Hana know anything about anything?

Martha returned to her empty boxes by the bookshelf. "Now you're being silly. Besides, if I ran off with Mr. Jensen, what would you do without me?" She scrunched her nose at Hana, who forced a laugh before responding.

"You'd be surprised."

James stormed into the room and stopped short, looking around, searching the corners.

"What are you looking for?" Clarissa wiped beads of perspiration from her forehead.

James ignored her and squatted near one of the boxes of already-packed books.

His mood had been testy at best the last few days. Martha hated the hurt on Clarissa's face each time he snapped at her or ignored her altogether. She couldn't help butting in.

"James. I think your mother asked you a question."

He looked up at Martha, blankness in his blue eyes. He looked so much like William these days. His lanky limbs were strong and muscular now. Martha's heart lurched to wonder if Clarissa saw it too.

He turned to Clarissa. "Sorry. I wanna make sure you don't pack my Jenny manual."

Clarissa tipped her head. "Your what?"

"My Jenny airplane manual. I, uh, might want to read it on the train." His face flushed just like Clark's had last night when defending his love for flying. She wondered if they held the same secret passion. For his parent's sake, she hoped not.

She reached behind her back and grabbed the tattered bound book. "Here it is. I was about to seal it up in this box. Lucky you said something." She searched his face. He avoided her eyes and snatched it from her grip.

"Thanks. I'll put it in my satchel."

"Welcome."

He opened the front cover, fanning the pages with his thumb. His eyes brightened just as Clark's did when he talked about planes. Clarissa should have another talk with her son. Or maybe *she* should. He might listen to someone other than his mother.

Martha stood and shoved a wood crate with her foot. "How about helping me carry this box out to the porch with the others, young man?"

He looked up from the book. "Sure."

She jumped over a pile of books to be by his side. "I'll take one of these smaller boxes and go with you."

James's brows lowered. He hesitated, but then manhandled the crate to get a good grip, and marched toward the door. Martha scurried to keep up, her lighter load in tow.

She caught Clarissa's eye as she walked by her. "Get back to work, ladies. I shall return."

Clarissa's hesitant nod and pleading eyes were confirmation she had the right idea, even if James didn't think so.

He plopped the crate onto another one that had been nailed shut. "That it?"

Martha planted herself in his path. "No. Sit down."

Wide-eyed, James leaned on the porch rail and huffed a sigh. His eyes rolled with that annoyed expression shadowing his face.

"Okay, lean then." Martha took a seat on top of a side table. "I just want to chat a bit about what's bothering you."

"Nothing's bothering me."

"You mean right this second? Sure. But what about every other minute of the last several days? You're acting like you can barely contain your anger. Am I right?"

James looked off toward the barn. *He must be wishing his dad would call him over.*

"I'll get over it. One way or another. Sorry if it shows too much. I'll try harder."

He pushed himself off the rail. "Gotta go."

Martha held out her arm. "Hold on. I'm only concerned about your feelings and how they might be eating at you. I know you don't want to leave here, and you're dreaming of flying. I know someone else who has the same dream. But he's older and you still have parents who need you. Especially now. Will you try to remember that, and be more understanding of their feelings?"

His silence rattled her own temper. She loved this kid, but he was acting like a spoiled brat. "Can you?"

He jerked his head toward her to meet her gaze. "Sure. I'll try." He took one step and then softened his voice. "For as long as I can."

His boots pounded the dry dirt as he made his way to the barn. Martha shook her head, wondering what he meant by his last statement. Something twisted in her stomach, that small twitch that made her want to run after him and make him promise he wouldn't do what she suspected.

Mama walked from the driveway over to Martha.

"Hi, Mama."

Mama's brow glistened with sweat, following the deep wrinkles on her skin and down her temples. "You got a letter from Sister Clatilda." She held it out to Martha.

Martha's stomach tightened more as she fanned herself with the envelope. The possibilities of what Sister might have to say in a letter raced through her mind. Permanent termination. More enlistment physical duty. It had to be bad news.

Mama wiped her brow with the bottom of her apron. Martha looked her over and smiled at the sensible shoes Mama always wore, no matter how warm the weather. Even in the heat of this week, she would never dare wear sandals.

"Are you all right, Mama? Is the cottage cool enough for you?"

"Oh yes. I'm fine. Have to go finish my baking. I hope it's good news."

Martha frowned. "Good news about your baking?"

"No, no. Good news from Sister. Tell me later." She turned and hurried to the cottage, her apron ties waving behind her.

Martha shouted after her. "Don't get over-heated."

Mama waved over her shoulder.

Sitting on the steps, Martha leaned against the porch post. She flipped the envelope over in her hand. "Get it over with."

The plain hospital stationery wasn't fit for Sister's beautiful cursive. For a nun who taught simplicity and plainness, she had a flare for exquisite handwriting. Martha's eyes scanned the first paragraph. The usual greeting and inquiry into her health. Then the last paragraph grabbed Martha's composure and shook it.

We are so short of nurses, the board has determined it would be in the best interest of the hospital to reinstate you to duty, effective immediately.

It will be necessary for you to meet with the disciplinary panel to go over procedure and remind you of the rules regarding subordination and surgery room conduct. I hope you are able to report to me by Thursday.

Sincerely,

Sister Clatilda

Mama's wish came true. It was good news—at least it would be if she could be sure her self-control had permanently won over her bad temper and trembling hands. The image of that day in surgery flashed before her. Her knees threatened to buckle. What if they asked her to get right back into the operating room with that doctor? The thought of facing the panel made her knees buckle. It had to be done. She had created the situation and she had to face it.

Only humility would help her now. And maybe some prayer.

Chapter Five

May 1941

The children's ward bustled with activity, and Martha's uneasiness racked her body. She called upon her best concentration skills to get through each minute. Even though she was grateful to have her job back so soon, the unsettling of life still needled her. The fact that she had been reinstated at the hospital didn't remove the stain from her record. Although the panel didn't grill her extensively, the reprimand came in no uncertain terms. Sister Clatilda seemed to be satisfied after the meeting.

"I think it went well, don't you?" Sister Clatilda had asked Martha. The word *well* wasn't exactly the feeling, but she had nodded in agreement. Sister's next words had caused more anxiety than the panel's rebukes.

"You'll need to fill in on the children's ward the rest of the day."

Sister had walked away before she could see Martha's hands clench. The shaking that had caused her so much trouble returned, distracting her all day as she tried to focus on caring for sick little ones. The measles made the round at the schools the week before, but this week, severe stomach flu demanded more help from the nursing staff. The poor nurses could barely keep up with bedpans and emesis basins, the acrid smell overwhelming the large room and flowing like a fog into the hallway.

While Martha gave one eight year-old girl a sponge bath, she took a closer look at the attempt at décor around the room. Peeling cut-outs of large paper dolls and balloons covered one wall. The opposite wall held a long shelf lined with teddy bears and rag dolls. The thought occurred to her that the children might wonder why they could only look and not touch the temptations. They couldn't possibly know the toys were nothing but germ spreaders. A shame to tease sick kids with untouchable toys.

"Time for a break." A nurse coming on shift slipped alongside Martha and pulled the bowl of warm water toward her.

"Thanks."

In the break room several tired nurses took slow bites of sandwiches and sipped on coffee to keep them awake. Martha sat next to two new graduates she recognized from working at this ward before. They chatted about children and motherhood—about how terrible it must be to tend two or three sick kids at home.

Martha listened until that strong feeling bubbled up inside. "I don't want children," she blurted out. "I couldn't stand to see them die."

The statement caused a curious look from both nurses. One set her coffee cup down and frowned. "Why do you think a child of yours would die?"

Why indeed? It was a strange thing to say, and now Martha had to punt. "Because it seems like a lot of children drown—I mean die." She felt her face redden. She hated the glaring lack of logic from her own mouth.

The girls changed the subject and didn't include Martha in the rest of their conversation. She cringed, wishing she hadn't made the remark. She had to stop this nonsense. Thinking about children dying would only start her shaking again.

In another hour she was breathing fresh air, driving toward

the airport with the window rolled down, glad to be off duty. She felt on the brink of something, and wasn't at all sure the place she was headed would be a welcome change, but Clark had insisted.

The car bumped over a dried up rut in the road, reminding her of her present course. The steering wheel vibrated in her numbing hands. She loosened her grip and searched the dirt road to the airport about one or two miles in front of her. Sage brush and dried tumbleweeds lined a wire fence on one side and a six-inch stand of rich green alfalfa lined the other side of the road. She could smell the fresh cool aroma of the field. It seemed familiar.

"You shouldn't have agreed to coming out here. Why did you let him sweet-talk you into it?"

Her decision to break it off with Clark hadn't stuck. He was his usual persuasive self, asking for more time together. His happy personality and irrepressible positive outlook had convinced her he was worth overlooking her own insecurities, even though she knew full well about his chosen career—which could change if she had any say about it.

Still, the knot in her stomach grew with each turn of the road that brought her closer to the small airport. She had never been on this side of town. The low hills and blowing dust seemed a good place for an air strip, like something out of a movie.

Right now, the sun shone in her eyes, glaring off the windshield. Clark was up there somewhere. What if the sun were in *his* eyes? She stopped her thought process before she talked herself into turning around.

Hana was right, it was just a little plane, and flying lessons were no big deal. The instructor was always right by his side. What was there to be afraid of? Lots of men take flying lessons. It didn't mean a thing.

"Then why do you have the urge to step on the brakes? You

could find yourself a nice young man who wants to stay on the ground, couldn't you?" Her voice rippled in the wind whipping through the window.

The huge hangar structure came into view. The windsock hanging off a pole on the rusting metal roof puffed with air and stiffened in its warning salute. Wind. Wasn't that a bad sign? What if it blew that little plane right to the ground?

She pulled into the parking area and rolled up her window against the dust sifting in swirls through the flat acres. She shielded her eyes to look at the sky. There was the baby blue and white plane Clark had described, about to make a landing. How could two men possibly sit in that tiny space? As the aircraft approached, she could see that there was only one person in the cockpit. She stepped closer to the hangar to get a better look at the pilot. It couldn't be Clark. He said he had an instructor.

"Come on, son! Watch your cross wind."

The voice came from a hundred feet to her right. She turned to see an older man, gray hair sticking out of his cap and one pant leg rolled up half-way to his knee. She stared at him, but he didn't take his eyes off the plane for one second, like a moth to a flame. Martha stepped closer, glancing back and forth between the plane and this gentleman. Soon she was close enough to see the *Instructor* insignia on the back of his shirt.

"Up, man, up!"

Martha turned her gaze back to the plane just as it wavered, its wings dipping from one side to the other like a kite playing in the air. Her legs wobbled. The roar of the sputtering engine muted the hollering of the man who had now jogged toward the airstrip. His fists were clenched at his side.

The face of the pilot came into clear view.

Clark.

The man flung his hands into the air and made some sort

of large motion, a signal of some kind. Why didn't he do something? The sputtering worsened, and the wind picked up another cloud of dirt, sending it into the plane's path. Clark was going to crash. Martha could barely stand, and wished she hadn't moved so far from the car.

The man waved another signal and soon the plane's wheels had screeched onto the dusty strip. She covered her ears with her hands. Her blood drained from her face to think he had invited her to witness his own possible death. What was she thinking? Her instinct had been right all along. If she stuck with this guy, she would end up a widow.

Even though the older gentleman whooped and hollered, Martha didn't stay to join him in congratulating Clark. Biting her lower lip, she pulled open the car door and plopped into the seat. She would leave this ridiculous scene just as she had left the operating room that day. This time she didn't care what the repercussions would be. She never wanted to see Clark again.

The dust swirled behind the car as the tires spun, picking up pebbles from the road and pinging them against the back of the car. She moved the rearview mirror so she didn't chance seeing him. Her eyes stung with moisture. If she weren't hanging on so tight to the wheel, her hands would shake visibly.

She would certainly dream tonight—of planes crashing and bursting into flames. It would be *his* fault, but he'd never know, because she was done with him for good. This daredevil would have to find another female admirer.

Her heart fluttered at the thought of him chasing someone else. No matter. She didn't care. Or if she did, she would rid herself of that feeling as soon as possible.

When she pulled into the long driveway to the vineyard, her jaw ached from clenching. Mama sat on the porch, snapping her first small harvest of peas into a bowl. Pop sat next to her, a newspaper in front of his face. As she passed by them to park the car, neither looked up. That meant that neither saw her tear-stained, dust-caked face. All she needed was a minute to re-powder her nose.

After doing her best to look refreshed, she stepped out of the car and walked fleet-footed to the porch. Pop had left, leaving Mama with her small bowl of produce.

"Hi, Mama."

"Hello, dear. How was work today? You're later than usual."

"Work was good." In her present mood, she didn't regret telling a little white lie. She grabbed a snap pea and popped it into her mouth. "Nothing like fresh peas from the garden. I can't believe how early they came on, even though there aren't many yet. Good thing you planted early."

"Mm hmm."

Her rambling must have given her away. Mama's familiar question-laced face made Martha relent. She at least needed to tell Mama about breaking it off with Clark. If she got it over with quickly and decisively, there would be no prodding and no more discussion. If she spoke it out loud, she would have to stick with it, and could move on. A good plan.

"Mama, I won't be seeing Clark anymore. You know, the young man who took me to the dance? Nice guy but he's not my type."

Mama stopped snapping peas. Her hands rested on the edge of the bowl in her lap. "But I thought you really liked him. I was hoping to have him for dinner soon."

"I know. That's just the way it goes. These things happen. I don't need someone around who risks his life taking flying lessons and wants to go to war and probably get killed…" The tears burst through her dam of stubborn pride. She reached in her pocket for the already soaked hankie.

Mama set the bowl on the porch floor and folded her hands in her lap. "You're afraid of him dying? Just because he is taking flying lessons?"

Martha swallowed down tears. "Yes. You should have seen what happened today at the airport. He almost crashed. Well, it looked like he would anyway. I can't live like that. And didn't you hear what I said? He wants to join the army and fly big planes."

Mama peeked at Martha's hands.

"Did you work the children's ward again today?" Mama leaned back in her chair.

Martha sniffled. Mama obviously hadn't heard a word she had said about Clark. A dumb idea to bring it up, but next to God, Mama was always her most understanding confidant—the one who never pushed her to change who she was at her core.

"Yes. I did."

"You've been upset ever since. Before you went to the airport. Is that right?"

Come to think of it, Mama guessed right. "Yes. I suppose so. At the beginning of my shift there was a little girl who came into the special care ward. She almost drowned in her grandmother's swimming pool. It was very sad. I guess that's what set me off." She frowned at Mama, but couldn't shake off the amazement at almost forgetting about the little girl. "Can you blame me?"

The answer to that questions was obvious, but her instinct told her she wouldn't get let off the hook. There was something else, something that would bother her even if Mama supported her reasoning.

Mama bit her lower lip, a tear in her eye.

"I think I may know what's behind your worry—your night-mares. Been thinking about it all day."

Martha studied her mother's face. It never occurred to her that there could be a simple explanation to her problem. It didn't seem likely Mama would have any answers, and she wasn't in any mood for old wives tales.

"What do you mean?"

"I think it's all related to a childhood experience you must have forgotten. I don't know much about how the mind works, but I've heard that some memories can hurt you."

Martha stilled. It wasn't like Mama to entertain this kind of notion. Her education and worldliness were limited in scope, a simple woman who usually didn't put much stock in science or psychology. Yet, Martha wanted to hear more.

"What memory?"

"Do you recall that summer on the farm in Nebraska when Uncle Martin tried to teach you to swim?"

"No. Why?"

Mama rested her arms on the sides of the old rocking chair. Martha waited a moment for her to reveal what seemed to be an important secret. One she doubted could have any bearing on her dreams or whatever else had been haunting her.

"He meant well, but it just turned out bad." Mama's gaze was fixed on the bowl on the floor.

"What are you talking about, Mama?"

"You wanted to know how to swim and talked Rebecca into coming along. Uncle Martin agreed to take you through the alfalfa field by the house, out to the irrigation ditch. He told you both to jump in, but Rebecca was too scared."

A nervous twinge wiggled in Martha's gut.

Rebecca. The name sparked a vague picture of a younger Uncle Martin standing by the bank of a churning waterway. He had on dirty blue overalls and a blue shirt with the sleeves rolled up to the elbow. The water below him bubbled and sparkled the reflection of a hot sun.

"I don't remember anyone named Rebecca. Mama, I don't think I ever had a friend by that name."

"She lived down the road from us. You were both seven years old. She was a sweet thing and the two of you were inseparable." Mama's gaze seemed to be pleading her to remember. "Uncle Martin finally coaxed you both off the bank and into the water. He didn't know the current was so strong until it was too late."

Martha squeezed her eyes shut. Her temples throbbed as images flooded past her eyelids. She could hear a little girl's high pitched squeal. No, it was a scream. The images grabbed her senses. She could feel swirling frigid water pull her legs as she flailed her arms to get back to a muddy shore. Once she did, the sun warmed her cold wet limbs. Rebecca's voice shrieked her name, piercing her ears. In her mind, she scanned the murky water to see Rebecca's head slip beneath the rippled surface.

Why didn't I get off the bank to save her? Why didn't Uncle Martin move faster?

Mama continued the story as Martha tried to make sense of the memory as the terrifying scene flipped on and off in her head.

"Little Rebecca wasn't strong enough to stay above the water. Uncle Martin went in after her, but she disappeared. You ran with him down the side of the bank, but after several minutes, found her limp body wedged against the floodgate."

Mama stopped talking, but Martha couldn't open her eyes. If she did, she would break apart. Perspiration dripped from her temples as she finished reliving the scene. She could remember her small body shivering and shaking uncontrollably, and she felt the pebbles pressing on the soles of her bare feet as she ran.

Please, God, stop this horrible feeling. I remember her. Please tell me Rebecca lived.

Then the last few memories of the ordeal flashed through her mind as if on a flickering movie reel. Uncle Martin trudged toward the house with Rebecca's body in his arms, her dangling legs swaying in the momentum. He huffed and puffed as he hurried though the yard next to the barn. Martha could see herself running after him, pleading.

"Please put her down!" She had screamed. All she wanted was to stroke Rebecca's blond curls and tell her to wake up.

Uncle Martin laid her little friend on the sofa in the living room. He dashed to the wall phone in the kitchen. It jingled like a sleigh bell as he cranked the handle. Mama knelt by Rebecca as Pop pulled Martha away. She fought Pop's grip until they both fell to the floor. Hot tears dripped down her chin as she listened to Mama slapping Rebecca's back. Hard. Again and again. She buried her face in Pop's side for a long moment then turned to see if Rebecca had roused. Mama was crying as she pulled a patchwork quilt over Rebecca's gray face.

"Martha?" Mama's voice interrupted the horror, but Martha kept her eyes closed.

"I have no more memories of Rebecca after that day, Mama."

Tears flowed again when she finally dared to look up. Mama held her hand.

"I'm sorry, Honey. I hadn't realized you didn't remember the accident, but it might explain your problem. I suppose we should have talked about it over the years."

The porch had darkened in the shade of the Hawthorne tree's low-hanging branches. The sun had moved behind the house. They had been on the porch longer than Martha realized. A peculiar shiver tingled her arms.

Mama whispered. "Are you all right?"

"I'm not sure. Poor little Rebecca." She rose and pulled open the screen door. The cottage smelled musty from the swamp cooler. She hated that smell—wet and cold. Just like Rebecca.

Mama called after her. "Do you want some supper?"

"No thanks, not hungry."

As she closed the door to her room, her thoughts raced back to her conversation with the nurse in the children's ward. She knew now why she didn't want children, and she knew why she wanted to let Clark go. She would always worry—hiding from tragedy and death, but now she knew where the deep-seated fear came from. Little Rebecca—an accident that was no one's fault.

She opened the door again. She had to know something. Mama was in the kitchen when she went to look for her.

"Mama? I don't remember anything after—well after Rebecca died. Did her parents blame me? What did they say?"

A tear rolled down Mama's cheek. It would seem Martha wasn't the only one to be moved by that day and the memory of it. This was the worst part of Martha's fear—how long a death stayed with you, haunting your dreams, making you cry—and shake.

"We called someone to come and get the child. Her parents were there with her, kneeling beside the sofa where she lay. When they took Rebecca, her mother stayed behind. She pulled you onto her lap and held you while you both cried."

Mama wiped her face with her apron. "You kept saying, *I'm sorry, I'm sorry.* She just rocked you and said it was all right, not to worry. She said they knew Rebecca was in heaven, and that she was happy. She said Rebecca was probably dancing up there, twirling like a feather on a breeze. I can still see the mother's far off look."

Martha nearly choked on her emotion. "I don't remember that."

Mama nodded and reached for the coffee can. Her hands moved in slow motion, scooping coffee into the percolator. Martha shuffled back to her room. She sat on the edge of the bed and stared at the barn through the window—the barn that had burned, taking William with it. James's father—dead. How did her friend Clarissa deal with all the death she had endured over the years? Maybe like Rebecca's mom did. Martha wished she knew.

Perhaps she had found her own answer. Her hands were still. Maybe they wouldn't bother her anymore. Maybe death wouldn't taunt her now.

Clark fidgeted on the wood bench near the tree down the block from the hospital. The poplar leaves above him quaked in the warm breeze. His guts fluttered as if he were a boy again, waiting for his dad to take him behind the woodshed for a talking to. Funny how there was always more than just talk in those days. This was different. He hadn't done anything wrong, but he knew Martha would be upset with him just the same. He should never have asked her to come to the airstrip. Unlike the woodshed, this place might bring understanding, and this time he would have a chance to get out of trouble. A small one, but a chance.

He caught a glimpse of her trekking down the path. He stared at the ground and waited to look up until she was close, then the sun blinded him from seeing her face. Only the silhouette of her uniform distinguished her identity. Once she took a few more steps, he could see she wasn't smiling. He would have to fix that.

He jumped up to meet her. "Good morning."

"Morning."

"Thanks for agreeing to meet me." He gestured to the bench and brushed off a spot for her to sit. "How are you?"

"Good."

It was as if they were starting over again. As if the arduous effort of winning her the first time had been wasted and he sat here with a stranger. He opened his mouth to say something brilliant and clever, but she grabbed the moment for herself.

"I'm sorry for racing off the other day at the airport. I was pretty upset and I should have at least said goodbye." She crinkled her nose. "It was rude."

Her confession threw him off. He would have to change tactics. If she was in an apologetic mood, he would need to be smart about his response. Anything he said could be misconstrued.

"Well, I'll admit I was concerned when I saw the dust flying behind your car as you sped away. I thought maybe you had an emergency."

That was a lie. He knew exactly what had alarmed her so much. Letting her off the hook completely wouldn't solve anything, but carefully done, it could open the lines of communication.

"No. No emergency. I just… I didn't like seeing what I saw. You in that plane, looking as if you were going to crash. It just made me realize—"

"That you don't want to date a guy who risks his life in a plane. I get it." He prepared for another blow of rejection. Martha wasn't one to hold back.

She stared at her lap and nodded. "Clark, we are very different, you and me. You like to be in charge, take risks. I don't like being bossed around, and I like my safety nets. You like thrills and danger, and I like playing it safe at all costs. Knowing you're enlisting in the army and flying planes frightens me. When I saw you wobbling all over the sky, I knew your passion would be a deal breaker for me."

Clark leaned into the bench back, wondering if a debate would do any good.

"Martha." He cleared his throat. "I know it sounds cliché, but I'm more likely to be killed walking across a crowded city street. Aircraft accidents don't happen that often anymore. What you saw was something that occurs every day with pilots. We have to navigate the winds, and learn how to fly in all conditions. That's what eventually will keep me safe—learning to handle situations like you observed."

Martha's eyes narrowed. "I knew all that before I went out there. It's still a risk, and you can't tell me otherwise. I'm smart enough to know that lots of pilots get killed. And on top of that you want to fly for the army. What if there is a war? You'll be dropping bombs or something more dangerous. Being a war widow doesn't fit into my plans for the future."

Her face flushed as she broke off the last sentence. She looked away. *War widow?* Just the sliver of hope he needed.

"Maybe you should let go of *your* plans for your life, and ask God what He wants for you. I know I've had to do that."

She jerked her head to glare at him. "You think God wants you to go to war in a plane and kill people?"

His heart sank to his feet. He could take her remark one of two ways; she was crazy with paranoia, or she was fonder of him than he realized. The third option would be that something had her scared of death to the point that she couldn't abide by even the smallest of risks. Perhaps it was all three.

He leaned forward to rest his elbows on his knees. "I see where you're coming from. I'll warn you. I am what I am, and that includes going through with my enlistment. Boot camp is in a week. I'll be gone till Christmastime. I'm hoping you'll not give up on me. I care about you. A lot. I didn't expect to—especially after that day in the gym when you were so mean to me."

She threw her head back laughed. "Like I said before, you deserved it for disobeying me. I told you, I don't like being bossed around."

It was time to make his wish known and accept whatever answer she gave.

"I wish you would reconsider not seeing me again."

She turned sideways to face him. He braced himself for her brush off, but there was no armor against rejection of the heart.

"Clark. I have reconsidered—several times. It's been a long

couple of days on an emotional merry-go-round. Let me just shorten the story by saying I'm working on overcoming a fear due to something from my childhood. I want very much to get to a place where the fear of people I care about dying doesn't control me."

She raised her brows, her expression still.

What should he say? He had to understand her exact meaning. To his delight, she kept talking.

"I came to realize in the last few days that death can haunt you if you ignore it—pretend it never happened. My little friend Rebecca drowned in front of me when we were seven. I pushed the memory down until it ate away at me. It was dormant for years. Then it affected my ability to be a nurse, and apparently my ability to love anyone who could be a risk-taker." She tipped her head. "Does this make any sense?"

"Of course it does. How terrible that you had that experience."

"It's over now."

He couldn't suppress a grin. "I bet you were a spitfire of a kid."

She smirked. "That's a whole other issue. An understatement if you talk to my Mama and Pop. I have a temper you know."

"Not obvious at all."

She laughed and all the tension in his neck melted.

"So, are you giving up on us?"

"I wasn't aware there was an *us*. I don't know if I'm ready."

His heart ached. She was right next to him, yet seemed so far away. His efforts with this woman could all have been wasted time.

"I don't want to pressure you, Martha. I just wish you would give *us* a chance."

She looked away, and he waited until he thought he would run out of patience.

"I can't promise anything right now, but let's take it one day at a time." She stuck out her hand. "Deal?"

A hand shake just wouldn't do as far as he was concerned. His kiss would demonstrate he could turn her one day into a long gig. He placed a hand on each of her arms, but before his lips could touch hers, Hana called to Martha from down the path.

"Martha, come quick. It's your mom." She waved frantically and turned back to the hospital entrance.

Clark touched Martha's hand, but she pulled away and sprinted to follow Hana down the path. He grabbed the sack of untouched lunch and ran after them. His heart beat against his chest to think of the words just spoken about Martha's fear of death. The timing couldn't have been worse. Or was it perfect?

By the time he caught up with Hana and Martha, they were rounding the corner of the hallway behind the nurse's station. He stopped short, wondering if he should follow. He turned to find a chair. Hana whispered his name as loud as she could.

"Clark. Martha wants you to come."

The door to the exam room was open, and Martha was at her mother's side, her posture straight and face without emotion. Martha's father stood by Mrs. Watkins's bed. The room was cold and bare except for the bed and a small rolling metal cabinet.

Clark had never been fond of hospitals—so sterile. He had only met her parents briefly the night of the dance. How awful to meet them again under this cloud. He stepped back to listen to the conversation between Martha and a white-coated man he presumed was a doctor.

"We've removed the stinger. As you know, that's the first thing to do. Cold packs should bring down the pain and swelling. We didn't have to surgically intervene to ease her breathing. The oxygen mask seemed to be enough."

"Prognosis?" Martha's voice cracked.

Clark wanted to jump between her and the doctor to hold her and tell her not to give in to fear.

"I'll be honest. This was a close call. I understand she has had a few smaller reactions. It's wise not to tempt fate and to keep her away from anything that attracts bees."

Clark knew exactly what Martha and her dad were thinking. A vineyard and orchard was no place for a woman who could die from another run in with a bee.

And not the environment for Martha to get over her fear of death. Waiting for the next bee sting would get on his nerves if he were in her position. How terrible it must feel to know your parent was near constantly at risk. It was the very thing Martha had tried to explain.

He supposed most grown children start to worry about their aging parents sooner or later. Someday he would be in that place. At least he could go off to training in a week without worrying about his folks. Three months away from them—and Martha—would be his first real test as a soldier.

Chapter Six

July 1941

The porch chair creaked as she rocked. Martha pulled off her sweater. The summer sun had worked its magic on the rising thermometer. Spring had left in a hurry this year, forging a steamy wet path to summer. The dryness of the last few weeks touched the leaves on the apple trees and vines, leaving them thirsty for a good soaking rain.

Martha gazed at the empty windows in the big house. The tearful goodbyes from last month still ached in her chest. Soon, the harvest help Frank had rounded up for Pop would be roaming the vineyard and climbing the fruit-laden trees. How she would miss helping Clarissa serve meals under the big white oak in the yard. Her friend's departure left an empty lull at the farm Martha hated. The yard in front of the big house, now void of Hope's toys and mud cake station, was once again lifeless. Clarissa and her family had made it a home. Now it towered over the cottage like an institution longing for occupants.

Even Clark couldn't fill the place in her heart left by the family from Kansas, but her feelings for him were of a different nature. She just had to decide how strong they were. He had left her too, and over the last two months she had wavered over the risk she took falling in love with a fly-boy. There were times when she regretted letting her emotions run away.

She fanned herself with her first letter from Clarissa, still unopened, waiting to be cried over.

As she stuffed the sixth letter she had gotten from Clark in six weeks back in its envelope, she smiled. His promise to write every week had not been an empty one. She had written back each time, telling him of her progress at work, and how much she missed Clarissa and the rest of the Wildings. Her next letter would be news of Pop and Mama's decision to leave the vineyard after harvest. She'd be homeless—and very lonely.

She spoke aloud her hopes. "Maybe not for long if all goes well at Christmas. We'll see if Clark has a solution for that."

A deep rumble in the distant sky made her smile. The farm might get the much needed rain after all. She slit open Clarissa's letter and devoured its contents.

June 28, 1941

Dearest Martha,

How I miss you already. I meant what I said about coming to Kansas for a visit.

We arrived home after a long train ride. It feels strange to say home. Like a picture in a tattered magazine, everything around the homestead looked unchanged. The only signs of life were tall grasses poking up from the shorter sand piles on the lea of the house. A few more shingles had blown off the roof, and the dunes in the fields to the west had grown taller, leaving no fence-line visible.

Had it not been for the miracle of the little picket framed grave-yard, the scene would have crushed me. James was the first to see it. The white crosses were not buried in sand, and not a weed bothered the area inside the white fence. It was as if a protective bubble had covered it all the years we'd been gone. The thought occurred to me that Elijah had come by to take care of my little ones, but of course that's silly. He must be far away from here by now.

That first afternoon was spent sweeping, shoveling, and fixing...

"Martha." Mama poked her head out the door. "You need to come to the phone."

"I didn't even hear it ring. I was so absorbed in Clarissa's letter—"

Mama pulled her by the arm into the living room. She looked into Martha's eyes and touched her hand. Martha knew that look.

"It's Hana. Mr. Jensen... well, you talk to her."

Martha's heart dove to her stomach. Something was very wrong. She grabbed the receiver.

"Hana? What happened?"

"Clark's father was brought in early this morning. Heart attack. Martha, he passed away just a little while ago. You'd better come."

Her throat tightened as she tried to speak. "Sure. I'll come right now."

The phone jingled once as she slammed the receiver down. She slipped her hand into Mama's. "He died. Mr. Jensen died."

"I know. Hana told me. Do you want us to drive you?"

"No." She broke away from Mama and snatched her purse from the table by the sofa. "Mama, I barely know them. To them I'm just a girl Clark has been seeing. How can I help?"

"Just be there. It's all you can do."

"Right."

The soaking rain she had predicted pelted the windshield all the way to the hospital. Martha tried to rehearse in her mind what she might say to Clark's grieving mother. Was there family that would come? Did Clark know?

She pulled into the employee section of the parking lot and jumped puddles to race up the stairs to the reception desk. Nurse Ginny waved her on. "Room 115."

Martha's sandals squeaked on the white floor. She scanned her casual clothes. She hadn't even taken the time to change into a nice blouse. Hana appeared in the hallway.

"I'm glad you're here. Mrs. Jensen is alone in the family room."

Martha hugged Hana tight. Leave it to her thoughtful friend to arrange for someone to be with Mrs. Jensen. It would be a test of Martha's bedside manner, only in a different way this time.

Hana took Martha's hand. "The daughter lives in Portland and can't get here till morning. Their other sons aren't close by, and she didn't want me to call anyone. I thought Clark would want someone with his mom."

"Does Clark know? Is he coming? Maybe they won't let him out of basic training to come home."

Hana walked with her down the hall. "He was called right away by the chaplain and he indicated he could be here late tonight. I think his C.O. offered to fly him home."

"What's a C.O.?"

"Commanding officer."

Martha shook her head. "That's how much I know about the army. I'll be here when he comes—if Mrs. Jensen wants me to stay."

"I'm sure she'll appreciate you being here. She didn't want to leave until the funeral home came to get her husband. It will be at least an hour or two. There were several other deaths in town today."

Hana opened the door to the family room. Mrs. Jensen was not there.

"I thought you said she was waiting in here." Martha peeked around the door to see the corner of the room. How strange that worrying family members had to sit in a room as sterile as the rest of the hospital. No comfy chairs, no pretty drapes. Martha was glad Mrs. Jensen wasn't there.

"This is where I left her. I'll go check with the nurse's station. Hang on."

"I'll check the ladies room."

Hana's petite frame vanished down the hall and Martha headed in the opposite direction. The restrooms at the end of the corridor would be the likely place to find Mrs. Jensen. After a few strides, Martha passed room 115—Mr. Jensen's room. The door was ajar and low light lingered inside. A quiet murmur caught Martha's attention. She inched to the door and pushed it open. Her breath caught.

Mrs. Jensen lingered by her husband's sheet covered body, her right hand tentatively resting on his exposed arm. The dim light above the gurney skirted the shadows on his lifeless form. Martha couldn't move, watching her trying to bridge the gap between life and death. The woman's murmuring stopped and she reached for her purse sitting on the floor at her feet. As she did, she locked eyes with Martha's.

At first there was no recognition in her expression, then she squinted in the dimness before straightening up. A pensive smile spread gracefully over her face, and she took one step closer.

"Hello, Martha." She looked back to the body for a second. "I just had to make sure he was all right. He's really not here now. On to a better place." Her eyes pooled.

Words caught in Martha's throat. How could anyone who had just lost her life's companion look so peaceful? Any idioms of comfort she could conjure up wouldn't suffice. The moment seemed to call for a deeper expression. Martha crossed the gap of empty space and wrapped her arms around Mrs. Jensen's thin frame. The purse dropped to the floor as the woman embraced her with a warm response.

After a long moment Martha pulled away. "Let's go to the family room. I'll get you a cup of coffee." She took Mrs. Jensen's arm and led her out. Hana met them in the hallway and took the woman's other arm. Together they made their way to the waiting room. Mrs. Jensen stopped and stared at the window. Rain rippled its way down the glass, blurring the view of the cloud-darkened sky.

Martha wondered if Mrs. Jensen was thinking it was a lousy

day for a loved one to die. The sentiment sat on the tip of her own tongue. She expected to hear her say something sad, but instead Mrs. Jensen made a request.

"May I have tea instead of coffee?"

The tears Martha had been holding back leaked out now. Hana pulled tissues from her pocket and slid them behind her back to Martha as she pulled Mrs. Jensen to a chair.

"Of course. Tea it is."

As Hana hurried out the door, Martha blew her nose and took off her coat. Mrs. Jensen had only a light sweater covering her shoulders. The room wasn't warm, so she draped her coat over Mrs. Jensen's lap.

"This will keep you warm while you're waiting for the tea." She crossed her arms over her chest. "Are you all right? Do you need anything? Do you want me to call anyone? I'm so sorry this happened."

Don't rattle on.

Mrs. Jensen patted the seat next to her. "Just sit with me and tell me what you've heard from Clark. I know he writes you much more than he does his parents."

Martha's heart skipped a beat, but there was no reason to feel guilty. Mrs. Jensen's tone was gently reassuring. Even as her husband lay in the room down the hall, she appeared calm and controlled.

Martha sat. "He'll be here soon and can tell you all his news. He's a good man, your son."

"All my sons are good. Henry and I are lucky that way. Our daughter Leola is a sweet one too. Did you know she had a baby girl a few months ago?"

Her gaze moved to the window still streaked with rain. Martha took her hand and leaned back, letting the silence take charge. The clock ticked to 1 o'clock. Hana returned with tea in hand, one for Martha too.

"You girls all right in here? Can I get you anything? I'm on duty till three, and I'll come sit with you then." She leaned down to Mrs. Jensen. "We're still waiting on the funeral home. I'll let you know when all that happens."

Mrs. Jensen set her tea on the table next to her. "Thank you, dear. You've been very kind and a good nurse."

Hana smiled and patted Mrs. Jensen's hand. "I'm happy to be of help. I'll be back soon." She waved at Martha before dashing away.

Martha welled with pride. Mrs. Jensen was right about Hana. "She's a dear friend. Her whole family is nice. I'm glad she was on duty today."

"Japanese, am I right?"

"Yes. Her folks are in the Seattle area. I think she misses them."

A twilight of sun twinkled through the droplets on the window. Martha hoped the day would brighten just enough to take the edge off the sad atmosphere. She closed her eyes while Mrs. Jensen sipped her tea, and thought about how awful it would be to lose Pop. The day would come, and she hoped she would have the strength of Clark's mother.

She glanced at her hands folded in her lap. No shaking. Her stomach wasn't in knots. Her mind hadn't been racing. Fear had not gripped her soul today.

Time slipped by in silence. Mrs. Jensen seemed content not to converse. Then a familiar voice broke into the quiet.

"Hi, Mother."

Clark hovered in the doorway, his jacket soaked and his satchel dripping on the floor. Even in his grief, he looked more handsome than when she last saw him. His face was wet with rain, or maybe tears too. His hair had been buzzed quite short.

Mrs. Jensen stood and reached for him. "Hello, son. I'm so glad you're here."

The last thing Martha saw as she left the room was a mother

and son clinging tight to one another. It seemed to her that death had little sting at this moment.

Mrs. Jensen's faith and Clark's muscular arms would make a good stronghold against the pain they both felt. She could hear his voice as she made her way to the nurse's station, but the aching in her gut wasn't just for his grief. She knew the minute she saw him in the doorway what had happened in his absence—through all the letters and occasional phone calls. Everything had changed and she wasn't sure of anything anymore. Except for one thing.

She loved him.

The usually quiet little house on Pine Street had been a hive of activity all afternoon. Clark sometimes imagined the walls would creak if one more visitor came through the door. He had opened the windows in the living room and kitchen, hoping a breeze would cool the small space. His mother had asked him to clear away some of the clutter of floor lamps and side tables to make it easier for guests to move around.

The extra folding chairs the pastor brought were filled most of the time with people he didn't know. Clark had no idea his parents had so many friends, a fact that shamed him. The day had been a comfort to his mother, he could tell by her relaxed posture and generous embraces. She would be fine, and he would go back to boot camp without so much concern.

Watching Martha take charge and help behind the scenes, organizing and preparing food, Clark grew fonder of her by the minute. Her attention to his mother and friendly ways with the rest of the family sealed his decision to propose. When he first saw her in the family waiting room with his mother, it was the confirming thought in his head. She was the one for him.

His brothers would certainly approve. She had teased them

and listened to their stories without the slightest hesitation. His sister even joined in the laughter at his expense when Martha retold the story of his fainting in the gym. It lightened the sadness for a little while. He admired her talent for making people at ease.

It wasn't until everyone had left that he felt the letdown pour over him like an ocean wave. His jaw ached from smiling through all the greetings, and his body felt bruised from a hundred hugs from the women and slaps on the back from the men. How interesting it was to see how people coped with death, each one carrying their own burden of discomfort and awkwardness. The end of someone's life somehow made others look at their own mortality. He could see it on the faces of the older folks who came to call.

Now that everyone except his sister had left, the house could calm again. Once Pastor had taken Clark's brothers to the train station Martha helped put the house back in order. Clark studied the framed photos on the living room wall. Fishing buddies lined up by a boat—his dad in the middle, holding the 20-inch trout he bragged about for most of Clark's childhood. The longer he stared, the more he sensed his father's eyes on him, drawing him into the picture. How many times had he held that strong hand as they made their way to the creek down Jefferson Road? Then the hug around Clark's neck when he caught his first big trout.

His mother's touch on his arm startled him back from the past. "How are you doing, son?" Mrs. Jensen's eyes drooped, yet her smile remained.

Clark put his arm around her shoulder and walked her to the bedroom door. "I'm fine, but *you* are going to lie down for a while. Don't try to argue about it."

"I won't. I'm tired—I admit it."

"Here's your sweater, Mrs. Jensen. I think the rain might

have cooled off your bedroom." Martha was by his mother's side, sliding the sweater over her back. "I'll be going soon, so you take care and let me know if you need anything."

Mrs. Jensen reached back and patted Martha's hand. "Thank you, sweet girl. You were a godsend today."

Clark nodded at Martha as his mother disappeared into the bedroom. She shut the door quietly and he wondered how she would feel about sleeping in the bed she had shared with his father all these years. He never wanted to feel that alone, and life seemed especially short today. He took Martha's hand.

"Let's sit on the porch."

Martha scowled. "Hear the rain? It might be a bit damp."

"I don't care. We'll be covered. I need to get out of this stale house air. All those people sucked up our oxygen." He didn't mean to be funny. He really did feel closed in, even though everyone had gone. The lingering heaviness of sorrow leaned in on him.

They found a spot on the porch swing his father had built, and snuggled in. He could breathe deep now. The rain had already thinned to a slow dribble, and the sun filtered through the lattice behind them, creating a checkerboard on the porch floor.

It felt good to have Martha next to him. Months of only men to sit with wore on all the soldiers at camp. "I'm grateful for everything you did today. You were great."

"My pleasure… well, you know what I mean. I just hope your mother is going to be all right. I could have my mom come over to sit with her when you leave. I would, but I have to work."

He leaned his head on the back of the swing. The cooling air felt good on his face. He pulled the blanket up around his shoulders.

"What was it the minister said today about sorrow?"

"Wait, it's here in the program. I kept it." Martha reached in her sweater pocket and pulled out the folded paper. "It says;

And God shall wipe away all tears from their eyes; and there shall be no more death, neither sorrow, nor crying, neither shall there be any more pain: for the former things are passed away. Revelation 21:4."

Clark looked into her eyes. "Is that comforting to you?"

"Yes. I've heard it before. My friend Clarissa memorized it after she lost two children back home. She said it showed her God cared about our sorrow."

Clark believed the scripture with his heart, but his mind struggled at how it all worked. "I don't know."

"You're just tired and sad. I need to go so you can get some rest." She put her hands on the seat of the swing and leaned forward.

Clark caught her by the arm. "Not yet. I have something to say. It may be a strange time to say it, then again, it's the perfect time."

She squinted. "What are you talking about?"

"Life is short. Too short to waste. I love you. I think we belong together, and I want to marry you."

She eased back into the swing. Her arm tensed under his grip, so he let go. He waited for her to respond, but her silence persisted. He had sprung it on her, and now she was upset. It didn't matter—she had to know how he felt.

"Don't jump into accepting. I can wait… for a few more minutes."

His joke hung in the air. Had he misjudged her feelings for him? He stood and loosened his tie and top shirt button, his heart in his throat. "I guess I messed up. I'm sorry if I shocked you."

She looked up, her face as white as her blouse. "It's… it's just a surprise. Not a shock. We have some things to talk over before I answer, and today's not the day to do that. Our hearts are somewhere else today. Don't you agree?"

She was right. What a dope he had been to bring this up now. His grief had turned his emotions to mush and made him go overboard with his need for her. He should have planned this out with more thought. He knew better.

"Yes. I agree. I need a day or two with my mother to settle things. Then I'll come see you before I go back to base. Would that work?"

She nodded. A smile appeared at last.

He held out his hand to help her up. "You go home. And tell your folks thanks for stopping by earlier. I didn't get to talk to them much, but it was nice to see them." He winked. "I thanked them for providing me with such a lovely girlfriend."

She jerked her hand away. "You didn't."

He chuckled. "Okay, so I just told them you had been a big help the last few days."

"That's nice. Let me get my purse."

She hurried through the open front door and emerged with her purse under her arm.

He pulled her into a long kiss. She didn't resist, but didn't exactly fall into his arms. His chest relaxed when he saw her blushing smile. That and the kiss were something he could hold onto for a few days.

She patted his face. "Your turn to go lie down. Tell your sister goodbye. She took the baby upstairs before I had a chance. She'll be a comfort to your mom while she's here."

Clark helped her down the steps and opened her car door.

"I'll call you tomorrow," he whispered to her. "Think about what I said?"

"Yep." She turned the key. "I will."

The rain dripped off the tree onto his head and a shiver ran up his back. He needed a nice sunny day tomorrow. He searched the sky for clearing. The dissipating clouds would soon let the sunset glow over the housetops. Someday he would be able to soar straight into a sunset as soon as the army helped him finish his flight training.

His eye dropped to the horizon, the Blue Mountains barely visible through the mist. They seemed a world away.

"Where are you Oma and Opa? You don't even know you've lost a son."

He could hear Leola playing with the baby upstairs. She would have to leave soon too. At least she would take their mother with her. His father would be at peace to know she wasn't alone. He gazed one more time to the bluing sky, and he wondered if his dad was off fishing up there.

"Night, Dad."

Hana fumbled the bottle of rubbing alcohol in her hand, but recovered before it hit the floor. "He what?" Her mouth hung open.

"Proposed."

"Stop teasing me."

"I'm not. We sat on the porch swing after his dad's funeral and he popped the question." Diving into a conversation with Hana about the proposal might bring to light the issue Martha wanted to share with her friend. She needed advice, and Hana would be brutally honest with her about Clark's future in the air.

Since the day of Mr. Jensen's death until now, she had handled her fears brilliantly. Outward manifestations were at a minimum and for the most part, she was able to concentrate on what needed to be done without dwelling on the fact that someone had died. Progress, but not complete victory. She dealt with death on a daily basis at the hospital, but those patients were strangers. The merry-go-round of reasoning sometimes wore her out.

The proposal had distracted her to the point she could think of nothing else but Clark's choice to fly with the army. She didn't know if she wanted a way out of his life, or wanted an excuse to stay in.

"The day of the funeral? Doesn't that seem a bit strange to you? Four bottles of alcohol. Two bottles of mercurochrome."

Martha scribbled on the clipboard. "Got it. Sort of strange. You have to know Clark. He's a decisive man. He takes stock of situations and chooses the best course of action. Very matter of fact, but I'll say he has a certain romantic flare. Then he talked about how short life is. He's very thoughtful about life. Very sensitive."

"Sounds like you like him. But do you love him?"

Martha stared at the cabinet in front of her. She had been questioning her feelings since he proposed. She knew the answer, she had known it when he came to the hospital. But saying it out loud would harden the concrete mush of her feelings.

"I guess so."

"You *guess* so? Martha, you can't just let this slide. Clark wants to marry you. It's decision time. You'll have to answer him from your heart." She slid a box full of aspirin bottles across the counter. "This is the last box."

"Good. Sister Mary Margaret will be pleased."

"So?"

"So what?"

Hana shoved the box away from her and touched Martha's arm. "Do you love him? Do you want to marry him?"

She willed the answer off her tongue. "Yes I do. But…"

Hana's brows raised. Her wise friend would be straight with her, but that wouldn't solve the main issue. Flying. War. Death. All the topics she hadn't yet discussed in depth with Clark.

She opened another cupboard door. Empty. Supplies were low. They had to get the inventory to Sister Mary Margaret this morning, and Martha's coffee energy had thinned. She re-focused on Hana's lecture.

"There will always be doubts in any big decision. You pray, you think, you feel, you make a decision based on what you know is the truth. You love him. He loves you. You want a life with him. He doesn't have any major flaws does he?"

"One."

"Really? What?"

"He is determined to fly. Even though we may go to war someday and he could die a terrible death, he can't think of anything else."

"That's funny. I know someone who risks their life every day in her job and doesn't think anything of it."

Martha leaned back. Who was she talking about? Hana's smile gave her away.

"How do I risk my life being a nurse?" Martha scoffed.

Hana returned to the aspirin box and tapped on the top of each bottle. "Twelve aspirin bottles."

"Got it. Now tell me." She glared at Hana while she stacked the bottles in the cabinet.

When she finished, Hana looked around the medication supply room. "Martha, we deal with chemicals, contagious diseases, delirious and violent patients, sometimes long hours that make us so tired we shouldn't be driving home, and sharp objects that could slice off a finger. I know that sounds trivial compared to flying a plane, but anyone could die from even the least of risks."

Martha pulled in a breath. The room smelled of disinfectant. If only she could sterilize her world—free it from obstacles and fear. It would be easy to say yes to Clark. The truth in Hana's words echoed his rationale. She could hear phantom agreements from Mama and Clarissa.

"Okay. I get it. I'm thinking. And praying. And feeling my way through. He's wants my answer tomorrow. I know he's anxious to know before he goes back to finish up basic. I should talk to Sister about it, huh?"

"Talk to me about what?" Sister Mary Margaret bounced

through the doorway. Her usual scowl made Martha's heart sink. She obviously thought Martha had mentioned her. It was Sister Clatilda she needed, not crotchety Sister Mary Margaret. *Now what?*

"Good morning, Sister," Hana broke in. If anyone could soften this nun's mood, it would be Hana Kato, queen of sweet talk.

"Is there something I need to know? Something wrong?"

Hana and Martha looked at each other, both knowing a lie would not go unnoticed. Martha took the lead. What harm could it do to tell Sister about the proposal?

"I was just telling Hana that my young man has proposed. I was going to get counsel from Sister Clatilda. That's what we were talking about."

Sister didn't miss a beat. "You're too young. Young men these days aren't prepared to raise families. You should wait until you're older. Sister Clatilda would say the same thing."

The look of disbelief on Hana's face sparked a giggle in Martha. She couldn't hold it back, even after Hana nudged her in the ribs.

"My point proven." Sister spun around and marched away.

Martha covered her mouth with her hand. Hana nudged her again. "What is the matter with you? You made Sister mad."

The giggles dissipated. Sister's words hung in the room, solemn and sharp. What if she were right, and what if Sister Clatilda agreed? Her stomach knotted to think she was on the brink of making the wrong decision. She felt as though the air had been sucked from her lungs. Then another feeling... sadness.

"Don't you mind what she said. You know better, and just remember the source. I think you know Sister Clatilda would say what I have said, what your mom would say, and Clarissa too. You already know your answer, my friend. You just need to give it life."

The heaviness lifted as she weighed the advice. It was

ultimately her call, her life, her emotions. "I know my answer. I'll tell Clark tomorrow."

Hana turned off the light and shut the door behind them. "There's a phone in the hall. Why wait?"

"How do you know what I'm going to say?"

Hana shrugged and patted her stomach. "I'm hungry. I'll save you a seat at the cafeteria."

Martha's feet felt stuck to the floor. The clock read 12:45. Clark's mother and sister would be on the train by now. He would be home.

She tingled from head to toe, and the sensation released her feet to move. She shuffled down the hallway to the phone on the wall by the elevator. The receiver was cold in her sweaty hands, and she held on to it for several moments before dialing Clark's number. The rings buzzed in her ear—two, three, four rings. He wasn't home. Five, six. Just as well. After thinking it over himself, he may not want to hear her answer. Seven, then *click*.

"Hello?"

She gulped in air at the sound of his voice. No turning back.

He repeated his greeting. "Hello?"

No, she had to do this. Now.

"Yes."

"Martha? Is that you? What did you say?"

"I said yes."

Clark took off his uniform jacket and draped it over his satchel. Only a few minutes to say goodbye. He had barely seen Martha since she had accepted his proposal. They were both busy—he with packing more things to send to his mother and Martha with her job.

Martha straightened his tie. "The next few weeks will go

fast. I hope I can get everything done in time for an August wedding. Won't be anything fancy."

He felt a twinge of guilt. "Are you sure you don't mind a small wedding? And we could still have it at the church if you would rather."

She shook her head. "Nope. I want it on the vineyard. I know the weather might be a little warm, but it's so beautiful—and handy. Do you think your mother will mind it not being a church wedding?"

He wasn't about to burst her happy bubble by repeating his mother's wish for the church option. "She's fine with it. Like you said, it's beautiful. I like keeping it simple and small since we don't have much time."

The train rumbled the ground like a small earthquake. Time had slipped away, leaving them with the same sadness as all the other couples at the station. Martha pulled her purse off her shoulder and dropped it on the ground. Her eyes filled with tears.

"Don't cry. I'll be back soon." He kissed her forehead. "I know everything has moved pretty fast. I don't want you to feel pressured about the wedding."

"I don't." She sniffled into her tissue.

The train had stopped and the rush of people getting off had slowed. He swallowed down his own tears and grabbed Martha by the shoulders. He kissed her hard and long, and then pulled away. Before she could say anything, he marched off with his coat and satchel swinging from his hand.

He turned on the run and hollered to her. "I love you."

"Love you too."

She was still standing there as the train moseyed away from the station. This would be the first of several goodbyes. He wondered as the landscape raced passed his window if one day he would be saying goodbye to her *and* America's shores.

Too many ifs to think about. He would sleep all the way back to base and dream of Martha, and a wedding overlooking the vineyard.

Chapter Seven

Aug 30, 1941

The minister droned on, talking about the institution of marriage. She was too nervous to listen, even though she knew his words were important. The rows of vines brought their own flavor to the event—a perfect backdrop. The fragrance of rich earth and ripening fruit created a festive atmosphere everyone could enjoy. Even now it captured Martha's attention as she pretended to look at the man in the black suit. Behind them sat family and a few close friends. Pop had taken great care to set up chairs in perfect rows. The grass beneath their feet came compliments of Clarissa's insistence that Frank plant a grassy area beside the big house.

Most brides would have dreamed of a big church wedding, white dress, and three-tiered white cake. But everything was perfect here, right down to her blue tailored suit and Clark's meticulous dress uniform. Martha savored the smell of lilacs and Mama's prized roses, then closed her eyes against the sun. In a few moments, she would be Clark's wife, his *co-pilot for life* as he put it.

"You may kiss the bride."

Her eyes popped open and Clark's grin made her giggle. He brought her close, grasping her waist with tenderness. His kissed her softly in a long embrace. She grabbed his lapels and kissed him back. They both laughed as the group behind them erupted with cheers and clapping.

As Clark took her hand and held it high with his, she noticed Pop wiping his nose with his white hankie. No tobacco stains today. Mama nudged him and headed straight for her newlywed daughter. Martha let go of Clark's hand and kissed Mama's soft cheek, so proud that her mother had stepped out of her comfort zone to buy a fancy dress for the occasion.

"I'm happy for you, honey. I'll get the food out now."

She broke from Martha's arms and hurried toward the cottage back door. Martha shook her head. So like Mama to worry about the food, and for Pop to take care of enough blubbering for both of them. Clark hugged his mother and then she reached for Martha, pulling her to his side.

Mrs. Jensen patted Martha's arm. "You're very lovely today, dear. A nice simple wedding in the perfect place."

"Thank you, Mother Jensen. I'm so glad Leola could join us and bring baby Carol."

"Yes, me too." She turned toward the cottage. "I need to go help your mother. You greet your friends."

Friends. The one friend there was her maid of honor and assistant wedding planner, Hana. If only Clarissa could have been here—how perfect the gathering would have been. At least some neighbors had attended at Pop's invitation. Someone standing behind her tapped her shoulder.

"Here's your bouquet, Mrs. Jensen." Hana's red eyes betrayed her. Until today, Martha had never understood why all the women cried at weddings.

"You were the ideal maid of honor." Martha took the small bundle of roses and threw her arms around Hana's shoulders.

"Did I tell you how much I'll miss you?"

Hana nodded. "About twenty times." She wiped another tear from her cheek. "I'm due at the punch table. See you in a bit."

Clark sauntered up to her side and reached around her waist. "I'm starving. I need some of your mother's potato salad. Now." He grabbed her hand and pulled her toward the cloth-clad table covered with all of Mama's special goodies and a large bouquet of white lilacs. The wedding cake sat off to one side—angle food with meringue frosting, topped with strawberries.

"Clark, there's a phone call for you." Pop waved from the top step off the back door. "Colonel somebody."

Martha set down her half-filled plate. Her heart pounded in her ears. Military life wasn't supposed to invade their wedding. They had five days of honeymoon before Clark had to start infantry training at Fort Knox. So far away. He'd be there for so many months, and she would be a lonely newlywed.

Clark kissed her cheek. "It's probably nothing. Be right back."

She wanted to run after him and listen to the conversation. It didn't matter. Whatever Colonel whoever had to say, Clark would tell her.

"When are you going to cut that beautiful cake?" Hana snatched a black olive from a bowl on the table.

Martha thoughts jolted back to answer Hana. "As soon as Clark is done with his phone call. Mrs. Jensen baked it for us. It should be scrumptious." She pulled off her jacket. "Whew. That is if it doesn't melt first."

Hana shifted from foot to foot, a sudden look of uneasiness covering her face.

Martha folded her arms across her chest. "Okay, out with it. What's going on behind those dark eyes of yours?"

"I didn't want to tell you today, but I don't have much choice with you rushing off soon for that thing called a honeymoon."

"Tell me what?"

"I'm leaving the states and moving to Hawaii. There's a clinic on one of the islands near a place called Pearl Harbor. Some of my family are there—mostly cousins. I wanted to do something different."

Martha's happy heart developed a sudden crack. Her best friend wouldn't be just a few states away. She would be clear across the ocean. Another goodbye to suffer through.

"But why go so far away? Why Hawaii?"

"Well, why *not* Hawaii?" Hana's plastered fake smile jarred Martha. "I just don't want to go back to the Seattle area. There's been so many changes there for our Japanese American community."

Martha knew what she meant. She had read in the papers how tensions were escalating among the farmers over there. She hadn't paid much attention, but now it had affected her, causing her friend to run so far away.

"I can't believe it. I don't know what to say. I'm happy for you, I think. Just sad for me."

Hana reached out and hugged Martha tight. She whispered in Martha's ear. "We could never be far apart really."

Tears stung in Martha's eyes as Hana released her. She grabbed a napkin from the table and blew her nose. Clark's arm was around her shoulder before she realized he had approached.

"What's going on here ladies? A sappy farewell?" He nudged Hana, who nudged him back.

"Sort of," Hana mumbled.

Martha wadded the napkin. "I'll tell you later. What was the phone call about?"

Clark looked back and forth between Hana and Martha. "I've been called to base a little sooner than expected. I'm afraid we will have to cut the honeymoon short."

Hana's hand pressed against her mouth.

Martha un-wadded the napkin and held it to her eye. "What are you talking about? They can't do that. When do you have to be there?"

"In three days. I've been chosen to help set up a new tank training area." He took a step back. Did he think she was going to hit him? Leave it to the stupid army to ruin her honeymoon.

"It's kind of a good thing. Gives me a leg up for Officer Candidate School, and the Colonel left tickets for us to take the train tonight. Better than driving." He wrapped his arm around her. "I'm sorry. It can't be helped. But they got us a nice bunk suite for the trip. That's something at least." He grabbed her hand and squeezed it. "We could get room service."

She saw right through his attempt to butter her up. "Do I get a nice bunk suite for the ride home after you report to your tank thing?"

"I'll see what I can do."

Hana touched Martha's arm as she inched toward the punch table. Martha thought her chest would burst. She could feel the pulse in her neck. She walked away—slowly at first, then marched around the cottage to the front porch. She passed Mother Jensen—her mouth open to say something.

Sitting on the porch, the tears came in full force. She hated crying. What good did it do, except relieve the tension she had penned up all day? She didn't believe in omens, but if she did, her newly diminished fears would be at an all-time high soon. *Why can't things just stay the same?*

A small blue flowered plate with an enormous piece of anglefood cake invaded her space. "You missed the cutting of the cake." Clark's voice didn't help to calm her, but she huffed and took the plate.

"Nice." She scooped up a bite and shoved it in his mouth as he opened it for what she expected would be a rebuke for disappearing. White frosting dripped off his chin. He slid his finger over the goo and planted it on her nose.

A low giggle was all she could muster. "This has been a most unconventional wedding, Mr. Jensen."

"I don't mind. I'm just sorry we'll have to make do with an unconventional honeymoon. Two days on a train isn't what I had in mind. I say we get going. We can stop by your place and unpack all the things we don't need to take now."

She wanted to whine, but thought better of it for Clark's sake. He must have sensed her inner complaints.

"Maybe we'll find you a nice hotel to stay an extra few days before you come home. I might be able to sneak away to spend some time with you. It's only orientation for the first few days. Then I'll put you back on the train for home."

Home? It wouldn't be *their* home. And what a lousy prospect—holing up in a hotel waiting for her man to steal time for her. Then it would be a long train ride home to an empty bed. Not her ideal beginning to a marriage, but it was all she had. Her mother and friends would tell her to make the best of it.

She looked up at him, his face still smudged with frosting. She pulled him close and kissed it off. "I say we get out of here before someone else throws another wrench into our day."

They hurried arm in arm to the yard where everyone mingled around the food table. Pop waved them over and said something to the rest of the group she couldn't hear. They were probably hoping to gather around and take turns wishing the newlywed couple well, but there wasn't time.

Mama edged over to stand by Pop. Martha recognized that look. Something was up.

"Mama?"

"We have an announcement to make," Pop said. Everyone turned to face him. "Mama and I have bought a farm in California. We'll be moving right after harvest. It's what's best for Mama and her bee allergy, and we would like a change now that our daughter is leaving us."

The oohs and ahs from the small gathering were nothing

compared to the shock jagging through Martha's stomach. She froze for a moment, then raced to Mama to hug her.

"Good decision. I'm glad, but I wish you'd told me. Is everything in order then?"

Pop answered for Mama. "Everything is arranged. George has a new man coming soon to take over. We didn't want to bother you with all you had going on."

All she had going on. She looked around the group wondering when she would see any of them again. Hana would be in Hawaii, the folks in California, Mother Jensen in Portland, and her dear friend Clarissa back in Kansas. How scattered she felt at this moment. When she returned, she would only have a little time to spend with her folks.

As well-wishers hovered around Mama and Pop, Martha whispered to Clark.

"I'd like to go now. Please?"

He pressed his forehead to hers. "You bet. I'll get the car ready."

Hana pulled her elbow as Clark jogged off. "Let's get you ready. Want to change?"

Martha looked down at her new suit. "No, don't want to take the time." She blew out a breath between her lips. "And I'm exhausted already. A quick change would do me in."

Hana gave her a quick squeeze. "I'll miss you, but I'll be busy getting ready to leave myself. We'll talk more when you get back. I'll meet you at the train."

Hana leaving. She always knew this day would come, but couldn't have imagined Hana would be on a tropical island.

Clark returned. "All packed."

The sea of waving arms in the rearview mirror made Martha laugh. If someone had told her six months ago that she would be driving away with a soldier to a honeymoon on a train for Kentucky, she would have scoffed.

"You okay, Mrs. Jensen?"

117

Mrs. Jensen. "Yep. Just tired. How about you?"

"Tired and hungry. Your mom's potato salad has worn off. Steak on the train?"

The thought of spending energy to eat in a train car brought out a smirk. "Only if it's from room service."

"You got it. Only the best for an army wife."

Her heart skipped a beat. Yes. She was an army wife. Just what she said she'd never be, but *had* to be if she wanted Clark. And she did.

Martha jolted awake at a sudden movement. Grabbing Clark's arm in the darkened train car, she sat up straight.

"What happened?"

"Train jerked a bit coming into this town."

"What town?"

"Not sure. Somewhere in South Dakota, I think."

Martha tried to look at her travel clock, but as dark as it was, she could barely see her hand. She sat up and pulled Clark's watch to her face.

"Five-thirty? Why are you awake? Are you all right?"

Clark laughed. "You've been snoring. I didn't wake you because I knew how tired you were, and I'm fine. Any more questions?"

"No. Some wedding trip. At least we get steak every night."

She snuggled close to him. The army had already infringed on their lives and they'd only been married two days. She gritted her teeth and dismissed the fluttering in her chest. Sooner than she expected, Clark would be playing with guns and tanks—probably every day. This train ride was as good a time as any to find the courage she needed.

She switched on the overhead light and grabbed her purse from the floor. Finding a compact, she examined her mussed face. It was worse than she thought.

"Nice look for a honeymoon. Sorry, husband."

"No need to apologize. I'll have to get used to scruffy looking faces if I'm going to live in a barracks."

She slugged his upper arm with her fist. "Thanks a lot."

She sat up and pushed back her black waves of hair from her forehead. He fluffed the pillows behind her and lifted the shade on the window. She gazed at the shadows of landscape whizzing by. Ribbons of wispy clouds played around the full moon lighting the sky. The train had crept out of the station in wherever-town and moved fast enough now for the clip-clap of the track beneath them to start its rhythm.

"Martha, I want to talk to you about some things."

"What things?"

He sighed hard. "Well, like what you're going to do while I'm gone. I worry about you."

She tipped her head. What was he worried about? He should know by now she could take care of herself. Her face felt hot.

"Don't get all man-has-to-worry-about-wife on me. I can manage on my own. Just because I have a husband doesn't mean I'm dependent."

He scowled. "I didn't mean that exactly."

She sat up straight. "Then what did you mean?"

His lip curled up on one side. "Martha. Why are you so defensive? I'm just making sure you have a plan and will be all right."

It never occurred to her that he would want to have a say in what she did and where she went. It struck a sour chord, and she had to bite her lip. She had to let him feel a part of her life, no matter how much she didn't like suggestions on what to do. But it was the same in reverse. She had insisted in knowing his track for the military, hadn't she?

"Okay, tell me what you see me doing while you're away."

Clark cleared his throat. "Well, I had hoped you would help

my mom pack her things when she moves permanently to Leola's place. They will still be at the house when you get back. And we do need the extra money if you could continue working some. Then you'll come to see me at Christmas at Fort Knox. Maybe even come in early December and stay for a while. That's where the extra money comes in."

He rubbed his chin. "Then you can…"

"You sure have it all worked out, don't you." She crossed her arms. The fact was that he had called it as she saw it too. She should have said so first to have the upper hand.

Clark leaned away from her. "What don't you like about my ideas?"

She threw her legs over the mattress and grabbed her robe from its hook. She rested her hands on her hips. "Probably nothing. I can live with it." *Let him think he runs the show.*

The truth was, she liked the way he wanted to take care of her, even though it pressed against her sense of independence and control. Then once he was out of the army and they could live a normal life, things would even out again. For now she could do this army wife role.

She slid her feet into the slippers Hana had given her as part of her trousseau. The train waggled a bit, throwing her off guard. She found herself sitting next to Clark again.

"Okay, I can go with your suggestions. I just can't wait till we set up housekeeping somewhere. You know… build a home of our own."

Clark smirked. "Like out in the country, right?"

"Sure. Why not?"

"I don't mind as long as we have room for an airstrip."

There it was. The pilot in him invading their happy little place in the country. All she could do was hope he would grow out of that phase before his mandatory one-year stint was up. She opened her mouth to change the subject when the train squealed against the track, obviously coming to a quick unscheduled stop.

Clark jumped off the bed and grabbed his robe. "What in the world?"

Someone rapped on the door of their cabin.

Clark opened it to see a porter ready to bolt down the corridor. "Train wreck down the line. We'll be delayed. People hurt…"

His voice faded as he reached the next door and issued the same edict for a shaken older woman.

Martha immediately began to dress. She threw clothes out of their suitcase to find trousers and a blouse.

Clark touched her shoulder. "What are you doing?"

"You heard him. People are hurt. I'm a nurse. I need to go." She pulled on the wrinkled trousers from the case and slid into some brown loafers. She grabbed her sweater from the end of the bed.

"You can't go out there. Who knows if it's safe? Let's find out more about it."

"I'll find out more when I get there." She paused and looked into this eyes. "Clark. This is what I do. I'm obligated to help someone in need, and I want to."

Clark took a step back, frowning. "I know. I just don't like it. It could be dangerous."

She stopped moving to stare at him and touch his arm. "Now you know how I feel."

He opened his mouth, but looked away. She had struck a nerve. He sat on the bed and pulled his robe off his shoulders. "I need to find out how long we'll be delayed. Will have to call my C.O. if it's very long. Sure hope it's not too serious." He held her in his gaze for a moment.

"Me too."

While Clark dressed, Martha stepped into the tiny closet-like bathroom and looked in the mirror. Her white face betrayed her emotions. What if there was a child among the victims? She closed her eyes. *Don't think about it.*

"I'm ready. You?" Clark looked her up and down. He hugged her tight. "You'll be a great help, nurse Jensen."

Martha mumbled a plea to God for mercy as she headed for their door with Clark. Surely there would be a doctor aboard to assist the wounded. They ran down the hall to the outside landing between cars. Once down the steps, Martha could smell smoke and gasoline. Her nose burned. Clark covered his mouth with his shirt collar and bolted off in the direction of the conductors standing away from the tracks.

Martha made her way toward the steaming wreckage several cars ahead of the engine car, on a perpendicular set of tracks. Her shoes slid on the slippery gravel between the iron railings. She moved forward until she reached a small crowd of onlookers and porters. She had a strange urge to laugh at the passengers from the train who stood in their pajamas in the cool evening. The picture would have made a good headline, an irony of imagery.

She heard shouting from within the group. Something about not moving someone and needing more help. Martha's heartbeat ramped up as she pushed through several stunned people lingering close by. They parted for her until she halted at the sight of the wreck. A train on the other rails crept to a stop, and a car smashed to bits lay on its side just off the tracks. A crossing sign still blinked its angry red warning, and to her left a broken red and white guard arm lay in pieces—strewn across several yards. The light from the engine car blinded her when she turned.

"Is there another doctor here to help me?" A familiar voice broke through the clamor of train noises and conductors hollering instructions.

No. It's impossible.

Martha inched forward, keeping her eyes on the man crouched next to the victim. She crept around pieces of greasy metal to face him. Her knees buckled to see Dr. Turner working feverishly to tend to a chest wound on a young woman. The same Dr. Turner who had kicked her out of his operating room all those months ago, the cause of her suspension. Of all the trains in all the states tonight, he had to be on this one. She pulled some air into her lungs, nearly choking on fumes and smoke.

She knelt beside him. "I can help, doctor."

He tore at a white shirt someone had tossed his way, then threw it at her without looking up.

"Rip this into strips for a bandage on her arms and legs. I really need a doctor." He looked up and searched behind her into the crowd.

"I'm a nurse."

He jerked his head to look at her face and paused before answering. "Well, that's at least something. Help me get her blouse off and give me your sweater."

She scrambled to pull it off. He rolled it up and placed it under the patient's neck. "I checked for spinal injury as best I could. I have to get this bleeding to stop or it won't matter if her spine is involved."

Martha nodded, her throat clogged. She ripped at the shirt until she had all the bandages she could tear from it. Her insides jiggled as she handed them to Dr. Turner. "Doctor, will these do?"

"Yes. Follow my lead and I'll show you where to apply pressure. You know what to do, right?" He looked at her again, with his brows knitted.

"Yes. I know what to do." He hadn't recognized her. Yet.

They worked together for what seemed hours. Martha didn't know where Clark was and didn't have time to look for him. After a while, Dr. Turner shifted position.

"I think she's stable." He pulled out a pen light from his pocket and lifted the woman's eyelids. "So far anyway."

A siren blared in the distance. Martha sat back on her hip, resting with one arm on the ground and the other hand on the women's wrist to monitor her pulse. She kept her head down, hoping he wouldn't figure out she was the nurse who bailed on his amputation procedure.

Dr. Turner rose from his position. The woman groaned and Martha leaned in close. "You're going to be all right. The ambulance is here."

The woman's eyes fluttered open. A tear dribbled down her temple onto Martha's sweater. She stroked her patient's blood-streaked arm, wondering if she had little ones at home waiting for her.

"You had a doctor right here with you. He saved your life."

The woman nodded slightly and shut her eyes again.

"With your assistance, nurse." Dr. Turner stared at her for a moment, then waved the stretcher bearers to move into position.

Martha held the woman's hand while the attendant tried to start an IV. The poor young man shook so hard, the needle wouldn't hit a vain. Martha's patience waned. She grabbed another needle set and gloves out of his bag and nudged him away.

"Let me do it before you poke her to death."

The attendant stared at her, frozen. He couldn't have been more than 20 years old and probably very inexperienced. Tonight was not the time for him to practice his skills.

Dr. Turner knelt beside the wide-eyed young man and spoke low.

"Better get out of her way. I have a feeling she might smack you."

Martha held her breath as she inserted the needle. Blood on the first try. The attendant handed her the tubing and tape, then moved out of the way. The patient groaned again.

Dr. Turner leaned near her. "It's all right, miss. You're in good hands."

When Martha finished, he was nowhere to be seen. Within moments the young woman was being carried off to the ambulance. Martha searched the dissipating crowd. Clark waited a few yards away, staring at her with a half-smile. She maneuvered the wreckage to reach him. He shook his head slowly.

"You were amazing. I didn't know..."

"You just do your job. I'm glad I was here." She surveyed the crowd. "You won't believe who that doctor was."

Clark took her by the hand and pulled her toward their car. "They said we can leave in a few minutes. The truck is here to haul away the wreckage."

"Clark—that doctor—"

"Nice work, nurse, uh—" Dr. Turner called behind them.

Martha clutched Clark's hand and clung to his side before turning her head.

Clark jumped in. "It's Nurse Jensen. As of yesterday."

Martha plastered an insincere grin on her face. The doctor would never recognize her married name. *Thank the Lord.* And it was dark enough that he might not see her face clearly.

Dr. Turner nodded and backed up a few steps. "Nurse Jensen. Sister was right. You are good, despite your temper."

He grinned and walked away. Martha stood, breathless. Clark put his arm around her.

"See? You *are* amazing. The doctor said so."

She stared straight ahead. Dr. Turner knew. He *knew* and he still let her assist him. Maybe she was the one who was hard on others, not him.

Naw. He's still an operating room bully.

October 1941

Packing was officially her least favorite thing. Especially for people she loved about to leave her behind. If everyone would just stay put, life would be as it should be. It had been hard enough to say goodbye to Clarissa, then Clark, then Mrs. Jensen. Now her parents and best friend were moving to greener pastures, against all her efforts to keep them here.

"Hand me that stack of newspaper, Martha." Mama sat at the kitchen table wrapping her china and her precious tea cup collection. Each one she held up to the light and inspected. Each one had a story, and Mama told it out loud today as if she needed Martha to remember. And she would remember, for Mama's sake.

Martha sat back and studied her mother's expression. Once in a while, the wrinkles around her mouth would tighten as she pursed her lips—her way of stopping the tears. No use in trying to comfort her. *Just let Mama work out her sadness so she can let go and move to California with a fresh heart.*

Pop stomped into the kitchen from the back porch. "What am I supposed to do with all these mayonnaise jars and lids, and pickle jars too? You never throw anything away, Ruth."

Martha couldn't contain her chuckle, especially when Mama scowled at Pop.

"Put them in a box for Martha. She might want those someday."

Martha stopped laughing. "Oh no you don't. I'll have no use for those." She hollered after Pop as he marched away. "I mean it, Pop. Throw them away."

Mama jumped up. "Just wait a minute. Mrs. MacGregor down the road preserves food, and she'll use them." Mama disappeared down the box-cluttered hall, and Martha could hear a soft argument between her parents.

Someday she and Clark would be fussing over each other's quirks like this. All he had to do was get through with the army, and forget about being an officer and a pilot. This time next year they should be settled into their own place. Just no children for a while. A long while.

Mama shuffled back to the kitchen chair mumbling something about a stubborn man. A car pulled up the drive. Martha found an empty spot to put down her newsprint and went to the door.

Hana was at the bottom of the porch steps with a box in hand. "I brought lunch."

Martha held out her arms in a shrug.

"You're supposed to be packing, not making lunch for us." She motioned for Hana to come in. "But I'm starving."

"Hello, Hana," Mama called from the kitchen.

Hana held up the box. "Balogna sandwiches and fruit salad."

"How nice. Ed! Hana brought lunch!"

"Coming!"

Martha pushed aside a pile of books on the table and Hana set down the box. She pulled out enough for Mama and Pop before Martha held up her hand. "Let's eat on the porch where there isn't so much stuff."

"Good. I want to hear all about the honeymoon. Well not *everything*."

Martha led her to the porch and sat next to Hana with the small wicker table between them. The fruit tasted fresh and sweet, reminding her of the summer already lost. October's chill wasn't icy yet, but enough to let everyone know winter hovered, waiting to pounce.

Hana took a bite of the sandwich and spoke with a full mouth.

"So? We haven't had a chance to talk for weeks. You never finished telling me about the train wreck. You have to tell me today."

"Why such a rush?"

Hana swallowed her bite and rested her hands in her lap. She gazed out over the yard, searching the big house and leafless vineyards beyond.

"Because I'm leaving this afternoon."

"What? Not next week? Why?"

Martha's lip quivered as Hana pulled her coat tight around her chest.

"They want me at the clinic in Hawaii sooner than expected. They're short-handed and I don't have anything tying me here since I gave my notice to Sister Clatilda. I'm ready to go. Except for saying goodbye to you. Saving the worst for last."

Martha's appetite was instantly replaced with an overwhelming grief so strong she couldn't muster a tear. Staring at Hana's sad face didn't spark any particular desire to hug her or hold her hand. If she did that, it would set the world turning, and she wouldn't be able to be strong like she had the last few weeks.

"Are you mad at me?"

Martha leaned over and wrapped her arm through Hana's. "Certainly not. I'm just thinking about how much I'll miss your laughter, your advice, and your jokes. Well, least of all your jokes."

Hana's cheeks streaked with tears. Martha always thought *she* would be the one heading off to some big adventure. Nothing in life was as she had planned it. Yet, it seemed right and fine. Until this moment.

"I'll miss you too. Let's write often. I'm not sure how heavy my duties will be at the clinic. I hope I get a couple days off a week to see the island. I hear it's beautiful. Anyway, I'll send you my address in Pearl City. There's lots of military bases and hospitals around there, but I don't feel like joining up at the moment."

Her face shone as she talked and Martha hoped her dreams wouldn't collapse. Her friend deserved the best, and if Hana thought this was it, she would pray it all worked out.

"You'll probably find some handsome Navy guy to fall in love with. What do your folks say about you going so far away?"

"Papa-san is sad, and I'll probably get a lecture from Mama-san when I stop to see them for a few days. She'll have my bags packed full of everything she thinks I'll need. I wish they had the money to come visit me. I hear from friends that it's more welcoming over there—you know, for Japanese Americans."

Welcoming. Martha would never understand how Americans born in America wouldn't be welcome in their own country.

"Well, Hana Kato, you're welcome back here anytime. Don't get so attached to palm trees and tropical sunshine that you forget about us."

Hana put the rest of their lunch in the box, and pulled on her gloves. "I have to go now. It's time to say goodbye."

Another goodbye. Martha's numbness had blossomed into blubbering. She stood with Hana on the porch, hugging and sniffling. Neither said a word. Hana pulled away and got into her car. She turned to blow a kiss and wave before edging the car down the driveway.

Mama touched Martha's shoulder. "I heard. She'll be far away but still in your heart."

Martha wiped her cheeks. "Why do things have to change? Why do people want to go off to strange places and leave the ones they love? I don't understand. I'm afraid for all of them."

Mama took Martha's hand—a rare gesture.

"There's no need to fear. The world is more than we know. Clark and your friends sense that. It's what draws them. That must be where their destiny is… out there."

Mama let go of her hand and went into the house.

Shivers ran up her arms. Not from the cold breeze—from within. "I don't want to know, I guess. I'll have to let the rest of them tell me about it."

Chapter Eight

December 7, 1941

Martha crossed off another day on the calendar with a red X. Only 12 more days and Clark would be home on leave from Kentucky. He could see her new place for the first time. At least the army had sense enough to allow suspension of most training during Christmas. What was it Clark had called it?

"Christmas exodus."

An odd phrase, but she was grateful for a few short weeks together, and it was better than her having to take time off work to go visit him. Working extra days to earn enough for decorations, a tree, and several presents she had already wrapped, gave her a leg up on her plans. She had each day of leave filled with something special; someone to visit, a restaurant to try, and lots of time just laying around listening to the new radio she had bought.

The early morning sun tried to break through the gray clouds, and Martha guessed this particular Sunday would not be bright, except in her heart. Skipping church would give her a chance to rest up for the six-day work week and write a long letter to Clark. So many details to work out about his transportation home.

Toast popped out of the toaster and landed on the counter. Her tiny kitchen was a mess—another small chore on the list of today's activities. After finishing her breakfast and letter to

Clark, she would dive into the two thick novels calling to her from the sofa table. Nothing like a cloudy day to snuggle up and read.

She clicked on the radio and scanned the channels for music. Her ears caught a few confusing words. *Bombed... Pearl Harbor... Japanese.* Her heart slammed her chest as she tuned in a clear station.

"President Roosevelt said in a statement earlier that the Japanese have attacked Pearl Harbor from the air."

The rest of the broadcast fought for clarity in Martha's mind. What did this mean and why would they do such a thing? As she listened to several more stations, the terrible announcement was confirmed. Her stomach churned and she tossed the toast she had just buttered in the sink. Through the front window she could see others had heard the news. One woman ran down the street screaming to call her children into the house. Another woman met her in the street and they hugged each other, crying and talking loud.

"Clark."

Did he know? Had he heard the same broadcast she heard? The phone rang. She jumped and then grabbed the receiver and just listened.

"Martha? Honey? Are you there?"

"Clark. What's happened? What should I do?"

"Don't panic. It's all very far away and there's no need to be afraid. I only have a few minutes before they suspend communications. We've been called to a briefing, but I won't be able to call you for a while. We were just about to leave on a three-day—well, I only have time to say all leaves have been canceled indefinitely. I don't think it will lift before Christmas. I'm sorry."

"You can't come home at all?" She wanted to crawl through the phone to see his face. This couldn't be real.

"Not now. We're likely going to be at war with Japan after

this. I have to do what the army tells me. I'll call again when I can. I love you."

"Clark, wait." Her words caught in her throat. "I… I love you too."

The line went dead, then clicked several times. "Hello? Can you get off the line now? We all have calls to make you know."

Old Mrs. Harvey barked her usual nasty rebuke. Martha slammed the receiver down hoping it would resonate in the woman's ear. She couldn't have held it longer anyway. Her hands shook so hard she couldn't hold a tissue.

"I can't believe this. I need to call Mama and Pop." She reached for the phone again, but pulled back knowing Mrs. Harvey would still be rattling on, spreading fear and gossip. She would try later. She sat on the sofa and pulled her robe tight around her aching chest. All at once it hit her.

"Oh no. Hana."

She jumped up and reached to the top shelf on the bookcase for her world atlas. Her shaking fingers thumbed through the pages until she came to the Pacific Ocean and Hawaii. The print was too small to read. She had to find Pearl City on the map. Maybe Hana was far out of the bombing area. She carried the atlas to her desk and rummaged through the drawer to find her magnifying glass. Skimming the page, the name came into focus. Pearl City.

"It's on the harbor." Her knees buckled. "She could be dead."

The room spun. The phone rang again. Maybe it was Clark calling back.

"Hello?"

"It's your dad. We just heard and wanted to see if you were okay."

Her dad hated talking on the phone. He *must* be worried.

"Hi, Pop. I'm all right, but pretty confused like everyone else. I'm scared for Hana."

"That's why we called. We knew you'd be worried. Just let us know if you hear anything. Have you heard from Clark?"

"Yes, his leave has been canceled. I probably won't see him for a long time." She choked back tears. Pop would start to cry if she did.

"That's too bad. Well, you call us soon. Don't worry too much. Good bye."

"Bye, Pop."

She wanted to laugh at their abrupt conversation, but it was typical for him. She should have talked to Mama. She didn't even get to ask how things were with them. It would seem her parents' world was growing smaller, while hers was exploding, like her head.

She put the receiver down before Mrs. Harvey could start scolding her. If only there was some way to find out about Hana. Everyone else she loved was safe.

A knock at the door made Martha groan. Who could possibly be here to see her? She looked out the peephole to see the face of the neighbor from across the hall. Martha couldn't remember her name. They had only exchanged polite good morning greetings. The woman seemed strange and aloof at times.

Martha opened the door just enough to show her face. "Hi."

The woman's eyes lit up. "Did you hear? I can't believe it. Are you scared? I am. Can I come in?"

Great. The last thing she needed was a lunatic in her living room scaring her half to death. Avoidance was paramount, even if it meant a white lie.

"Gosh, I'm sorry. I've got the flu and I wouldn't want to give it to you. Thanks for checking on me. I'm all right."

The woman stepped back. "Oh. Well, I just hope they get all the Japs out of here. There are a couple families down the street. I'm locking my door and you should too."

Martha's chest tightened. "I don't think we have anything to fear from those nice people. You're jumping to conclusions."

She started to shut the door. The woman mumbled something derogatory. Martha pulled the door open again.

"You are a ridiculous person. Go home and lock yourself in."

She slammed the door and turned the lock. It was people like this who made trouble for people like Hana. A new energy rose inside. This country would come together now, and she had to be ready to join in.

The rest of the day droned on, peppered with intermittent updates on the lives lost and ships sunk in Hawaii. Evening finally came, along with Mrs. Roosevelt's usual Sunday radio address. Martha hadn't listened to the first lady's broadcast for a long time. Perhaps she would have something to say about the bombing.

The radio screeched until she found the station. Listening to Mrs. Roosevelt squeak out her speech gave Martha a ray of hope. She turned up the volume.

We know what we have to face and we know that we are ready to face it. I should like to say just a word to the women in the country tonight. I have a boy at sea on a destroyer, for all I know he may be on his way to the Pacific. Two of my children are in coast cities on the Pacific. Many of you all over the country have boys in the services who will now be called upon to go into action. You have friends and families in what has suddenly become a danger zone. You cannot escape anxiety. You cannot escape a clutch of fear at your heart and yet I hope that the certainty of what we have to meet will make you rise above these fears.

Martha wiped her face with her sleeve. It was as if the woman spoke right to her. Her words couldn't have sunk deeper into Martha's cracked heart. She had to rise above the fears—battle them with everything she had left. When Clark got home, he would see a wife who could wholly support him.

She would make him proud. She pulled the afghan over her and curled up in a ball. Her stomach fluttered as she dozed. Scattered dreams of nursing school and Hana—of Clark up in a plane, trying to land. Images that should have comforted pushed her deep into sadness.

She woke to complete darkness. She hadn't even left a light on. No point moving now. Her bed was too big without someone to share it—the sofa would work well for tonight.

And maybe from now on.

Martha hurried to Sister's office. For once she wasn't in trouble, so she couldn't imagine why she had been summoned. Only one reason entered her mind. Hana. Perhaps the channels of the church had managed to get word about her friend. After weeks of trying after the bombing, all her personal efforts had come up empty. Hana's last letter told of her putting in extra hours to fill in for nurses at some hospital nearby. She'd been working the night shift on weekends, no doubt wearing herself out.

The office door which was ajar, so she knocked.

"Sister?"

The room was empty. She checked her watch—a few minutes early. She had just enough time to read Clark's letter. The sun shone in the window and she hovered there, unfolding a few pieces of coffee stained pages.

January 13, 1942

Dear Martha,

I finally have time to sit for a few minutes and jot down a letter. I'm sorry you have to be there alone with all the commotion going on around the world. I sure feel it here. The men are mad as can be at the Japanese, and I hear all kinds of talk about what we ought to do to them. Personally, I don't have time to think of such things. I just want to get done here and come home to you, even if it's just for a ten-day leave, which brings me to my news.

We have so much to talk about. I want to tell you that I've been accepted into flight training. I know that doesn't thrill you, but it's my dream, one I'm especially passionate about after Pearl Harbor.

She looked up and out the window, resisting the urge to wad the paper up and throw it. Despite her determination after Pearl Harbor to support his decision, her resolve had weakened when war was declared on Japan and Germany. Her prayers for Clark to be denied flight training had been overridden by his prayers to be accepted. Her only hope now was that he wouldn't make the cut. A pang of guilt squeezed her enough to scold herself.

"Shame on you, Martha Jensen."

"What have you done now?" Sister's voice sang across the room. "At least you have a conscience."

Martha turned to see a slight smile grace the nun's face. She knew Sister Clatilda wasn't much of a kidder, and Martha assumed she was serious.

"I do. Most of the time."

Martha folded her letter and returned it to her pocket. She sat in the chair opposite Sister, just as she had done dozens of times. Their talks weren't always pleasant, but she hoped today would be different.

"I asked you here to tell you I have news of Hana."

Martha gasped. Shivers danced across her arms.

"When you asked me to use the church channels to look for her, I was very doubtful anything would come of it. Hana is not affiliated with our faith and we don't usually have connections in cases like this. However, I can tell you she is alive, but injured."

Martha's hands flew to her face. Alive was good enough—unless—

"She is expected to recover physically."

Martha's tears flowed freely. She tried to speak through her emotion.

"What else, Sister?"

Sister moved around to the front of the desk, hands in her sleeves. How many times had Martha watched her stand like that? This *was* serious. The shaky line between wanting to know and not wanting to hear the rest wrestled in her mind.

"She had head and other injuries. I wasn't able to ascertain what else. The priest who visited her in the hospital explained that many of the wounded from that day struggled with deep emotional trauma. He believes Hana is experiencing that. She was withdrawn and seemed angry."

Angry? Hana? Impossible.

"He must have her mixed up with another patient. That doesn't sound like Hana."

"He was quite certain in his identification, and his description of her fit. I'm sorry to worry you with this news, but she *is* alive. We can be thankful for that. I just wouldn't expect to hear from her for quite a while. She will need time to recuperate."

Martha shook her head. Poor sweet Hana. She must feel so alone.

"Thank you for finding her. I'll give it some time and hope she contacts me. What else can I do?"

"Pray. As I will."

Martha nodded and shuffled from the room. Her energy drained, she had no desire to go back to work, but if Hana could endure, so could Martha and all the other overworked nurses.

She stared down the hall at the bustling young volunteers from the high school. Since that terrible day in Hawaii, women and girls had heeded the call to give their time for the war effort. Martha could see the shining dedication in their eyes, the same look she once had. Hard times and experience with tragedy had stolen that gleam. She wanted it back, but today wasn't the day to reclaim it. Her dear friend was hurt, and she had no way of helping her.

"Nurse Jensen?" A young girl appeared behind her and Martha turned.

"Yes?"

"Would you have a minute to show me again how to work the autoclave? The small one in the surgery supply room doesn't seem to like me."

Her sweet smile softened Martha's anxious heart. If anyone could restore enthusiasm for nursing, it would be a girl like this.

"Well, let's see if we can change its mind. Lead the way."

Martha could swear the girl was about to skip down the hall. She chuckled. Sister Clatilda would never approve. Martha followed her, trying to keep up. From the back, the dark-haired girl almost looked like Hana—but without the oval eyes.

She briefly wondered what any children of hers and Clark's might look like, then shook away the thought. *Not for a long time, if ever.*

He would be home from infantry training soon—she struggled to wait for the day. She hoped he would come back with a new determination—not to fly, but to do his service in some other job. A safer one.

The young girl waited at the door into the supply room, her brows raised.

"I'm coming. No need to be impatient."

Martha knew all about impatience.

March 1942

Clark lay in bed listening to Martha breathe. He didn't want to open his eyes for fear of seeing it was still dark outside. He had missed the slight dusting of snow Martha wrote him about, as well as missing Christmas together. The holiday had been swallowed up with the start of war. He and Martha weren't the only couple to be separated for months following Christmas. Her letters kept him going, hearing about her efforts to stay busy and not think too much about him being gone. He was proud of her for not complaining, and he knew she worried about Hana.

Since coming home from infantry training last week, his sleep patterns had been turned upside down, and he felt the settling of his racing thoughts he had been accustomed to. The lazy rain pelting the window helped slow his mind, but meant a second day of cold, wet dreariness. At least he had taken time to fix Martha's car at the garage yesterday. He enjoyed the memories associated with the musty oil and old tire smells. The new owner would take over soon and Clark wouldn't have a workspace to fix anything, let alone grinding and welding on Betsy.

Betsy. Who names a car?

The wind blew a blast of rain on the side of the apartment. Martha would sleep through it, but he felt the urge to get up and start the coffee. He opened one eye, but the other seemed to be stuck shut. He swung his legs around the edge of the bed and raised his brows to try to open the stubborn lid. It let loose with a searing pain. Even looking at the dim light of dawn through the window felt like a blazing flame. He shut both eyes and rubbed the sticky one. Opening it again brought worse agony than before—pain he had never experienced. He couldn't hold back a loud groan.

Martha sat up straight.

"What's the matter?"

Clark headed for the sink. He had to flush out his eye before the pain worsened.

"My eye. It's killing me."

Martha's feet hit the floor and she followed him into the bathroom. He felt his way along the wall until his hands touched the porcelain sink. He turned the cold water faucet and cupped his hand, splashing as much water as he could into his right eye.

"Is something in your eye? Let me look."

Martha flipped on the light which shone in Clark's face. He shielded his face.

"Turn off the light!"

"How can I look in your eye if I don't have light? Does it hurt that bad?"

"Yes, it hurts that bad. I can't see much out of it, and the light is making it worse."

Martha shut off the light and grabbed his arm. He had to let her guide him to the bed or his legs would buckle. His mind whirled with panic. What had he done to injure it? He rocked back and forth, taking deep breaths to calm himself, but pain burned back into his head. Martha sat close to him on the bed. After a few moments, he tried to open his lids again. The searing hadn't gone away, still rippling his vision. He grunted loud enough to make her jump.

"You're scaring me. I think we need to get to the hospital to see what's going on."

Clark could hear Martha rummaging through dresser drawers. He dare not open his eye. The burning unsettled his stomach as he mentally retraced his steps, trying to remember what could have happened to cause such a problem.

"Here, slip these on. I'll help you." Martha pulled him up by his arm and helped him put one foot at a time in his pants. It was like being a child again. He didn't care.

Together they made their way down slippery concrete steps and into the car in front of the building. Martha said little, only asking about the pain every few blocks. Clark held his head in his hands and concentrated on not moving his eyeball. If anything were seriously wrong he would have decisions to make.

"Can you think of something that might have gotten in your eye?" Martha's probing tone irritated his already frayed nerves. "What did you do yesterday while I was at work?"

"Worked on…"

That was it. He had welded and did some grinding, but he wore glasses and a welding mask. He knew to be careful, his dad had hounded him about it for years. There was no other explanation.

"I think I know. It just dawned on me."

"What?"

"Working on Betsy at the garage. You better step on it. This could be bad."

The car lurched a bit as Martha accelerated. Clark thought through every step at the garage, trying to pinpoint the possible cause. It had to be either a flash burn from the welder, or a metal fragment from grinding on the bumper. The latter would be his worst nightmare come true. His brother had a metal fragment lodged in his eye that caused a rust ring, but Clark couldn't let that happen to him.

"We're here. I'll come around to help you."

The cold air from her open door chilled him to the bone. He kept his eyes shut all the way from the car to the hospital door, then through a wheel chair ride to the exam room. Martha waited with him for a doctor to decide if his dreams had been crushed.

Another hour ticked by before an exam was underway. Clark's jaw hurt from clenching his teeth. After the initial introductions, the doctor looked over the questionnaire and raised his brows.

"You're lucky I was here today, young man. Got called in for an emergency eye operation. Was just about to leave the hospital."

The words hadn't comforted Clark in the least. Especially when the painful examination nearly sent him to his knees.

The lights, the eye wash, the numbing, all seemed endless. The doctor gave no indication of his findings through the process, but now sat across from Clark. Martha had kept her tongue, a feat he imagined must have been difficult considering her medical knowledge.

"You have a piece of metal in your eye, Mr. Jensen."

Clark had suspected as much, but the statement hit hard all the same. He focused on Martha with his unpatched eye. Even through the dim light he could see the concern written on her face. No doubt she had seen this kind of injury before, and knew more than he did about the ramifications.

"Can you take it out?"

"Yes, but I'll need a release signed."

Now Martha spoke up. "What kind of release? Is he in danger of losing his vision?"

The doctor rolled his chair to face her. "Because of the location of the fragment, yes."

Clark grew weary of the debate. "Just do it."

"Mr. Jensen, I need to tell you about the possible effects of this kind of procedure."

The man rattled on about infection, permanent vision loss, scarring, and a few other things Clark knew nothing about. He could feel his blood pressure rise, something the doctor said he specifically should avoid.

"Doctor, I am scheduled to start Officer's Candidate School in five days." An urge to cover his ears came over him. He knew the answer already, but it was best to know for sure. Flight training hung in the balance.

"That's out, I'm afraid. At least for a while."

The air left Clark's lungs. Martha's head was bowed, so he couldn't read her expression. This could be the end of his ambitions. What would he do then—sit behind a desk at some recruiting office?

"All right, I understand. Let's just get the metal out and then I'll have to contact my new commanding officer. Guess I am in some trouble then?"

The doctor handed him a sheet of paper and a pen. "I'm sorry, yes, at least for now. Have your wife look this over with you and I'll be back to have the nurse set up for the procedure."

"Thank you, doctor." Martha reached around Clark and took the paper.

Clark leaned into the back of the exam table. He had no choice. The fragment had to come out, and he had to take whatever followed. The realization pressed into his consciousness.

Martha slipped her hand into his. She would want to mother him. Exactly what he didn't want. He would beat this—no fuss, no crying. His eye would heal and he would be able to join the group of men who shared his dream.

"I'm sorry, honey. I looked over the form. It's straightforward and says everything the doctor already told you. Can you see to sign it?"

He snatched the pen from her and scribbled his name.

Martha touched his arm. "Is there anything you want me to do?"

"No."

His tone was sharper than he meant it to be. She slunk away and returned to the chair just as the doctor came in, followed by a nurse carrying a large tray of instruments. The nurse nodded to Martha.

Clark couldn't keep his eye open to see anymore. He grasped the soft leather chair arms and tightened his fingers around the end. He could only listen to the noises of gloves snapping, instruments tinkling, and soft-soled shoes padding the floor. The strange thought occurred to him that he would rather lose his hearing than his sight, but that would still keep him out of the air. Someone draped a sheet over his chest. He could smell something sweet—a solution of some sort on the tray close to his head.

She tipped the big chair back a bit and hovered over him, removing the gauze eye patch.

"Just some numbing drops first."

Within a few moments, his eye pain diminished, and a bitter taste settled on the back of his tongue. He concentrated on each sound in the room, trying to calm his churning stomach.

"We're ready to begin if you are." The doctor spoke low, leaning in on Clark's right side.

Clark wondered how Martha felt as she watched from the other side of the room. He hoped she would say a prayer.

"Do a good job, doc. I need this eye. 20/20 please."

Chapter Nine

*M*artha had done her best to keep Clark's spirits up. Her loneliness while he was gone had turned to frustration over her inability to ease his disappointment. As much as she wanted to help him, she fell short at every effort. She was a good nurse, yet couldn't sooth his doubts. He wouldn't let her take time off work, so her shifts were spent with half her heart and mind on her job and the other half worrying about Clark at home alone in the apartment. He would often overdo, she could tell when she got home.

His mood had fluctuated from angry to sullen to apathetic, then back to angry again. Keeping up had taken all her energy. For over two months, they had only gone out a few times. An infection had set in, delaying his recovery even more. She had counseled with Sister Clatilda to get suggestions about how to handle a man whose ego had been bruised and ambitions put in jeopardy. The army waits for no man.

"Just stay close and let him work it out," Sister had said.

If only it were that simple. If only Hana were here to lend her shoulder to cry on it would help her keep her patience.

The thought of Hana stung. Nothing could be worse than what her friend was destined to endure in the coming months. Martha had been so relieved to get Hana's phone call last week. After waiting for months to talk to her, she stayed mindful of the edge to Hana's voice, the unsaid wounds of her experience.

At least she was home with her family. Soon the two of them would be reunited once Martha could find a way to visit her. Or perhaps Hana would come back to work with her at Our Lady of Lourdes like the old days. Hana might want to get far away from whatever memories haunted her.

The radio blared through the door with an Andrews Sisters tune when she approached the apartment. The neighbor she had told off the day of Pearl Harbor's bombing peeked out at her through a crack in her door. Her dark hair frizzed out from under a stocking cap with a tassel at the top. Her cheeks were red, and she wore a pair of glasses low on her nose.

Martha had succeeded in avoiding her most of the time, but always the woman's beady eyes seemed to be watching her. As Martha slipped her key in the lock, the woman poked her head out into the hall.

"I don't think our landlord would appreciate you taking in soldiers. It's indecent. I have a mind to tell him about you." Her voice grated low. Cigarette smoke filtered through the opening.

Martha's grip tightened on her key. She let out a deep breath, hoping she could tame her anger down to simple irritation. She pulled the key out and slowly turned to face her neighbor.

"Well, I'm sure he knows about it, but you feel free to tell him anything you like."

Before the woman could respond, Martha was inside the living room, slamming the door behind her. She straightened her posture and spoke her thoughts aloud.

"Well done, Martha. Well done."

She spun around and nearly dropped her purse. Clark stood in the kitchen wearing her patchwork apron, flipping something in a frying pan. The radio on the shelf above the sofa still blasted, and he tapped his foot to the beat. Something seemed odd about his behavior, especially considering his terrible moods since his injury.

"Clark?"

He acted as if he didn't hear her. She moved closer.

"Clark, what's going on here?" She reached for the radio and turned the volume down to a dull roar. She couldn't possibly compete with the lively lyrics of "Boogie Woogie Bugle Boy."

"Hi. I'm fixing dinner. That's what's going on. Got a problem with that?"

She stepped back. He had lost his mind. After months of sulking inside, doing little else but studying flight manuals, he must have had a breakdown. Martha froze. *What should I do?* She slipped off her coat and eased onto the arm of the sofa. Her mind whirled with scenarios until Clark finally set down the pan and approached her.

"Sorry, I was being goofy. Dinner will be ready in about an hour. Gotta stick this in the oven. Hang on."

Her mouth hung open. He was clean-shaven, cheerful—and now that she looked closely, he wasn't wearing his eye patch. She'd have to scold him.

The oven door slammed and she jumped up.

"Where is your patch?"

He grinned. "Don't need it."

"Clark, you just *think* you don't need it." She walked around the room, looking through drawers and under magazines.

"Martha, stop. I saw the doc today. My eye is healed and my vision is back to 20/20 in that eye with only a slight stigmatism. I'm going to start OCS in a week with the new class. Just talked to my C.O."

Martha's legs wobbled. *No.*

"A week?" Her safety net fell from beneath her. Clark's eye injury was her ticket to keep him out of the army and safe at home with her. The plan that had been tucked in the back of her mind suddenly collapsed. She sat and clasped her hands together.

"Yes. Isn't that great news?" Clark turned his back on her and opened the icebox door.

Great news? No. One week and he would be on his way to an army career and then possible flight training. She wouldn't see him for months, maybe years if they made him go overseas. Her ice-cold hands trembled. She pulled them apart and stuffed them between her legs and the cushion. She would have to find a way to be positive—affirming. Where would she find the courage to face the situation without letting Clark know how upset she was?

She cleared her throat. "So, what about that little bit of blur you've been complaining about? Maybe you shouldn't jump into OCS so fast."

"The blur was from the drops I was taking. Doc said to stop. It's clearing up already this afternoon."

Martha's face grew hot. He wasn't being realistic and she had to talk some sense into him. She pushed herself off the sofa and marched into the kitchen. Clark had retrieved some chicken legs from the icebox and set them on the counter. He studied her face.

"You're upset."

Keep calm.

"I just want to make sure you're doing the right thing. I don't think you realize how important it is to take care of your eye. Maybe you should get a second opinion."

He frowned and tipped his head. "I will. The army doc will examine me and give me all the tests I'll need to continue with my training. But for now, I'm clear to go to OCS."

Her temper flared as she processed what he said. By the time she spoke, the level of voice volume had intensified.

"Clark, this is not fair to us. How can you think of going back? You shouldn't be flying. You might... it's not... they have plenty of other men who can do the job. You don't have to do this. You have an out."

Clark took off his apron and grabbed Martha's hand. She felt his grip tighten as he pulled her toward the sofa and pointed for her to sit. Perhaps he was ready to talk sense. He sat next to her.

"Listen. I think what you're saying behind all those words is that *you* don't want me to go—that *you* are afraid something will happen to me. Like little Rebecca you told me about? Am I right?"

She opened her mouth to answer him, but he held his finger to her lips.

He looked long into her eyes. "This really isn't about me, is it?"

Again she opened her mouth, but shut it at the sight of his fingers headed for her face.

"I thought you were over your fears about risk and death. Honey, you can't hold on to everyone you love and keep them safe. You aren't in charge. You can't control what happens to me, or your folks, or Hana. You can't even control what happens to you. I have a job to do, and it just happens it's something I love. Flying."

She offered one last option. "What if you don't get into flight school, or you don't pass in the end?"

"Then I'll do something else. The fact is that I've been drafted like so many others and in times of war you don't just say no. Wouldn't you rather see me using my talents and gifts rather than be in a foxhole on the front?"

"A desk job would suit me fine. Can't you understand my side of things?"

Clark threw his head back and groaned. "Of course I do. It's very normal to feel the way you do—to a point. Lots of other wives live with fear about their husbands. They learn to handle it. You will have to do that too."

Other wives. She hated being compared to them. She had

met some of those kinds of women at the hospital. They visited their husbands in final recovery from war wounds, and she had seen the pretense of support and pride. She knew deep inside they carried the same disdain for duty and service—that they had died a little inside. Patriotism was one thing, but worry about a loved-one's well-being was something universal.

She was too tired to argue anymore. If acceptance is what Clark wanted and needed, she would do her best to comply, at least for now. She could still hope he would not even get to flight school.

"I'll try. Sorry to spout off."

He frowned and she knew he didn't swallow it. Still, he wrapped his arms around her. The pang of guilt growing in her gut would have to be ignored as long as possible.

August 1943

Since he left Martha, the days and weeks had flown by. With hardly any time to miss her, Clark felt badly. Officer Candidate School was more intense than he anticipated, with all eyes on him to perform as an officer should. He'd always been told he had leadership qualities, and he enjoyed the organization and planning it took to put an idea into action. He recalled his days as a student at Pasco High. It always seemed to fall to him to keep class projects, games, and other activities going in a straight line. He liked it, even if he had to work with people he considered bumblers. His dad would tell him that even bumblers are needed in this world.

He had written Martha about his time here the last two months and sent pictures of all his new pals and comrades. She barely mentioned them in her return letters, keeping her topics to the weather, the other nurses, and any news from

Hana she had received. It was more and more clear to him that she hadn't dealt with their uncertain future well. Something he would try hard to understand.

"Not bad food tonight, eh, Jensen?" Jonesy emerged from the mess hall kitchen. His lanky arms seemed to hang to his knees, and his bright red-orange hair sparkled in the overhead lights. He gathered up a few dirty dishes from the table where Clark sat.

"Actually, it was quite good, Jonesy. Your culinary skills have risen to a new level. We all appreciate it."

Clark marveled at this kid's freckled face. He must have been a cute little boy. His disposition was a welcome change from the instructors who never seemed to let up.

"Gee, thanks, Jensen. Wait till you guys taste my cinnamon rolls in the morning. I've been practicing." He patted his stomach.

"That's great. My mouth is watering already." A pang of loneliness struck to think of home-baked goodies. Martha was always baking cookies or pies. Her mother had been a good teacher.

Jonesy walked away, balancing dishes on his arms, another skill he had become proficient at. All walks of life and personalities merged here at the base to make everything run smoothly. Clark imagined it would be the same overseas, if he got there. The all clear he had received from the army eye surgeon was no guarantee of a spot in the pilot's seat.

Matthews and Philips slid into the seats opposite him. He nodded to them and sipped down the last of his lukewarm coffee.

Philips leaned into Clark's space. "We just heard some interesting news."

Clark wasn't in the mood for gossip about the antics of his fellow students while on leave over the weekend. He tried not to look interested.

Matthews continued the conversation. "You know the 446th bomb group that was formed last April?" Clark nodded. "Well, they are looking for top pilots to join some of the squadrons. They'll be looking us over pretty hard if we make it that far."

Philips chimed in. "I plan to be one of those pilots. We'll see some heavy action. Gonna be based in a place called Flixton—Station 125. England's real pretty, I hear."

Clark's curiosity rose more than he anticipated. Being part of a new bombardment group for B24s would be a great assignment. He'd rather be with a B17 group, but the 446th would suit him fine. The RAF had been flying 24s for some time. He heard they were rolling off the assembly lines in the states faster than making furniture.

Clark stood and snatched his empty coffee mug. "Well, maybe we'll all make it. Gotta get through a few more weeks here. Then we'll know who's promoted and who'll make the 446th."

He backed away from the table thinking of Martha and how she might feel about him getting to command a flight crew of a B24. There would be many discussions to have between now and then.

He turned just in time to miss bumping into an instructor. "Excuse me, sir." He saluted as his face warmed.

"No problem, Jensen."

Clark saw the opportunity to ask a question. The answer could be part of his plan where Martha was concerned.

"Sir, may I talk to you about something?"

"Sure. I only have a minute. What's on your mind?"

Clark shifted from foot to foot, wondering if he should stick his neck out and risk humiliation. For Martha's sake he had to know.

"What would be the chance of my wife following me while I go through flight training?" He held up his hand. "I know wives can't stay on base, but what if she had an apartment so I could be there on my days off?"

The instructor raised his bushy brows. "Not recommended, but I know some men do that. You need to stay focused you know. Wives can be a nuisance in my opinion, but you can get by with it."

He walked away. Clark called after him. "Thank you, sir. I'll think on it."

Focused. He could do that. In fact, he would be able to focus better if he weren't worried about Martha all the time. It was the perfect solution. He would tell her as soon as he got home.

"Wait a minute. What if I don't make the cut? I might be stuck in a fox hole."

Someone grabbed his coffee mug. "What fox hole?" Jonesy tilted his head, waiting for an answer.

"Oh, just thinking out loud. Bye, Jonesy."

Clark jogged toward the door. He would pass, he knew it. He would be flying soon. He knew that too. Now he had to make Martha see it wouldn't be so bad. He shuddered to think of her reaction.

He would find out in a few short weeks.

"I'm sorry to be leaving you, Sister. I know one less nurse isn't what you need. But I have this opportunity to go with Clark, at least for a while."

Sister sat with her lily white hands folded across her desk. She hadn't said much, leaving Martha to fill the gaps in conversation. She couldn't tell whether Sister was in agreement with her resignation or if she were about to express angry disappointment. All the explanations had been shared, and the only thing to do was wait for Sister to respond.

After a few silent moments, Sister spoke. "I think you're doing the right thing. My only concern is that I sense you have never really reconciled your fears where Clark is concerned.

I know you must be proud of him for his new officer's status, and that he was selected to be a pilot, but he will be in harm's way from now on. How do you feel about that?"

Martha never liked being backed into a corner, and her churning insides told her that was exactly where Sister had maneuvered her. How was she supposed to explain how she felt, when she didn't know herself? It was time to bluff.

"I know God will watch over him. Flying is what Clark wants to do, and the army quite agrees. I just have to accept it and be grateful I can be near him."

The more she talked the more she relaxed. A strange sense of independence flooded her. She could go on pretending until she convinced Sister and Clark, and maybe by then she would have convinced herself.

"I see. I hope you're being honest with yourself, but I'm at least encouraged that you know the truth. It's another thing to apply it to your heart and life. I will pray you find that path. I'll miss you, Martha, but we'll survive. A new batch of nurses is graduating soon."

She came around the desk, reached for Martha's shoulders and kissed each cheek. "Remember these are trying times for everyone. God bless you."

Martha couldn't hold back her tears. She didn't deserve Sister's trust, but she would gladly take her blessing. Mama and Pop had been hard to convince, and offered for her to come live with them while Clark was gone all those months. As it happened, Martha had been able to sublet her place to a new nursing student for the duration of Clark's flight training.

"Thank you, Sister. I will miss you and Our Lady of Lourdes. Hopefully the war will end soon and we'll come back to the area. I'd love to settle down here, but I don't know about Clark."

"Time will reveal everything." Sister led her to the door and held it open while Martha shuffled down the hall. She turned once to see if her mentor still watched her, but Sister had shut the door. Probably taking time to pray.

Martha hugged the familiar white walls all the way to the locker room. These halls had been her home—the cafeteria her kitchen, the staff her only community. She would be back and Sister knew it. If Clark was sent overseas, she would have nowhere else to go. She couldn't stay with Mama and Pop. Their small farm was too far from any hospital, and Lady of Lourdes was her home away from home. It would be the only place she could wait for Clark's return—in the town where they met and fell in love. It would be her lucky charm.

The thought made her laugh. She didn't believe in luck. She only hoped God wouldn't be too busy to watch over Clark as she had proclaimed to Sister. It was probably time to start her petitions in Clark's behalf. And while she was at it, she would pray for mercy, should she end up with a husband in the thick of war.

She sat in Betsy, not feeling like going home. She had just enough rationed gas to take a drive by the river. Sister's words spun like a wheel in her mind. She had to figure out how to make them stick in her heart. This would be a battle as big as the war itself. Clark had called her stubborn many times, and he was right. Why, she wasn't sure. Some was her natural personality, but some of it inherited from a haunting she didn't know how to shake.

She pulled into a small gravel parking lot near a cove in the bend of the river. A single bench rested beneath a large willow tree. Several children romped near the gravely shore as a woman dallied nearby. The sky hinted of summer lost, and amber leaves on the trees across the river echoed the call of change.

She surveyed the spot. "Looks like a good place to ponder."

The warmth of the sun sang the song of possible Indian summer. Soon those amber leaves would crisp and fall, but she wouldn't be here to see it. The shade of the willow tree felt good on her back. The children splashed and played among the rocks, squealing with joy. As she stared at them, her chest tightened. The story Mama had told about Rebecca taunted her. She closed her eyes tight to break the onslaught of images. All at once the joyous squeals changed to match the screams in her mind.

Then someone shook her shoulder.

"Help me. I can't swim. My little girl is going to drown." The woman pulled on Martha's arm until she lifted her off the bench. Martha couldn't feel her feet moving, but she was near the water in a moment's time.

The woman cried. "See, she's hanging onto that branch." She pointed out to the water where a brown-haired girl clung to a branch that dangled over the swift edge of the cove.

Martha froze, but the woman pushed her toward the water. Feeling her blood drain from her face, she looked down at her white uniform. She was a nurse, and just like at the train wreck on her honeymoon, she had to offer assistance. The woman shrieked to the girl.

"Hang on tight, Cathy!"

Martha felt the sand slide through her toes when she kicked off her shoes. She waded in the water up to her knees. If the little girl lost her grip, what could Martha do to stop her from being swept away?

Just keep moving toward her.

The cool current swirled around her thighs now. She would be up to her waist by the time she reached the girl.

It's okay. You can swim.

The water got colder and pushed on her legs as she neared the crying child, so close she could almost touch her. The little girl let out a guttural sound as if she were vomiting. Instead, she slipped down the branch even farther. Martha's heart skipped beats. She thrust herself forward, trying not to slip on the rocks. Was she breathing? Her chest hurt more with each inch.

"Hurry!" She could hear the mother shouting. She had waded in to her knees, her shoulders shaking with hysteria.

With one more thought of Rebecca, Martha lunged at the girl and grabbed her thin slippery arm. She clutched her hard to her breast so the child could wrap her arms and legs around her torso. The force of it made Martha stumble, but she gathered her balance and turned to trudge through mud and rocks to reach the mother. Her feet were nearly numb.

"Take her before we both fall," Martha called out to the mother.

The child let go and wrapped her arms around her mother's neck. The mother backed away with her crying child while Martha drug her heavy feet to dry ground. She heard someone gasping for air. She barely made it to the bench before her wobbling legs gave out, and she realized the gasps had been her own.

The mother and child and other children ran toward her.

"Thank you so much," the mother cried. All the children were sobbing and clinging to the woman's legs.

Through sharp wheezing Martha managed a, *You're welcome.*

The little family waddled up to their car. The motor started and tires crunched against gravel. Time had stopped. Martha was alone on the bench. Had she dreamed this? No. Her shoes were lying on the shore and her uniform dripped.

How quickly a child can drown. How quickly someone had to act to save them. This time, she was able to be the rescuer and not just an observer. It was possible that Rebecca could have lived if an adult who could swim would have been there.

"I couldn't save you, Rebecca. I'm sorry."

The rushing water answered her. It was bigger than her, as Sister said. She had held on too tightly to everyone she loved. She was not in control of the water's current, or of life's current.

The ebb of life would come and go. She let out a long breath and closed her eyes. Months of flight training would be her test. She would go with Clark and know he was in God's hands.

Chapter Ten

September 1943

*I*t was a close call. All the weeks of studying gauges and maps had strained his eyes. The trouble started with dryness and irritation, and by the time he sought a doctor's opinion, he had experienced moderate discomfort and redness, along with periodic headaches. Across from him, the doctor scribbled notes in a file folder. Clark couldn't take the suspense any longer.

"What's my vision number, sir?"

"At the moment, you're still 20/20 in both eyes. But if we don't treat this problem now, you might have some vision loss. Just temporary, but a loss none the less."

Clark's heart dropped to his stomach. He had come too far to lose his status. He had kept up with the rigorous schedules, moving from base to base, and getting signed off on multiple types of planes. Now, he had reached the finale—the B24 he was destined to fly. From Curtis Field in Brady, Texas to Lowry Field in Denver, Colorado, he and Martha had been strong and focused. Every base in between had brought its challenges, both mentally and physically. If his eyes were affected, he would do whatever it took to make them perfect again.

"You know, young man, they lowered the vision requirement to 20/30 a few months ago. You could get by if your vision weakened, as long as it's correctable to 20/20." He raised his brows at Clark as if asking permission to settle for less. Clark laughed inside, thinking of the calm reaction to the new standard Martha had when she heard. He had expected a roll of protests for giving him more room for error—more chance to be accepted.

"Don't care, Doctor. I have to compete with men who have perfect vision. I need to be the best in all areas."

"All right. At least you're not grounded." The doctor approached with some small bottles and an eye dropper. "I have some medication you need to use once in the morning and once in the evening. Then use these drops in between if your eyes get dry. Don't take reading material home with you. Leave it for class time."

Clark huffed. "That will make Martha happy."

He would have to adjust to keep his eyes healthy, no matter what. He could at least spend more time inside the ships to memorize every station, every fuel line, and every defensive gun. His life and the life of his future crew would depend on him knowing each bolt and strap.

That is, if he passed his exams. A few more practice flights and he would be scrutinized for his flying skills and his knowledge. He had to make it.

He thanked the doctor and left the building. He remembered the note in his pocket from the duty officer. No doubt they needed a substitute pilot for a practice mission today. He opened the paper.

"Yep. Thought so. That's okay with me."

His steps turned into a jog. Adrenalin was always a help in these situations.

Each face could have been his face—each wound his. This haunted Martha daily as she stepped into the various wards of Fitzsimons hospital. She had made the conscious choice to choke down the fear triggered in her, and she had made herself a promise not to crumble every time she thought about the possibilities surrounding Clark's mortality.

Since rescuing the little girl months ago, the battle had been easier. Only lingering stabs of doubt made her stumble into old worry habits on occasion.

Sometimes she hid in the restroom and cried at the terrible atrocities she saw in the burn wards and the amputee wards. Even an occasional duty on the maternity ward provoked sadness at babies being born without a daddy. Yet, the more she analyzed it, she realized her emotion was more about compassion than fear over Clark.

Had she known how big a part of the war effort this hospital had become, she might have ignored the desperate call for nurses—civilian and military. Working side by side with army nurses had given her the education she hoped she would never get. Now, many had left to volunteer overseas. Some in the Pacific theater, some in Europe. Many never came home, and those who did were either injured or deathly sick with malaria.

Martha's outlook on service to country had taken a dramatic turn. If all these dedicated men and women could brave the horrors of war and come through with stronger patriotism, greater courage, and deeper faith, then she would strive to do so as well. For her sake, and Clark's.

"Good job on those bandages, Jensen." Martha did not turn at the sound of head nurse, Lt. Pawley's voice. No need to acknowledge praise around here. They all learned to give it and receive it as part of a coping mechanism—something she had developed and come to appreciate as the days and nights brought endless deaths and injuries.

She knew each one could have been Clark, but luckily for her, he was still here, still with her, as much as he had time to be while he finished his last month of training with the monstrous B24s.

Another patient a few beds away groaned. Martha finished bandaging Sgt. Joseph and opened his side table drawer to store the remainder of the gauze. On the bottom of the drawer was a photo. She looked at the soldier. He was well medicated and sleeping. She picked up the photo and studied the young woman and baby. It was signed; *love, Judy and Ronnie*.

"Such a darling little boy."

The Sergeant's response startled her. "Yes, he is. Takes after his mama."

She replaced the photo and scooted closer.

"I didn't mean to pry. Where are they? Can they come to visit you?" She stood and straightened his bed sheets.

"Don't want them to. I told her to stay away."

Martha had heard the same story before. Many of the wounded soldiers had lost their pride and feeling of usefulness. She knew not to react with pity or acquiescence. With a straight face she spoke truth.

"Well, that's your decision. I know your think you're doing her a favor."

He snapped back. "Who wants a husband without two legs?"

Martha leaned down closer to look straight into his eyes.

"I can tell you this, Sergeant. Judy does. Don't make her a war widow by default. It's not fair to her or a son who needs a dad's heart and mind. It doesn't take legs to raise a boy. It takes guts."

She pulled the rail up on the side of his bed and locked them in place. The patient down the row groaned again. Her words had likely not been received, but she felt good about saying them. She left him there with his eyes closed, a tear dropping onto his pillow.

She followed the groaning to a bed close to the ward door.

The young man lying there had gauze wrapped completely around the top of his head. One ear was also wrapped, and pink liquid oozed through the white bandage. She reached in his table drawer to find fresh gauze as an orderly burst through the doorway.

"Wounded coming in from Lowry. Plane crash."

Martha's heart leapt to her throat. Another nurse ran in as the orderly moved on down the hall. She grabbed boxes of supplies from the cupboard. Martha forced her feet to move and came up behind her.

"What kind of plane crashed? Military?"

The nurse shrugged. "Don't know for sure. All I know is that some of the crew died. Must have been a training flight. If you're not busy, you'd better come too." She hurried out the door, leaving Martha gasping for air.

If she were to find out which crew, she had to go, but everything in her resisted. She made it through the door in time to see several doctors jogging toward the emergency rooms in the next wing. She might be needed, whether it was Clark or not, but she could not move.

"Let's get down there, Martha." Lt. Pawley raced passed her, then stopped. She approached Martha and stopped in front of where was frozen to the floor. "Your husband is a pilot, isn't he?"

Martha nodded, tears forming around her eyes.

"I see. Would you rather I find someone else to assist until we know who it is?"

She stared down the corridor lined with carts and empty gurneys. This was her chance to beat her fears. This is what facing them looked like. She couldn't pass the job onto someone else.

"I'll go. Thanks, though."

She kept up with Lt. Pawley's quickened steps until they reached the triage area. Bloodied bandages and clothing lay on the floor. Six men lay on gurneys and six doctors hovered over them while nurses cut away pants and shirts. Her eyes touched on each body for a moment. No Clark.

Martha caught up with another nurse. "Where do you need me?"

She pointed a bloody gloved finger to the last gurney in the row. "There. He's probably not going to make it, but see what you can do to assist the doctor."

She nearly slid from the blood on the floor, catching herself on the edge of the gurney where an older doctor worked feverishly on the man's—no boy's leg. She grabbed a pair of gloves from her pocket and snapped them on. A box of gauze lay at the boy's head. She gathered a wad and dabbed at some superficial wounds on his forehead. His eyes seemed fixed, but then he blinked. He was still alive.

"Stay with us, soldier. We're going to fix you up."

She pulled back the shredded flight jacket draped over his chest to see his arm barely attached to his shoulder. A glance at the doctor did nothing to reassure her. She replaced the jacket and concentrated on his face and neck, trying to apply pressure to the bloodiest cuts. It seemed like a futile gesture considering his grave condition.

"I'm n-not going to make it." His whole upper body shook and shuddered.

Martha halted her efforts and leaned in close like she had with the Sergeant in the ward. "Who says so? Just focus on relaxing."

"I didn't even… get a chance… to make a difference." His voice crackled and faded.

She took hold of his chin. "No you don't, buster. Stay with us. You'll make a difference. I promise. Where you from?" She removed the jacket again and blotted off blood to make sure there were no foreign objects.

"Nashville… Tennessee. I'm… a—" He winced with pain. "…country boy."

"Nashville? Why that's my hometown. I bet I know your folks." She looked up at the doctor who frowned, then barked an order.

"Nurse, I need more saline flush."

"I've got it." Lt. Pawley stepped in with a bottle and tubing.

Martha continued her search for shrapnel. The boy's eyes rolled back and she touched his face. "What's your name, soldier?"

His eyes focused again. He swallowed hard. "W-Wayne. Burrows."

"Burrows. Well that name does sound familiar." She pressed on a deep cut with fresh gauze to see if she could stop the bleeding. "You know, I bet when you get home, your mom and dad will be so proud of you."

He followed her face with is eyes. She thought she saw the beginnings of a smile.

The doctor stepped back from the gurney. Was he giving up? No, he couldn't let this boy go.

"He's ready for surgery. Leg artery is stable." He searched the room. "Orderly, take this man to the first available O.R. Nurse Pawley, follow me."

Within seconds the gurney was slipping away from Martha's grip, the boy along with it. She didn't feel ready to let go. She walked alongside and locked eyes with him.

"See you when you're done in there, soldier. All right?"

He lifted his good hand and signaled a thumbs up. It was probably the last thumbs up he would ever give. He would probably never go home to Nashville. Her little white lie to cheer him probably did no good at all. She wished she could tell him that he had made a difference.

To her.

"It was terrible. I had to go off shift so I don't know if any of them made it. A nurse can feel pretty helpless sometimes."

Clark sat on the apartment sofa with Martha as she fanned herself with a magazine. He had been able to steal away a whole night with her. The training schedule had let up a bit after the accident, and many of the men were taking a few days leave. They had but few precious days together each week—sometimes only a few hours. Yet, she seemed content to just be near him while he completed his training.

He knew after dealing with the crash casualties she would be anxious to see for herself that he wasn't on the plane. He would never tell her that he was supposed to have been. A last minute change had kept him on the ground.

He nodded at her assessment of feeling helpless. "We're all busted up about it. It wasn't even on the base. They had engine trouble and had to crash land in a corn field nearby. I can tell you that several died at the scene. That's all I know."

She grabbed his arm and slung it around her neck to nuzzle into his chest. He could feel her tense muscles. He rubbed her arm and kissed her forehead. The fan sitting on the floor blew the hot air in the room around, and he pulled off his shirt. The heat here was nothing compared to the stifling air up in a B24. *His* B24. Until they reached high altitudes, the men always complained of feeling sticky hot.

Martha sniffled. "I was paralyzed with fear when the word first came. But after that, instinct kicked in and when I didn't see you on one of those gurneys, I did all right. It helped to try and comfort one of them. He didn't look much older than 18." She turned her head up to look at him. "Do you suppose he is one of those who lied about his age?"

Clark hated talking about this. It was like cutting off a finger to have a fellow airman lose his life. Each man lost to the group was felt by everyone. The mighty Eighth Army was a huge entity, but the new 446th was made up of individuals. He knew that being a part of it would mean grief on a daily basis once they entered active duty. It was something he couldn't explain to Martha. He wouldn't even try.

He scooted to the front of the sofa.

"He might have been one of the ones who lied. I don't like seeing the young ones come through, itching for a fight and thinking they will conquer anything that gets in their way. You should hear some of them talk about how they could stop the war single-handed. All they need is a plane and some bombs, they say. The cocky crew members are the ones to put the rest of us in jeopardy."

He turned to see the stunned look on her face. Clearly, she hadn't thought of that before. He wished he hadn't said it. Then again, she needed to know the realities if she were going to hold up during his deployment.

She leaned forward. "Clark, I know you worry about me falling apart. I want you to know things are changing for me. I can see the bigger picture now—of what it's like to lay down your perceived control over life. Seeing those wounded crewmembers made me face the fact that someday, you could be rolling in on a stretcher. I can't hold you back or stop you from going. But..."

"Oh there's the *but*." He tipped his head back.

She smirked. "I was going to say that I don't want you thinking of anything but flying that plane when you're up there. That's the only assurance I have that my fears won't harm you. Do you understand?"

He wanted to give her a robust congratulations for winning the fear battle, but he knew her better than she thought. Despite her confidence and proclamations of bravery under fire, he sensed something she had not faced. She never used the word death. She hadn't faced that if his plane was shot down, there would be no survivors.

He had to tell her about his commission now, and test the waters of her convictions. He placed his hand on her knee.

"I've been assigned to the 706th Squadron of the 446th Heavy Bombardment Group. I'll be deploying to a base in England as soon as the entire group is fully assembled and we gather supplies." Her eyes teared. "I didn't want to tell you this now, but it seemed the right time."

Martha plopped down in front of the fan, cross-legged. He could see her shoulders shake. It couldn't be helped. She must have known he would be deployed. Unless...

"Martha. Did you hope I wouldn't pass the flight training? It's okay if you did. I understand."

She spun around to face him. "I'm not sure. Maybe I did. I'm not perfect, and of course I don't want you to go off to a war. No woman wants that. She wouldn't love her man much if she were happy to see him go. Am I right? I'll be okay. Or at least I'll do the best I can."

He had to smile. Sometimes she seemed more like a child than a woman, flitting from one rationale to another, trying to convince everyone she was fine and the only one she convinced was herself. There wasn't much he could do for her at this point. She would have to find her own way.

Perhaps her stubborn personality and quick temper would be God's way of strengthening her through whatever was to come. He slipped off the sofa and joined her on the floor. The sun had moved from the front window, cooling the room. He reached for her hand and slid his fingers through hers.

"Martha, I trust you to handle your own emotions. You'll have many of them in the coming months. It's only natural. None of us know what's ahead of us. We all have to embrace the world God puts us in. It's just not fun sometimes to feel like you're in the dark."

Martha put her head down. "Like I said, I'll do the best I

can." After a quiet moment she shrugged. "So I guess I'm a pilot's wife, huh? I want to know what to expect. Can you tell me where you'll be going and what you'll be doing—besides flying a plane, I mean?"

He leaned against the sofa. This was the moment he had dreaded. She had the right to know as much as he could tell her. Piling on this information could make or break her resolve, and he couldn't lie. The other wives would be talking about it and Martha could get blindsided. She would hate him if he weren't completely honest.

"All right. Here's the scoop. Our squadron has been selected—the 706th it's called. We will be stationed at a base in Bungay, England and flying our missions from there. My plane is a B24 Liberator heavy bomber." He paused to assess her expression. She showed no signs of emotion.

"Go on."

"I have a crew already assigned. I haven't met them all yet. I know they'll be a great bunch of guys and we'll work well together. I'd like for you to meet them sometime. I have a little gathering planned for those wives who are here or coming to say goodbye to their husbands. I heard that one of the wives will be painting our plane's nose art. I have an idea of what to name our ship if the others like it. Old Faithful. Great name, don't you think?"

He wasn't sure how much more to tell her. She was either taking it much better than expected, or was in shock. The best thing to do was to let any more information wait for another time. He pulled her close to hold her. She didn't resist, but wasn't relaxed either.

"So you'll be flying a great big plane with great big bombs to drop on the enemy. Will they shoot at you?"

"Yes. But our guns are better. Our gunners are positioned all around the plane."

She slid down and rested her head in his lap. No crying, no more questions. Just the kind of stillness that said it was time to stop talking.

They sat on the floor for a long time. The room was dark now. Peaceful. Clark feared he would fall asleep if he didn't go to bed.

As soon as his head hit the pillow he was out, but he woke with a start, reaching for Martha. She wasn't in the bed. He turned on the bedstand light and shuffled into the living room. Martha stood at the front window, her arms hugging her chest, moonlight kissing her face. He stood behind her and wrapped his arms around hers, tight.

"You could die," she said softly, emotionless.

"Yes."

It was as if that was what she needed to hear to close the lesson on B24s, and war, and bombs. He nuzzled his face into her neck, wishing he could make it all better.

He couldn't. No one could.

Chapter Eleven

September 1943

The dull gray mass of metal loomed over him as Clark inspected the first plane he could call his own. Its massive wings stretched wide, with two propellers on each one. A strange tenseness touched each muscle in Clark's body as he stared into the cockpit high above. Shiny new leather covered the seat he would sit in, the pilot's chair. Surrounded by windshields, instead of puffy clouds or blue skies, he would see his enemy coming at him. He wouldn't be spending hours with a crew, laughing and telling jokes to pass the hours in the air. From now on, his crew would be on a mission—on many missions. From now on, his heart would beat a new kind of rhythm.

Three weeks to get to know the men who would be his companions, an extension of his arms and ears. They would all be attached by gut responses and focused duty. He would need the best of men, the keenest of committed teammates. This monstrous B24 would be the best in the sky—he and his crew would see to it. They would make their 25 missions count. No mistakes on his watch.

"She sure is pretty. Would love to get my hands around her belly—so to speak."

Clark looked behind him. A young man stood gazing up,

one hand on his hip, the other holding a smoldering cigarette. His face was taken over by a contagious grin.

Clark turned to step toward him. "Yep, she's a good looking ship. You're a pilot?"

The young man laughed. "Naw, ball gunner."

"Ah, I get the joke now. *Hands around her belly*. Good one." Clark stuck out his hand. "Clark Jensen. Pilot of this lady."

"Albert Wagner. Your ball gunner."

Clark took a step back. "You're on my crew?"

Albert saluted and Clark returned it. "Yes, sir. I'm ready to go. Got my assignment a week ago and they hurried me over here."

"Where you from, Albert?"

"Sunman, Indiana. Born and raised. Yourself?"

"Pasco, Washington state."

Albert tipped his head. "Played cards with a fellow from Washington the other night. Don't recall his name. The way he talked, sounds like a pretty place."

Clark stole another look at the cockpit. He would soon be far away from that pretty place, as Albert put it.

"It is beautiful there. My wife and her family used to live on a vineyard in the southeastern part of the state. Never saw a more picturesque place. Would love to live on a farm like that someday when this war is wrapped up."

"I'm going straight back to Evelyn and my boy, Bobby, in Indiana when I'm done. I want the best team to work with so I'll be sure to get back to her."

"We'll have the best, I'm sure."

Clark had no guarantees, but now was the time to start thinking positively and reinforcing good attitudes. This fellow did seem eager to do a good job, and since his was one of the most dangerous, might as well begin their relationship with optimism—something this guy would need in the days to come.

"Well, the rest of the crew is supposed to be gathering later in the barracks meeting room. I hope they're all as anxious to go as you are." He took one last look at the ship. "Let's let the maintenance crew finish up here."

"Lead the way, sir."

On the way across the field they chatted about their homes and wives and the foods they missed. Other crews passed by in easy conversations and pats on the back. Clark's chest tightened to think how different things would be once they arrived in Europe. This was a real war. No more simulation, no more leaning on the news reels and papers to create visuals of this war. The training films would be comprised of men he knew and liked, some who were already over there in B17s and fighters. Checking the casualty list every day had become a personal mission—one he hated, but couldn't avoid. It secured his resolve, and reminded him that defeating Hitler was crucial.

Crucial because the world was tired of bullies. And because Oma and Opa were over there. Were they in hiding? In prison? He had to believe they were safe—that they had escaped to another country long before things got bad.

"Do you have any family in Europe, Albert?"

"Only some distant relatives in Germany. We've never stayed in touch. Probably should have. Not the best place for anyone to be these days. You?"

"Grandparents and a few relatives I've never met. We're pretty worried since we haven't heard from them for a long time. They were supposed to try to leave Germany, but we don't know if that happened."

Clark's stomach churned. He patted his wallet in his back pocket where he kept his grandparent's picture. His boyhood memory of their visit to America had burned deeper over the last year. He would need that heritage of strong German determination in the coming months. With any luck, he and

Martha would someday be able to introduce a child of theirs to Oma and Opa.

"Sir?"

Clark turned to Albert. "Oh, sorry. Did you say something?"

"Just that I'm sorry about your grandparents. Must be a helpless feeling." He took off his hat and pushed back a strand of brown hair from his forehead. "I'll keep them in my prayers."

"Thanks, Wagner." Clark looked the man up and down. "Say, you'll fit fine in the little glass ball. Glad to have you on crew." He reached out his hand. Wagner gripped it tight.

"We'll get the job done, sir. And live to tell about it."

"I look forward to proving you right. Let's hope our first flight with the officer in charge leaves him thinking we're worthy of his confidence. I don't mind saying I'm nervous."

Wagner tapped his watch, then saluted. "I have to go before the new books are all gone. Nice to meet you. See you at the briefing."

Clark's gaze followed his ball gunner as he jogged toward the barracks. New books? "Let's hope the rest of the crew is as settled as Wagner." He scanned the sky. A formation of B24s drew near from the distance. Soon it would be his crew up there.

"Lord, bring me the best."

She couldn't believe the time for deployment had come. Clark would be leaving for England, and she would go back home to reclaim her apartment and job. She would probably cry all the way back to Washington.

The sick feeling in her stomach intensified the closer they got to the train station. She hated goodbyes and this one would be the king of goodbyes, and the one she had held out hope would never become a reality. December 7th changed all that—not just for her, but for the world of wives, mothers, and sweethearts reaching for that last touch, maybe for a final time.

This is what churned Martha's stomach, but she would spend her last ounce of energy trying to convince him she was okay. Convincing herself had already cost her a bucket of tears.

Their conversation lulled the closer they came to the station. She could feel Clark's apprehension through her skin as she cuddled his arm while he drove. His tense muscles twitched with each passing mile. She prayed he wouldn't make too much of it. Her emotional stability depended on it.

"You have my C.O.'s information with you, right?"

"Yes, in my purse."

"And you signed the paperwork for getting out of the apartment here?"

"Yes, Clark. Everything is done. At least on my part."

His lips tightened in a straight line. "You call me as soon as you get home. I'll be busy, but keep trying till you get me. I want to know you made it okay." He gave her a quick once over. "Are you all right? I'm sorry we have to be apart, Martha."

There. He did it. He said the words she had stricken from her mind. Being apart was the worst of it. Not knowing what he was doing from day to day, hour by hour would consume her thoughts. Right now, the realization of having over 4,000 miles between them felt like someone ripping out her heart.

She could only nod against his shirt-sleeve, breathing in his scent. How many other women had buried their red noses into their soldiers chests today? She knew she was asking too much of God to make this all go away. It seemed fair enough to agree to let go of her fears and have all the children Clark wanted in exchange for his deployment. God might be full up with bargains from women trying to hold on to their men.

"Here we are." Clark pulled into the parking lot and turned off the key. "I'll get a cart to put your luggage on. Be right back." He pulled his arm from her grip and kissed her forehead.

The nausea that had pestered her all morning suddenly crept

up her esophagus. "I need to find a restroom." She slid out the driver's side and scurried toward the sign on the side of the station that said *Women.* She burst through the door and raced straight to the trash can. The breakfast Clark had lovingly fixed for her came up in a violent eruption.

She splashed her face with cold water and stared into the mirror. "What in the world is the matter with you?" The face glaring back at her needed a makeup redo at the least. How could she wave goodbye to her husband looking like this? Red eyes, blotchy skin, and smudged lipstick.

"You let your anxiety get the best of you, Martha." She rummaged in her purse to find her lipstick tube and comb. A sprinkle of powder helped the blotches, and she managed to comb her waves in place before redesigning her lips. One deep breath in and she would have to get back to the station.

She flung open the door to find Clark on the other side, pacing. He stopped short and approached her.

"Are you all right? Why were you in there so long? I was afraid you'd miss your train." He touched her elbow and gazed into her eyes.

She blinked and brought on her best smile. "I'm fine, just freshening up." *Stay upright and don't throw up again.*

"You look upset. I'm sorry this is so hard on you." He pulled her so close and hugged her so tight, she though he would squeeze the air out of her.

"It's all right. Let's get my ticket."

"I've already checked your bags and picked up your ticket. You're set, but we only have a few minutes to say goodbye."

For the first time she saw his eyes fill with tears, and for the first time she felt the pain he must feel. She had been so wrapped up in her fears and dread, she had forgotten that he might have his own demons to deal with. She dare not make it more difficult for him—after all, he was the one heading into battle. She would remain safe and sound here at home.

Safe. What will it matter if something happens to Clark?

He whispered in her ear. "I see the wheels turning in your mind. I'll be all right. I will come home to you."

Before she could breathe a word of doubt, he pulled her hand and led her to the boarding area full of soldiers and loved ones. The air thick with emotion and trepidation, Martha metered her breathing to keep her stomach calm and tears contained. She would have plenty of time on the long ride back to Pasco to break down.

Clark took both her hands in his. "You'll have a tough time, Martha. I know you. You'll worry and worry until you're convinced of the worst. I'm asking you here and now to fight it. Lean on your faith, stay busy. Write me letters and stay with nursing. You have to find strength to let me go and do what I must do without…well, worrying."

Martha's rolling stomach settled at Clark's words—wise words with a pleading she had never heard from him. There would be only one thing to do—help the one person who needed her the most. She would find strength for his sake.

They walked hand in hand toward her train car. "I don't want you thinking about anything except that plane of yours—what did you guys name it? Old something."

He pinched her chin. "Old Faithful."

"Well, I'll be old faithful over here, I promise."

The train whistle blew and men and women threw their arms around each other. A woman standing by the next car wailed. Martha felt like doing the same. Instead, she grabbed Clark by the shoulders and kissed him hard. Her cheeks were wet when she finally let go of him. She didn't know if it were her tears or his.

"Goodbye, Mrs. Jensen."

She stepped back. "Goodbye, Lt. Jensen. Behave yourself."

"You too."

She stepped on the first landing and turned to smile.

"I can only try."

The train jiggled into motion as she found her seat. Clark stood exactly where she left him. She waved, he waved. It seemed so cliché, like a tragic novel. Her insides felt anything but cliché. This was personal and real. She studied his face. She wanted to remember every slant of his jaw, the swimming color of his eyes.

She leaned her forehead on the window, straining for a last look. His figure grew smaller and smaller as the train gained speed. She would have to build a life alone. For a while. She would have to let go of her fears and let God take care of him.

For a while.

Clark stood at the east intersection of the three runways of the Bungay airfield. The icy wind blew against his face, and once in a while he thought he saw a snowflake flitter through the air. The view over the Waveney Valley was much prettier from the ground. Studying it from this vantage point always helped him gain perspective for mission takeoffs.

He couldn't see the town of Bungay from here, but the village of Flixton just beyond the tree line was a mark for bearings when he landed Old Faithful. The hangars, HQ, sick quarters, and other buildings were his small world now. He had grown accustomed to their drab exteriors and musty interiors.

He turned and walked off the runway to trek back to base. Slipping around the back of Hangar 2, he headed for the mess building. The rest of the crew would be waiting. He shook his head in wonder at how he had been so fortunate with the bunch of men he commanded.

Clark sensed someone following him. He turned and saw

the same uniformed boy he had seen right after the morning crew meeting. Tall and lanky, with his Adam's apple bobbing each time he swallowed, this kid looked far too young to be on an air force base in England. He barely looked old enough to be out of high school. His intense stare spooked Clark at first, then he realized the kid had a way about him—a look that pleaded for attention. And a sort of familiarity in his features.

The young man obliged Clark's motion to come near. He ran toward Clark, stopping short directly in front of him.

"Are you following me, young man?"

"Yes, sir."

"Why?"

"Just wanted to meet you. My team worked on Old Faithful last week and I've seen you come by every day to check on her. I wanted to tell you what a great crew you have. They come by to see her too."

Clark stifled a chuckle to hear that his crew secretly worried about Old Faithful as much as he did. "I see. What's your name?"

"Jimmy, sir." He stood straight and saluted.

"Forget the salute from now on, Jimmy. Maintenance crews have enough to do with their hands. Agreed?"

Jimmy nodded. Clark couldn't help but wonder about the young man's name. Jimmy was a strange name for someone who was trying to be a grown up in a war. Regardless, Clark guessed he would have an admirer from now on. He didn't mind. It would be a refreshing distraction from this war.

"How's the work on Old Faithful coming along?"

"Oh, she's almost done. As soon as we finish repair on the last of the flak damage, she'll be fit. Sure wish I could go up in her. I'm going to be a pilot someday, just didn't pass the first round of tests yet, so I decided to at least learn them from the inside out."

Clark frowned. "How old are you, Jimmy?"

Jimmy looked off in the distance. "Twenty-one."

Not likely. "Twenty-one? Well, you still have time to fly. It's good you're getting to know the planes this way. Nice to meet you, Jimmy."

Clark took one step back and felt the young man's eyes lock onto his. He recognized that look of hunger—the obvious desire to do more than just fix broken vessels. He wanted to fly in the worst way. Staying on the ground would be safer for him, and increase his chances to go home to his family, wherever they were.

Clark could offer little more than friendship at this point. Or maybe some extra time now and then.

"Say, why don't you set aside an hour when I come to do her final check tomorrow? I'll show you around the cockpit and tell you what you'll have to do as a B24 pilot. Sound good for 0700?"

Jimmy burst into a smile reminiscent of a boy being given his first bicycle. "Sounds good. Thank you, sir. See you tomorrow. 0700."

"Jimmy! Get over here!" Someone shouted from the last hanger door.

"My crew chief. Gotta go."

As Jimmy ran in the direction of the shouting, Clark mulled over how many young Jimmys there had to be, rushing to be a man, taking on responsibilities too big for their age. Yet, he understood the drive to do something about the world's troubles, and not just wait for it all to go away.

The door to the mess swung open and Hank Kingsbery held it for Clark. "Where you been? The crew is waiting. We're at the end of the room in the corner. Pretty quiet in here right now. Good time for a pep talk."

His co-pilot had proved himself once again. He seemed to

know what Clark was thinking before they even had a chance to know each other very well. A pep talk was exactly what Clark had in mind when he asked Kingsbery to gather everyone. There was little time these days to do much in the way of uniting a team.

"Does everyone have their Dr. Peppers?"

"Yep. They said thanks."

"Least I can do."

His stomach twitched just a bit. They had already flown five missions without even much communication. Clark had deliberated then over each man's character and found them to be solid. Of course, there were a few off-base antics to deal with just before they left the U.S., but nothing he couldn't deal with or tolerate. Adjusting to life in the European theater of a world war had taken all their energy. Time to put some personality into this crew.

The other eight men nodded as Clark approached. Wagner wore the same smile he woke up with every morning, a comforting gesture.

The others seemed in good spirits as well, with the exception of a possible slight hangover with Keegan.

"Men." He shook his head. "Wagner, don't you ever stop smiling?"

Laughter broke out and Sgt. Nye slapped Wagner's back. "It's a sign of his high intelligence."

Clark held up his hand. "Okay, okay. Let's get down to business before we get called away. Old Faithful will be back in service in the morning. We won't have to take another plane up for tomorrow afternoon's mission. I know you prefer our ship just as I do. My new friend Jimmy assured me just a while ago she'll be ready."

"Jimmy? That kid in maintenance?" Sgt. Watson spoke up after guzzling the last of his Dr. Pepper.

Clark hoisted his foot onto the chair next to him. "Yes. You know him? Seems like a nice kid. Wants to fly pretty badly."

Watson nodded. "He *is* nice. Doesn't look much older than a little-leaguer though."

The other men chuckled. Clark had wondered about the age thing, but something about the boy haunted him.

"So, unless we get a surprise call for a mission, I'll be doing a repair check at 0700 and the rest of you should be able to run through your station check list by 0900. Then we'll be ready to go whenever."

The men talked among themselves. Clark took a seat. "I have some other things I want to say. We haven't had much time to get well acquainted, and although I think we're working like an oiled machine, I hope we can find time once in a while to connect. If you don't want to share personal information, that's fine, but I'd like to go around the table and see if anyone would like to say something about themselves."

He crossed his fingers behind his back. It was a risk asking them to open up. Not all men on base wanted to get cozy and personal. Strangers dying didn't pull at the heartstrings like losing a friend. Even in their short time here, they had all witnessed both sides of the spectrum. Some men parading a hard exterior after the casualty report, some breaking down in tears. Clark wanted to be sure his men felt they could open up about their turmoil.

Wagner was the first to speak. "You all know I'm from Indiana. I have a wife and baby boy. Well, he's not a baby anymore. Those of you who've played cards with me know I like to have fun and pal around. I'd like to be friends with all of you. So just know that. And I'm always up for a game of cards. Helps pass the time between missions." He lowered his head. "And keeps my mind off missing my family."

There was silence in their corner of the room. The crew in

the kitchen hollered back and forth, banging pots and pans. One other flight crew huddled together on the other side of the room. Clark could hear every other word of a soft prayer, a tradition he planned to institute starting tomorrow.

He looked around the table. "Keegan? Back? Anyone else?" Nye raised his hand. Keegan pulled it down. "This isn't school, Nye." Nervous laughter erupted, then all eyes were on Nye.

"Well, I miss family just like everyone here, I think. I'm not married, so I don't worry about anyone back home. I like my job on Old Faithful. We've been lucky and I hope we stay that way. There's a saying my mom says…"

A door slammed. The mail carrier hollered out. "Mail call!"

Keegan lurched from his chair, but Kingsbery grabbed his arm. "I think this is more important. Let's keep going with our introductions."

Keegan shrugged and sat again. Clark nodded to his co-pilot, grateful for the backup.

Nye finished his speech. "She says you have to accept whatever comes and the only important thing is that you meet it with the best you have to give."

Clark nodded. "Thanks Nye. Anyone else want to say something?"

Hause sat up straight. "I feel pretty good about our crew. I don't know any of you very well, but I've noticed we all have a keen sense of duty and responsibility." He turned to Clark. "And, sir, I want to say I have ultimate trust in your command. You have a level head and know your job better than any pilot I've come across."

Clark smiled, relieved to have at least one of his crew confident in his leadership.. "Thanks."

"Well, it does help that he looks like a movie star. Makes us look important," Back nudged Hause.

Clark laughed, but his face felt on fire. "Okay, that's enough of that, fellas."

Nye spoke up. "What about you, sir? We don't even know if you're married or have kids."

Clark thought of Martha, wishing they did have a child, but that would have to wait till he returned home.

"My wife is Martha. We don't have any kids yet. She's a nurse. Can't wait to get home to her. We didn't have much of a honeymoon and I intend to remedy that with a nice long trip when I get back."

The mood changed. Clark knew they had bonded enough for one day. He would make this a weekly ritual. One thing was for sure, he was confident in the character of his crew. His job would be easier. He would do his best to get them all home.

"Okay, men. Go get your mail."

Chapter Twelve

December 19, 1943

"*I*'ve heard that some men have stayed alive in dire circumstances because they knew they had a child waiting for them. Besides, he has a right to know." Sister Clatilda patted Martha's arm as she lay on an exam room bed, an IV imbedded in her left arm. Sister pulled open the drapes on the window overlooking the grassy area in front of the building. Martha couldn't see it, but she knew the spot of her first date with Clark would be in view.

The low gray clouds had hung around for days, threatening snow. Sister moved about the room straightening canisters of cotton balls and gauze squares, leaving Martha a moment to think of her response.

"I don't know. I don't want to worry him."

Sister stood at the end of the bed and cranked the handle to sit Martha up a bit. She checked the IV tube and took Martha's pulse. "I think he'll be more thrilled than worried. You don't need to tell him you've been down with morning sickness."

"Down? That's an understatement, Sister. I guess you could call fainting in the hallway and needing IV fluids being *down*. I should have known what was wrong when I threw up at the train station. I thought all this nausea was because I was nervous about him leaving for England. This wasn't planned."

185

Sister looked up over her spectacles. "You mean wasn't planned by you and Clark." She pointed up. "Someone else planned this. He knows best. Even about babies."

"But I'm not ready for children. I'm not even sure I wanted any at all. My mother says it's because I lost my friend when I was little. She says it must have traumatized me enough to be afraid to have my own kids."

Sister pinched off the IV tube. "You're done. Let me take this IV out. Feeling better?"

"Yes. I need to get back to work."

"No you don't. You're to go home for the day. Drink lots of fluids, and rest. You know the routine."

Martha slid her legs over the edge of the bed. "Fine. I'm tired anyway."

The thought of going home sounded good to her. It was time to write Clark and tell him he would be a father come summer. She shuddered. One minute her heart jumped for joy and the next minute her palms sweated like crazy. She had just gotten used to the idea of Clark's deployment, and now she was spinning at the prospect of being a mother. She had been on the maternity ward and seen the tragedies of young mothers with a new baby. Some of them had just buried their soldier husbands—the joys of birth overshadowed by death.

"Are you okay to drive? Shall I call someone to come get you?" Sister bandaged Martha's IV site.

"No, I'm good. I need to call my folks and tell them about the baby. Don't want to scare them, but I could use some of Mama's home remedies about now. They'll be pretty excited about all this. Can't say I blame them, but…"

Martha bit her lower lip. She had to stop any negative talk, but there was one question Sister could answer from her vast experience.

"But what?"

Martha sat on the stool by the bed and reached for her shoes. "I guess I'm too sick to be enthusiastic about this baby. Is that normal?"

"I would say yes. Especially under these circumstances."

Martha groaned. This would be another test of her character while Clark was away. A little life depended on her and she had promised Clark to be strong. Today she needed grace on that account.

Sister glanced her way and then finished cleaning up. She pulled off the sheets from the bed and looked Martha up and down. "Are you steady on your feet now?"

"Yes, thank you for everything. I'm glad you were around today."

"I'm a permanent fixture." Sister juggled the sheets to turn out the light.

"I know. It feels like everyone else has left me. Clark, Clarissa and Hana, and even my folks. I'm all alone."

The hallway echoed with the chatter of nurses coming and going. Sister nodded in their direction. "You're not alone. You have all the other nurses here. And I'm sure everyone you mentioned will write you letters."

How terrible it was to live her life through letters, waiting each day for the mailman to stuff an envelope into her little apartment door mail slot. She had nothing else. Clark said to lean on her faith, but even God seemed far away, as if He were busy with the war and other more important things. Words on a paper would have to be her solace. Her world was about to get very small.

"One thing you're not thinking of. You have a baby coming now—that should keep you quite busy."

A baby. It wasn't real yet. The morning sickness that lasted all day and fatigue to go with it were the only signs she had of her coming motherhood.

"What if I'm a bad mother?"

Sister opened the supply room door and tossed the sheets into a laundry hamper. She moved to face Martha, her arms tucked in her huge sleeves, her eyes fixed on Martha's.

Uh oh.

"Martha, it's time to take hold of your worries. You must find that place in you that knows God is in control. You have a lot on your emotional plate. Don't let it choke you. Stay strong for this little one. Do you understand how important that is?"

Martha's eyes opened wide. Sister had never scolded her quite like this before. There was a firm affection in her voice, yet authority too. She was right. Where was the strength she had promised Clark she would have?

"Just concentrate on loving that child. Our Bible tells us that love casts out fear. I believe you can apply those words to yourself while you wait. Now go home."

Sister floated away, as if on a breeze of purpose. Mama would have said the same things. How she could use her mother's comfort now. If only California weren't so far away. She was tired of train rides.

She opened her locker door and removed her purse and sweater. On the shelf above lay Clarissa's letter she hadn't had time to read this morning. Maybe now would be a good time for some news from her friend. Clarissa always had funny anecdotes about the homestead to cheer her. And she must have received the letter telling her about the baby. No doubt she would have a lot to say. Martha sat on the bench and ripped open the envelope.

Dear Martha,

I am so thrilled about your news, but also sorry that you are there alone. I wish you would consider coming to Kansas, or at least go to be with your folks in California. But I know how stubborn you are. I hope you are well and taking good care of yourself.

I hadn't wanted to share our news with you. I was holding

back hoping to resolve our problem. I didn't want to add to your worries. James ran away several months ago. We suspect he joined the army but have not been able to locate him. The army won't tell us anything since he is legally of age. I'm not the only mother who thinks a 20-year-old is too young for war.

We have decided to accept his decision. I wanted you to know about it so you could pray for his safety as you pray for Clark's. We are heartbroken, but you know James. He is stubborn like you, and has a passion for flying much like your Clark. We can only hope that someone sees his immaturity and looks out for him wherever he is. No one in the military offices around here will tell us if he has enlisted or not. We contacted the state recruitment board and they say there is no one listed under his name and age. It could be he lied about both. For all we know, he could be overseas. They send them so young these days.

If you're still alone when it comes time for the baby, I would consider coming up there if Frank doesn't need me here. Please take care of yourself and keep me informed about your situation. I will let you know if we hear from James.

No more news for now. Take care of yourself and get plenty of rest.

Love,

Clarissa

She could barely read the last few lines as her throat clogged. James. She thought she had reached him all those months ago about not hurting his parents this way. He was no longer a boy as his mother said, but Martha suspected a child never really grows up in a mother's heart.

"Oh, James. What have you done? I hope you're not in Europe with all the action. It's bad enough Clark is there."

If anything happened to either one of them it would devastate her and Clarissa. Sister had to be right. God just had to be in control—watching over both of them. Only He would decide about their lives… or deaths.

She put on her coat and hat and made her way to the parking lot. A light drifting of snow had covered her windshield, so she dusted it with the envelope still in her hand. The car warmed and calmed her shivering. Daylight had almost disappeared. The roads could be slick and she would take it slow to her apartment. Clarissa was right—she needed to take care of herself now.

The narrow streets to her building twinkled with Christmas lights from rows of houses adorned for the season. She hadn't even put up a Christmas tree. What was the point? Clark wasn't there—not even Mama and Pop. They would be disappointed to know she wasn't going to celebrate the holidays. Maybe hearing about the baby would be their extra Christmas gift. She was waiting for Christmas day to make the phone call and surprise them, just to make it extra special news.

Four days until Christmas and she didn't own a single decoration. Tomorrow she would raid what was left of the Christmas merchandise at the Rexall Drug store. Feeling sorry for herself wasn't going to get her through the holidays. Everyone she loved would be saddened to know she had sunk so low as to ignore the holiday.

She stopped the car in front of her building and headed up the steps to her 400-square-foot home sweet home. There was a light in her front window. She didn't remember leaving any lights on, but she might have in her state of extreme nausea.

She stopped at the apartment door. The thought crossed her mind that there could be a burglar inside. Her mind whirled with images of someone rummaging through her drawers looking for valuables.

Don't be ridiculous.

Her key turned the lock and she opened the door to see Mama and Pop standing in the living room next to the tiniest Christmas tree she had ever seen. Pop's nose was red, and Mama's eyes moist with tears.

"Merry Christmas," they said in unison.

Martha dropped her purse and ran to them. She didn't care about being over-emotional. She just needed hugs.

"What are you doing here? When..."

Mama giggled. "When you told us you couldn't come to us for the holidays, we decided to get on a train and come to you. The landlady let us in and when we saw you didn't have a tree, we walked to the Boy Scout lot down the street and got the last little tree they had." She tipped her head to admire their handiwork. "Turned out nice, don't you think?"

"It's beautiful. I'm so glad you're here. I want to give you my Christmas present right now. I think you should sit down for a minute."

Martha slid her coat off and draped it over a chair.

Mama turned toward the kitchen. "I've got stew on the stove..."

"Mama, Pop. Sit down. I need to tell you something important."

Her parent's faces sobered. They inched over to the sofa. She had to blurt it out before they worried something had happened to Clark. A strange happiness tickled inside her as she said the words.

"You're going to be grandparents."

The small room off the hanger was so cold Clark had to plug in the heater he brought from the barracks. The mess had become too crowded with the insurgence of new crews as the 446th Bombardment Group grew to meet the needs of a war with Germany. Meeting with his guys was a crucial part of his plan to unite them. With Christmas happening tomorrow without much hope for anyone going home soon, he devised a surprise for the crew of Old Faithful.

Jimmy had helped him round up pseudo-decorations and had scoured the countryside near the base for a bush that might pass for a Christmas tree. The army had a big dinner planned for the entire base, but Clark didn't feel like a major production and hoped his crew would appreciate a smaller, more intimate gathering. A few bottles of Orange Crush, a beer or two for Keegan, and some broken Christmas cookies Clark stole from Wagner's goodie box stash would be the party fare for the day. He'd managed to raid the peanut and pretzel supply from the officer's mess. He even added Martha's caramel corn to the menu.

Jimmy poked his head in the door. "All set, sir?"

"Yep. Thanks for your help, Jimmy. You've been great."

Clark's heart sank to think he wouldn't be able to invite the kid to the party. There were things he needed to discuss with his men that couldn't be shared. He reached into Wagner's cookie box and found one that was nearly whole.

"Here you go. Merry Christmas, my friend."

Jimmy's face lit up. He took the cookie and nodded. "Merry Christmas, sir. Thank you."

Jimmy was too young to be here—in a war—without his family. Clark saw the sorrow written on his face. The look reflected his own feelings at being away from Martha. So many men on base were really just older boys, too eager for a chance to fight.

He watched Jimmy survey the room. He knew what the kid must be thinking.

"You wishing you were home for the holidays?"

Jimmy's face reddened. "Yes, sir." He picked off a small bite of cookie with his fingers and placed it on his tongue. A half-smile graced his face. "Good cookie."

"Well, maybe tomorrow we can play a game of cards. Don't think there will be a mission on Christmas Day."

Jimmy grinned wide. "I would like that, sir." He turned to leave just as Kingsbery and Nye came through the opened door.

Kingsbery threw his hands in the air. "I thought we were to report for an emergency meeting."

Nye stole a few peanuts from the bowl. "Looks like a party to me."

Clark pointed toward the table of drinks. "Help yourself. Save a beer for Keegan. I wouldn't normally offer alcohol, but it's a special occasion, and I know Keegan."

Sgt. Hanna stood in the door, his mouth hanging open. The rest of the crew wandered in and dove right into the refreshments. Someone ran out and then came back toting a portable radio. Christmas music was both a blessing and a curse to the emotional atmosphere. Keegan put down his beer after a few sips. Clark could tell the mood was turning from festive to apathetic. Maybe even sad.

"Have a seat, guys. I need to go over some changes to be made to procedure before our next mission. Didn't want to bother you with business tomorrow. Our last several flights were good, but I want better. We have a long way to go in this war, so let's brainstorm after I show you some of my ideas."

Kingsbery smiled as he pulled out his chair. "You're the perfectionist. We bow to your brains, sir."

Clark chuckled. "In know. It's my dad's fault. Just like him."

Jimmy burst through the door with only a single knock. Clark frowned.

"We're about to start a meeting, Jimmy. What…"

"A telegram, sir. Just came." He panted like he had just run a marathon. "I wanted to get it to you before—before the meeting. Sorry."

"Who is it for?" Clark reached for the envelope while the room hushed. Telegrams weren't always a good thing. Every man in the room stared at Jimmy, waiting for an answer.

Jimmy looked at the other men, then at Clark. "It's for you, sir."

Clark slipped the envelope from Jimmy's fingers. The relieved faces around the room left a pang of envy in Clark's heart, wishing it would have been for someone else. He slid open the flap and unfolded the tan paper. It seemed as though everyone stopped breathing.

Dear Clark,

Had to tell you before Christmas day. I'm pregnant. Morning sickness. Thanks a lot. I'm happy. Hope you are too. Merry Christmas. Love, Martha.

His hands fell to the table and he bent over it. He felt his mouth gaping, but was powerless to move.

"Sir, are you all right?" Jimmy leaned down face to face.

Kingsbery stood and moved close to Clark's side. "What it is, Clark?"

Clark swallowed to find his voice. "It's… a baby."

Hause piped up. "Whose baby?"

"Martha's."

Laughter bounced off the steel walls of the small room, echoing into the hanger. Kingsbery laughed through a question. "Just Martha's?"

Clark's hands went to his cheeks to cool them. "Mine too. So that means I'm going to be a father. How about that?"

Wagner stood and pointed to Jimmy. "We'll need more Orange Crush to celebrate, kid. Can you find us some?"

Jimmy responded with a broad smile. "I know where to pilfer some. On my way."

The pats on the back and handshakes shook Clark to the core. "I'm having a kid. What do you know?"

The meeting dissolved into a sentimental walk down memory lane for the few men who had children back home. Stories abounded about diapers, cravings, long nights, and cutting teeth. The single guys all agreed they were glad the telegram wasn't for them. Clark wondered when Martha was due. His own child would welcome him home from this terrible place. He loved flying, but not like this—not what he had in mind. He had another passion now—watching a son or daughter grow. Clark sat staring at the telegram, praying he wouldn't miss any of it.

January 15, 1944

Clark, in his letter, had rattled on about his crew, his plane, and some young man named Jimmy. He told her again how awful it was to be without her on Christmas, but that the telegram had saved the day with a distraction for him and the men.

He was always honest with her about his feelings in his letters, good and bad. She wished she could tell him how her fears came to her in the night and that the dream she thought had finally left her had returned of late—ever since she found out she was expecting. He would only worry about her, and he had enough on his mind—more important things than her dreams.

She folded this letter, more like a note, and returned it to the envelope to read the next one on her stack. This morning she had hit the jackpot with three letters in her mailbox. It had made her heart leap and lifted the fatigue she fought the day before.

"Aren't you the popular one?" Maggie stood over Martha with her hands on her hips.

"Why?"

"I wish I got letters," she giggled. "I guess I need to get me a boyfriend who's overseas so I get some. How's Clark?"

The silly girl had no idea what she was wishing for. Martha would gladly give up all letters just to have him home with her.

Martha's jaw twitched. "He's fine. Dropping bombs, you know."

Maggie's expression drooped. Martha knew she shouldn't have said it. It was cruel and sarcastic. Maggie knew it too.

"I'm sorry, Maggie. I'm just tired and cranky I guess. Clark is fine. He misses me, but he's happy about the baby."

Maggie leaned down and hugged her. "That's good news. Join us for lunch?"

"No, you all go ahead. I'm not hungry, and I have another letter to read. It's from Hana."

Maggie turned to the table where the other girls sat. "Be sure to tell her hello from us girls. She must be enjoying Hawaii."

Stupid girl. Martha opened her mouth to say something mean, but decided against it. What good would it do? They had all forgotten where Hana was now. Not in Hawaii, but an internment camp for Japanese Americans. It would shock these girls to know about it—as it did her when Hana first informed her. Hopefully, Hana's family could cope and be home soon.

January 10, 1944

Dear Martha,

I'm so happy to hear of the baby. What a joy it must be to you and Clark. I hope this war will be over in time for me to be there for you.

Sorry not to have written more often. Sometimes it's hard to get paper and envelopes. And I'm not very confident of the mail system here. I hope you get this before summer! We are doing all right, or at least okay. I can't believe we have been here for so long. We all thought we would be returning to our homes long before now. Some have lost hope, but Mama-san keeps us all in good spirits whether we like it or not. Papa-san hasn't been in the best of health lately, like many men who don't have enough to do or have lost their pride altogether.

It's surprising what things some of the people here have come up with to pass the time. The boys have a basketball team and the girls have several clubs going. Chiko will have none of it. I think she needs a stronger hand from Mama-san, but I'm only her big sister. There's been talk that they will re-open the draft for Japanese Americans. Some men here are already volunteering, but some are resisting, including my father. There has been some trouble, and my friend John is right in the middle of it. I'm praying it doesn't get out of hand. My father has been warned he could go to prison if he doesn't stop interfering. It scares me to think what might happen.

I told you about the armed guards here. Some of the boys spend their spare time, which they have lots of, thinking of ways to play jokes on them. My brother Martin has pulled a few pranks, but Papa-san found out and threw a fit.

I'll be glad when winter is over, although we do have fun stuffing the holes in the walls with wet newspaper—when we can find it. You would be surprised at how my decorating skills have improved. This place forces you to be creative.

Sometimes I wonder what would have happened if I had not volunteered to escort that wounded important dignitary back to the states after my recovery at Pearl. If I hadn't done that I might still be sniffing the island breezes. But then my family would be here alone. God knew best.

I have considered your request to come visit me. It's allowed, but in your condition, I forbid it. I'll see you when we are free.

I have to go now. Chiko needs help with school work.

Much love,

Hana

"Forbid?" The word riled Martha, but deep inside she knew Hana was right. Visiting her friend there could be a traumatic experience. Besides, she had been feeling so tired and achy the last few days.

The other nurses at the table were laughing and joking. They had no idea what was going on in some places of the world. She bet that most of them didn't know anything about internment camps or air bases in England. All they thought about were the good things in their small world. She wished she could escape like they had.

A sharpness seared through her abdomen, making her gasp. The letter slid off her skirt to the floor. She bit her lip to keep from groaning. After a few moments, the pain subsided. She sat very still and tried to relax. It must be the flu. Her pelvis had ached all morning and she felt like going back to bed instead of coming to work.

"Bye, Martha," one of the nurses waved as several of them skirted out the door.

"Bye, Paula."

She gasped for air as a cramp radiated around to her lower back. She felt warm liquid oozing from her.

No!

She stood to see a small spot of blood where she had been sitting.

"Martha!" Becky Norris cried from the other side of the room. "Someone get a doctor."

Now the blood ran down her leg and into her nice new white shoe. The room started to spin and Becky grabbed her arm.

"Sit down. Here's a towel. Breathe deep, girl." Martha tried to press the towel up between her legs.

Becky took Martha's chin in her hand and looked deep into her eyes. "Hang on. You're all right." She took the towel, lifted Martha's skirt and shoved the now red-stained cloth where it would soak up what was now a stream of blood.

Martha grasped Becky's hand. "Get Sister Clatilda. I need her."

The last thing she heard was the thumping of gurney wheels getting louder and louder, then stopping.

In the silence she relaxed. Sleep was what she needed and she could feel it take her.

Chapter Thirteen

*T*he screeching of the bare willow branches against the window grated on her nerves. The gray skies may as well drop their rain to make the dreariness complete. It had gone on for days—the cold darkness outside. And inside Martha too. It didn't seem right that someone else should be fussing over her, but Clarissa had insisted, showing up on her doorstep the day she came home from the hospital.

She shouldn't have come, but Frank had paid for a train ticket as soon as Mama called them about the miscarriage. By the time the doctors decided Martha was out of danger from the hemorrhage, three days had passed and she was weary of staring at white ceiling tiles. She had been tired enough of that hospital room to think of leaving on her own, but Sister would have been most unhappy.

"Are you ready for some soup?" Clarissa carried a tray into the room and set it on the coffee table.

"Sure. Thanks."

Clarissa pulled the rocker over and sat closer to her patient. "You look better today. What do you say we go to the grocery store together tomorrow? If you feel up to it."

"Sure. We can do that. My strength is almost back to normal."

She took a sip of the soup. If it weren't for Clarissa sitting there she would simply not eat. She had no appetite. She cried a lot, and couldn't seem to feel anything. Losing a baby certainly gave her a new appreciation for the women she had cared for over the years. She had just gotten used to the idea of being a mother, and now she suffered the heartbreak of losing a faceless, nameless child she had already come to love.

"Martha, when are you going to write Clark? The longer you put it off, the harder it will be."

"I will. Soon."

Clarissa sighed and leaned back in her chair. "I'm so sorry you're going through this. I know you were apprehensive about the pregnancy, but it really is a wonderful experience. You'll try again when Clark gets home and someday have a house full of kids."

Martha set the bowl on the tray and turned to face her friend. The question on her tongue had to be asked.

"How can you be so positive about motherhood after all you've been through? Losing two babies, and nearly losing Morgan to dust pneumonia. Then James runs away and you don't know where he is. What's so wonderful about all that? It seems to me God is not a mother's protector. I don't know if I want to risk having another event like this. I still have a husband who is in danger every day clear across the world. Is God looking after him? Why can't we just live a safe life?"

Clarissa smiled. "Well, that was some tirade of doubt, anger, and fear. I hope that felt good to get off your chest. Let me tell you something, Martha Jensen."

Martha bristled at her reaction. Didn't Clarissa know she needed sympathy and comfort? She should be polite and listen, but her friend had overstepped. Perhaps it was time for her to go back to Kansas.

"Yes, I've been through a lot with children, my marriage, my father, and endless years on the dried-up Kansas prairie. We are *in* the world, not *of* the world. This is a temporary home for us, Martha. We don't get too attached, and we don't bury ourselves in one place where we can indulge in self-pity. We go where we're supposed to go, no matter what the perceived dangers or inconveniences. The world has little to offer us compared to God's plan. There's more life to experience. It would be a shame to be paralyzed by fear for the rest of your years."

Martha felt like the air had been sucked out of her. Each word rang true. Like Mama's words, Sister's wisdom, and Clark's deepest hopes. She had tried to change her heart after each epiphany, but nothing had stuck. Leave it to Clarissa to drop the pretense of friendship when there were more important things at stake. Martha didn't know what to say. If only her fractured feelings could catch up to the honest sentiment.

Martha slid her legs off the sofa and sat up straight. "I'm speechless."

"Well, there's one good thing."

"No, really. I have no argument. I'm so numb I can't feel anything. I don't know how to move passed this, but I know what you say is true. Mama says the world is more than we know. I suppose that's what you were talking about. And that maybe if we knew the future, we would all be afraid."

Clarissa nodded. "Your mom is wise."

"I keep wondering what I would do if Clark didn't come home—how I would carry on. I wouldn't be able to if I was full of fear all the time. So what should I do?"

"One day at a time. Like the rest of us mortals."

Clarissa reached for the bowl and handed it to Martha. "Now finish this. Then I think you have a letter to write."

Poor Clark. If there was any way she could soften the blow, she would give her right arm. His last letter contained a picture of himself signed, to Mom, love Pop. He was about to be terribly hurt, but it couldn't be helped.

She cleaned up the bowl of stew. Clarissa took the tray to the kitchen. One more day and Martha would tell her to go back to Kansas where she belonged. Not because she didn't need her or was mad, but because there was a family there who needed her more.

She shuffled to the desk and pulled out a piece of stationery. *Dearest Clark,*

He scrubbed the controls and seats until they shined. Outside, the rain took care of the dust and dirt on Old Faithful. Clark had worked his way from the tail to the cockpit, rags and soap and hot water as his tools. Here he had solitude. Here he could yell at God and no one would hear. In the belly of his plane he could scrub away the grief and sadness that consumed him.

He should be there with Martha. She was all alone except for Clarissa. Thank God for her. He had never met this woman, but Martha spoke so highly of her and Frank and their children… he couldn't remember their names.

His biceps ached from reaching up to wash the sides of the plane around the hydraulic hoses. He stopped and threw down the rag and sat hard on the floor of the waist. If only they had a mission today—something to blow off some steam. He crawled up to his seat in the cockpit. A mission to help his grief?

"Well, now that's a stupid thought. Dropping bombs that could hurt innocent children to help ease my pain. Insanity. We should all be home with our wives and children instead of warring with people we don't even know. What's the purpose, God? Where are You in this terrible thing?"

"My mother always says that God knows best."

Jimmy stood in front of a line of men hovering below him, staring up at the cockpit. When had they climbed up into the ship?

Wagner stepped forward.

"We heard your sad news. We're all very sorry, sir. If there's anything we can do, please tell us."

The other crew members mumbled and nodded. Clark could barely hear them through the ringing in his ears. He crawled down to join them, all crammed together in the small space meant for only a few men at a time. A few of them backed up toward the tail section. Clark kicked a box of ammunition with his steel-toed boot. It clanged and the lid popped open.

"Thanks, guys. It's a sad thing, but Jimmy's mother is right. God knows best. I have to move on and get on with this stinking war. We have a job to do. Those idiots in Berlin have to be stopped so the world will be a better place for my future children. And your future children. Right?"

Words of agreement echoed through the belly of the machine they had all come to depend on. Like any friendship, the hours spent together cemented them in unity and comradery. How fitting a place to show support in sorrow.

Hause raised his hand. "Sir, the cloud cover will be with us today and tomorrow, reports show. Wagner here has an idea about a card game tournament. Some guys from one of the other squadrons are in. How about joining us?"

Clark shook off his emotion and smiled. "Wagner always wins, so how much fun is that?"

All laughed except Wagner, who looked confused, yet shyly aware of his talents. Clark patted him on the back as he maneuvered by him and down through the bomb bay doors.

"Uh, sir?" Jimmy called down to him.

"Yeah?"

"Are you finished cleaning?"

"Pretty sure I am, Jimmy."

The rise of chuckles from above relieved his low spirits. Even in sorrow there is always something to laugh about. He could only hope that Martha had found a distraction from her pain.

I should have been there.

He pulled on his flight jacket and zipped it, turning his face down and away from the pelting rain. He would hurry back and answer Martha's letter. No words he could say would comfort her with so many miles between them. He missed her and the baby he would never meet.

Clark heard footsteps running up behind him. Jimmy was at his side, holding onto his cap and meeting Clark's steps stride for stride until they reached the mess hall. Jimmy held the door open for him and they both hurried inside to brush the rain from their jackets. The room was full of men, and some looked up at Clark with knowing expressions. The word had obviously gotten around. Hopefully no one would make too much of it. His crew had relayed enough sympathetic sentiments to last him a while.

"Sir?"

Clark turned to his shadow and raised his brows. The kid was so eager to please, Clark didn't have the heart to dismiss him.

"Is there anything you need before I go back to the hanger? One more patch left on Old Faithful and then I move on to Satan's Sister. Then I'm done for the day. I can sure…"

Clark held up his hand. "You go ahead. But tell you what. You come by my quarters when you're done and we'll talk about flying. Okay?"

Jimmy's face didn't light up this time at the mention of flying. Clark knew it was only out of respect for his sad news. Who was this kid and how had he gotten here? His Peter Pan attitude charmed Clark, and he didn't mind being a surrogate father to such a nice young man.

"I'll come by. Thank you, sir."

"No, thank you, Jimmy. See you later."

Jimmy saluted and Clark returned the gesture with a grin. The rest of the crew had gathered at a table with Wagner. The cards were already flying across the tabletop. They all deserved a little diversion from the pending mission over Pas de Calais, France. If the clouds cleared tomorrow, it would be a *go* for the big mission.

Once in his quarters, he picked up the engagement picture his mother had insisted on. Martha smiled so happily next to him in his uniform. She had been so brave to follow him around and swallow her fears about his flying.

Clarissa had probably gone back to her Midwest home by now. "Martha should go be with her folks in California."

He would write and tell her he would send some extra cash he had put away and inform her it was to pay for her bus ticket. No. Train. It would take less time and be more comfortable.

He pulled a piece of typing paper from his typewriter and penned his suggestion.

Dear Martha,

I am full of sadness at the loss of our baby. I so wish I were there to hold you and take care of you. I think about you day and night. I would like for you to go see your folks. Would that make you feel better? I'm enclosing some cash to pay for the trip.

Don't worry about me here. Things are going well, and I have the best crew around. They help keep me safe and we have completed over half our mission quota already. It won't be long and I'll be home. We can make plans for our future—one without planes and war. Then we can talk about trying again for a child.

Please take care of yourself and when you write to Clarissa again, please tell her thank you from me for being there. She is a special person, and I would love to meet her sometime.

Enough for now. I want to get this in the next post. Weather has been bad here so not sure when the mail will go out.

All my love,

Clark

He sealed the envelope and held it to his chest. The grief

had faded, but the helplessness he hated still hung over him. It was the same feeling he had about his grandparents. Not knowing if they were dead or alive ate away at him. Here he was, just across the North Sea from them, and he could do nothing to help them, or even know if it was too late for help.

There must be someone who can make inquiries. Perhaps the chaplain would know of an agency he could contact. He put his cap on his wet hair and stuffed the envelope in his jacket pocket. A trip to the post and then the chapel. He would say a prayer while he was there.

That was all he could do now.

Martha lifted her head to eye the doctor. "So I'm completely healed up?"

She sat up on the exam table and wrapped the white sheet around her bare back. She hated being poked and prodded, but knew how important post-trauma exams were. Since the miscarriage she had fought to get back her joy and sense of emotional wellness. Clarissa had been so wonderful to stay with her for the week after it happened, but since then, it was a daily battle to regain her life. Yet, she was determined.

"Yes, I'm happy with what I see. It looks like you have been doing everything I said to do. I give you clearance for another try at pregnancy anytime you wish. It's been two months."

Martha didn't feel like reminding him that her husband was a zillion miles away fighting a war this doctor was too old to fight. She was grateful he had been so efficient and matter-of-fact. The younger doctors tended to make a philosophical point over things like this. She rolled her eyes to think of some of the well-meaning, but thoughtless counsel she had overheard while attending exams. She would be a better nurse from now on, especially on those occasions.

"I tried to behave myself."

"Please feel free to come see me if you need anything." He plucked his glasses from his head and slipped them into his shirt pocket.

Sister Clatilda had been sitting on the other side of the curtain in a chair along the wall, not uttering a sound. She had insisted on coming along to this appointment. Her attentiveness over the last two months had overwhelmed Martha. Her care reminded Martha of a mother's love, a sister's friendship, and an angel's spiritual guidance. All of what Martha needed and more. It reminded her of Clarissa's stories of how Elijah had always seemed to show up just when she or Frank needed him.

The doctor washed his hands and left the room. Sister let Martha dress while she cleaned up the exam room. Martha buttoned her skirt, which hung loosely these days. Clark would be upset with her for losing so much weight.

Sister stood next to her. "How did you feel about the doctor's prognosis?"

"I'm glad things are back to normal physically."

"And how about in here?" Sister placed a finger on Martha's chest above her heart.

"I'm fine in there. Couldn't have said that a few weeks ago. You've helped me so much."

They walked together out the door. The halls of the hospital echoed with organized chaos. The whole hospital had been busier these days. Many wards were full of men recovering from battle wounds, transferred to their home town to finish getting well. Martha had learned that some wanted to be returned to service—to go back overseas to finish what they started. That kind of reasoning she didn't understand, but she had not been a witness to the kind of unified determination these men experienced across the ocean. Clark had tried to explain it in his letters. She would ask him to clarify this when he got home.

"I can't have one of my best nurses fall by the wayside. It was my duty—and pleasure." Sister paused a moment. "Especially since you refused to go see your parents. Don't you think you should have?"

Martha looked away for a moment. "My folks are trying to get their farm going and if I had gone there, I would have been tempted to do too much. I get pretty stubborn sometimes, and I didn't want them to see how discouraged I was. I just told them I didn't feel like traveling. Mama protested a bit, but I think she understood."

Sister nodded.

"So can I return to full duty?"

"Starting tomorrow."

Martha nodded. "I have one request though. I need a few days to go visit Hana Kato in Wyoming. You know she's in an internment camp there. I want to go and see her with my own eyes. To make sure she's all right. I would take the train when the weather warms a little. Maybe in a few weeks?"

"I'm sure I can spare you for a few days. Especially for Hana. Poor girl."

Martha wanted to hug the woman, but knew better. She had something to look forward to now. It wasn't the trip to her folk's place that Clark had sent money for, but it would do her just as much good to see Hana.

Unless things were worse than Hana had let on.

Chapter Fourteen

*C*lark limped his way off the tarmac after talking to the chief mechanic. The mission had been rough and he felt unusually fatigued. A jolt of flak had thrown him and Kingsbery against the side of the cockpit. When Clark braced himself with his foot, he felt a twinge in his ankle. He had already decided not to visit the infirmary. They would only tape him up, but he'd run the risk of being grounded for a day. Not a risk he was willing to take. He would do his best to disguise his limp as he met with the crew.

The briefing room smelled of sweat and hydraulic fluid. Watson had stepped in a puddle of the murky liquid when a bullet punctured the line. Clark and the rest of the crew were just happy that none of *them* had been punctured. Each mission they all survived was a blessing and a curse. The old superstitions about luck and numbers always hung over the crew, no matter how Clark tried to dispel such nonsense. Even though it wasn't verbalized, the expressions on the faces of men crawling out of their beat up planes said it all.

Luck had no place in Clark's life. If he gave in to that rationale, his faith would suffer. His goal was to be an example of confidence to the men under his command. Sometimes he failed, but he would take God's provision over the luck of the draw any day.

"Well done, men. Old Faithful took a couple bad hits today.

The mechanic tells me it will be grounded for a couple days."

The men groaned in unison. They were as attached to their ship as he was. Like a familiar hat that fit well, she had been comfortable and covered them well under fire. Clark hated that she was in bad shape, and he didn't like flying other planes on base, no matter what the protocol was for resting a crew.

"I know, I don't like it either. I'll talk to Jimmy about speeding up the process."

The guys quieted one by one. They looked at each other until Wagner stood up. "Uh, sir?"

"Yes."

"Jimmy's been injured. He's at the infirmary, but someone said he's being transferred out soon. I guess it's bad."

Clark's heartbeat jumped. Not Jimmy.

"Okay." He eyed Kingsbery. "I'll need you to finish the briefing. I need to see Jimmy before they take him." He shook his head. "Tough break for the kid."

Kingsbery came to the front of the table. "Sure. Tell him we're all rooting for him. He's a great mechanic."

Clark nodded. "I'll inform you more about Old Faithful later today. Hopefully she can go up if we're called out anytime soon."

As he walked to the infirmary, Clark contemplated what kind of injury Jimmy might have had. He entered the front doors and remembered his limp. He pursed his lips and strode as straight as possible to the desk to find out where his young friend was. He couldn't think of Jimmy's last name. Hopefully they could tell him.

"Hi. I'd like to see Jimmy, uh…he's a mechanic injured here today. I don't know his last name. Sorry."

The nurse flipped through papers on a clipboard. "Oh, yes. Jimmy." She blushed slightly. Had Jimmy won someone's heart? "He's in recovery. Had a short surgery. I'll see if it's acceptable for him to have a visitor."

She disappeared down a hallway. He paced in front of the
desk until the nurse returned. She had a smile on her face, a
relief to Clark. She reminded him of Martha—dark wavy hair
under her nurse's cap.

"You may see him if you're Lt. Jensen. He's been asking for
you. Nice kid, but I'll warn you—he's hurting."

"Which way do I go?"

She pointed behind her. "Down that hall and take the first
right. His bed is the second on the left. He might be a bit
groggy, but he'll be happy you're here."

Clark meandered to find a large room with tall rounded
ceilings and beds sectioned off between white sheets hanging
from the ceiling. He had forgotten that the infirmary wasn't
really a building, but more like a huge glorified tent. Only a
few beds had patients in them. Most injured in the last mission
had been either discharged or taken away on a transport to the
nearest army hospital. Another nurse pulled back one of the
sheet partitions to reveal a sleeping Jimmy.

Clark leaned over to whisper to her. "Should I wake him?"

"Not asleep, sir." Jimmy spoke even though his eyes were closed.

By the time Clark reached his side, Jimmy had stirred and
turned to look around. Clark clutched the rail on the bed
trying to be discreet about searching for wounds. The boy's
head wasn't bandaged, nor were his hands. The only thing out
of order was the raised bedsheet over Jimmy's feet. A surgical
tube hung from the bed just below the area with red fluid
bubbling down it to a bag.

"I'm done here, sir. I really messed up this time."

Clark placed his hand on Jimmy's arm. "I doubt you messed
up, but what happened?"

The nurse checked the tube and then flitted away. If Jimmy
was injured enough to be done here as he said, there must be
a severe wound under that sheet.

"Lost most of my foot when a jack failed and let Old Faithful's wheel land on me. Guess I'm lucky it didn't get my whole leg. The doctor here says I will probably lose my foot. I'm sorry I won't be around to fix her up for you. They say I'm going home."

Clark gritted his teeth. Sending him home meant he wouldn't be back. He had come to like this kid very much. Actually, it was time to stop thinking of him as a kid. He was a man to take such a hit while trying to fix Old Faithful. What could he say to make things better?

"Jimmy, I don't know what's in store for you and that foot. I do know that the crew and I think you're pretty special. You're good at what you do. We appreciate it, more than you know."

Jimmy looked up at the ceiling, his eyes full of moisture. "What if I never get to fly?"

"Then you'll do something else worthwhile, no matter where you end up. Say, you never told me where you're from. Can I call your folks or someone?"

Jimmy continued to stare up. "No. My folks moved around. Not from anywhere you would know about. Just a small town in the Northwest. I'll call them when I get to the states. No hurry until I know what to expect."

"Northwest? That's where I'm from. Isn't that funny we never talked about it? We might be neighbors for all we know."

Jimmy's eyelids slowly closed. He would press him for more information about his home, but he knew it was time to leave.

Clark squeezed Jimmy's arm. "I'll go and let you rest. Let's get together when I go home. My wife and I can come visit. You'd like her. She's a nurse…"

Jimmy's eyes opened again. "Sure. That'd be great." He smiled at Clark and lifted his hand to salute. Clark grabbed it and shook it man to man. Friend to friend.

"I won't forget you, Jimmy. You really made a difference around here. The guys all said to say hi. They'll miss you. I will too."

"Thank you, sir. That means a lot. You take care."

"I will. Safe travels, son."

He turned before going through the door. The sheet hid Jimmy, but his face would be etched in his mind forever. As he passed the nurse's station he tried to think of a way to make a reunion between them really happen.

Clark stopped in his tracks. "Northwest. He could take something to Martha when he gets well. Who knows when I'll get home."

"Lieutenant?"

The same nurse who had led him to Jimmy stood beside him with a puzzled look.

"Oh, I was talking to myself. I have a question. When is he shipping out?"

She looked at her watch. "Forty-five minutes. He will need a better facility for the foot amputation."

The word tore through him like a hot knife. It was worse than he thought. This would mean Jimmy would never reach his dream of flying, at least not for the military. Perhaps his own plan might give him a mission to look forward to. A small mission.

"Look, I need to give him something to take along. Would that be possible?"

She shrugged. "Sure, I don't see why not."

He saluted her with a smile and hobbled as fast as his ankle would let him to his quarters. He unpinned his pilot wings pin from his flight jacket, rummaged in his desk for an envelope, and scribbled a note.

Take care of my wings until I come home. I love you.

He wrapped the pin in the note and stuffed it in the envelope, sealed it and printed her name on the front.

Mrs. Clark Jensen, Our Lady of Lourdes Hospital, Pasco, Washington

Martha would like Jimmy. Both were spunky and full of life. He picked up the note and headed back to the infirmary. The timing couldn't have been more perfect for a chance to send something special to Martha. How nice for him that Jimmy would be the one to deliver it.

"Don't let me down, Jimmy boy."

March 1944

Clark bolted up from his bed when he felt someone grab his socked foot. The darkness disoriented him, until he saw a dim light streaming through the open doorway to his quarters. For a moment he thought he was at his childhood home. His mother always woke him by tugging at his foot, signaling he would be late for school if he didn't get up. He strained to see a figure against the glow in the blackness.

For a moment Clark thought it was Jimmy standing there. Instead, Corporal Hansen's face came into view. "Lieutenant Jensen, sir. Sorry to wake you before dawn but I've received orders for you and your crew." The young corporal's words jumbled in with a conversation Clark had in dream just before he woke.

"What did you say, Corporal? What's wrong?" He threw off the wool army blanket and slid his legs over the edge of the bed.

"Sir, I just got the dispatch for you to gather your crew and be ready to take off at 0500. Sorry, sir." The young man held out the familiar brown envelope containing mission orders. The command center would have been busy for hours now, organizing and sending out communications.

"Don't worry about it, Corporal. I'm used to the routine. You will be soon too, and no more apologies for early mission calls, got it?"

"Yes, sir."

Clark pulled out the contents and read the first page before reaching for his watch. *Only 20 minutes till briefing.* "Okay, turn on the light. Hurry and wake up Kingsbery and then Ed Hanna. They can find the rest of the crew. We won't have time to go to the mess hall. We'll go straight to the briefing room. Grab us something from the pantry will ya?"

"Yes, sir." The young man disappeared through the door after turning the light switch.

Clark called after him. "And get some coffee brewing *now*! Bring the first cup to Keegan."

Clark could barely keep himself from crawling back into bed. He had only slipped under the covers a mere four hours ago, thanks to Johnny Keegan. The kid had to choose last night to get in a scuffle at the pub. At least they had saved him from a week in the stockade. Hopefully he had shaken his intoxication enough to do his job at the ship's radio this morning. Clark would size him up at the briefing and give him the boot if he wasn't in top shape.

The sound of engines turning over in the distant field started Clark's heart pounding. The corporal poked his head through the door again as Clark pulled up a trouser leg.

"Crew is up, sir. Oh, and you'll be taking up Satan's Sister since your ship is still down for maintenance."

"Oh, yeah. My ship. Shoot! Jimmy's accident must have slowed down repairs." He held up a hand. "Better get Keegan a couple extra cups of coffee a.s.a.p." Corporal Hansen gave a thumbs up.

His co-pilot stumbled through the door, rubbing the stubble on his chin. He squinted at Clark. "You look like you've been up all night. What's wrong?"

"I was, but that's another story. You'll have to ask Keegan sometime. We're taking up Satan's Sister up this morning. Old

Faithful is still in the hangar. All that flak we took yesterday must have damaged her worse than we thought."

"Well, at least we've flown this one before. Wish she did better on takeoff, especially if we're going to be loaded." He stared in the small mirror nailed to the wall.

"Hey, you don't need to worry about your hair. It's only a mission."

Kingsbery turned and raised his brows. "Funny. You're the glamour boy, not me."

"Cut it out." Clark grabbed his sheepskin-lined flight jacket from the bed post and rummaged through the inside pocket.

He ran down the checklist in his head as he stepped into the cold predawn air. Nye would need to bundle up in the waist today, just to keep from freezing. Not that the cockpit was warm and cozy, but Nye tended to show up without long underwear.

The briefing was short and sweet. The entire squadron would be headed for Wizernes, France to knock out German V-1 rocket sites. Wagner had unfolded his cloth map and found the target for his own notes. Clark had looked over his shoulder and studied it for a few minutes, checking to see how close civilian life was to the target.

"I'm going to have to get one of those maps someday, Wagner."

"It's the one from an extra escape kit, sir. I carry it with me every mission."

Clark shook Wagner's shoulder. "I'll put you in charge of getting our kits today if you promise not to eat all the chocolate bars out if it. I've heard tell they disappear on occasion."

Wagner threw him a half-salute. "I'll resist the temptation."

Clark forced away thoughts of escape kits, civilians, and any other negative chaos swimming in his head. He couldn't think about those things while trying to fly a different ship loaded with bombs.

JAN CLINE

On the jeep ride to the field of growling planes, he stuffed a small picture of Martha in his coat pocket.

The jeep stopped 300 yards from Satan's Sister. Clark joined the other members of the squad scurrying to their ships. He hated these rushed trips, but weather was on their side and that meant go.

The crunching of gravel stopped his hurried stride toward the plane. "Lieutenant!" Someone shouted from behind him. "Your coffee, sir."

Clark turned to see Corporal Hansen jump out of a jeep and clip along with a large mug in his hand. Even though he guarded the mug, some liquid slopped out each step he took. Clark held back from laughing. Poor kid. So much like Jimmy who always had a mug of coffee for him after the jeep ride. He would wait as close to the plane as he dared and wave to Clark before takeoff. It didn't seem right without him there.

The least Clark could do for the corporal would be to stop and taste the coffee he had ordered and forgot. He remembered what it was like to dream of flying—wondering what it would be like to hang out with pilots and planes. Now he was the pilot being admired by the young man who could possibly follow in his footsteps if this war continued. All he had to do was finish flight training.

"Thanks." Clark took the mug and peered into it. Only half of the coffee remained after the jolting jaunt from the barracks. He took a deliberate sip. "Mmm. Hits the spot. That'll keep me going. Thanks again." He handed back the mug and smacked the corporal on the shoulder. "See you later."

Clark could feel the eyes on his back as he jogged toward the row of ships in the distant runway.

Clark paused to look over the ship before hoisting himself into the plane's belly. The gunmetal curves of Old Faithful's massive frame served as a comfortable blanket each time he pointed one to the night sky. This felt more like he was borrowing his brother's car, never sure of the fit.

Wagner, Watson, and Hanna piled into Satan's Sister after Clark stepped into the cockpit. He surveyed the interior. Despite the perfume of fuel and hydraulic fluid, she was clean and well equipped. A fine ship even if she was a slow ascender. He pulled the clipboard from the back of the pilot's seat. Everything corresponded with the orders in his coat pocket. Now for the routine checklist.

"Where's Kingsbery?"

"Here."

Clark focused on paper. "Let's get through the list. Won't have to do this for many more days, my friend. I'll miss our precision pre-flight routine."

Kingsbery nodded and grabbed a pencil. "Sorry, but I'll be glad to go back to normal life without this."

Hause hollered from the back of the plane. "What's our load, sir?"

"Eight." Clark shouted back and then confirmed the size of the bombs as listed. "Thousand-pounders."

Kingsbery shook his head. "A maximum load of bombs, and a belly-full for this plane."

"We'll be fine."

The crew bantered jokes and passed a thermos of coffee. Clark stepped down and checked on Nye who was settled in waist position, cradling a steaming mug, and without a coat.

"Where's your flight jacket, Nye? You'll rock the ship with your shivering."

"I'm sitting on it. My butt is colder than the rest of me at the moment."

"Yeah, yeah. I know the feeling, but get your jacket on now. I can't have your brain locking up because you're frosted over." Clark checked the time. Five minutes.

Clark counted heads and returned to his chair to finish takeoff preparations. He took his time manning the expansive control panel, flipping switches and setting gauges. Kingsbery slapped him on the back as he always did when he settled in just before takeoff.

Clark returned the gesture. "Can't break ritual just because she'd not our ship, right?" The engine vibration numbed his hand as he pulled the throttle. His stomach fluttered—as usual. It was the same each time they traveled the pot-holed runway. Maybe more so this time with so many bombs to lift off the ground.

The sun had released just enough light to color the horizon with a burst of gold. Time to go. Time to do the job he had trained for. Time to pray aloud the prayer he had prayed each mission. The same kind of prayer he knew every pilot prayed each time before a bombing raid.

"Dear Lord, keep us in the shelter of your wing, and forgive us for any malice. Amen."

Several of the crew echoed, "Amen."

The mass collection of bombers never failed to take Clark's breath. Today the mission had enough aircraft to darken the morning sky by sheer numbers. Flying a plane this time of the morning felt like taking control of the heavens. The mighty Eighth would show its force today.

Satan's Sister rattled down the rutted runway like a peddler's cart banging and clanging. Clark steered the ship around pavement fissures and jockeyed for appropriate position. Carrying incendiary bombs supplied incentive for caution. He aimed for the horizon's edge. His heart thumped hard against his chest. He concentrated on the tops of the trees two miles straight ahead, until his stomach fell, like dropping in a rollercoaster.

Lift off.

The bulging plane creaked and moaned. After this job, he and Old Faithful would only have a few more missions together. Then he would be on his way home to Martha.

He guided Satan's Sister, hugging the ground to gain speed. He would start to pull her up when the other planes gained altitude. He could hear the rhythmic hum of B-24s coming alongside, then moving ahead, chomping at the bit to soar. He'd kept his distance from the other squad planes in formation. Time to ease up and follow them.

"Come on, Sister. Let's get some air."

Kingsbery busied himself in the co-pilot's seat, watching gauges and adjusting his headset. "You better give it a little more. Look at the altimeter. It's time to get her up."

Clark caught a glimpse of the controls. Barely 200 feet off the ground. *Yes, more air.* "Come on!" He pulled on the bar but couldn't raise the massive machine much above 250. It seemed all the ship could do was coast at this altitude, like moving in slow motion, afraid of going higher.

Clark's jaw twitched. "The extra weight isn't doing us any favors."

Kingsbery leaned into the window, then tapped on the engine power gauge. He grabbed Clark's arm and pointed out the window. "Number three prop is running up. I'll toggle it down."

Clark shifted in his chair. "It's taking too long." The treetops loomed close below them, some tickling the plane's belly.

His stomach churned at this scenario from his worst nightmares. "I don't want to dump any of the bombs, but stand by."

Kingsbery wiped perspiration from his face. "Even though they're still pin-locked, something could go wrong. Let's see if we can fix this."

Clark hollered over the roar of the faltering engine. "We aren't climbing. Cut the fuel to that engine and feather it. Hurry up, Hank!"

A shrill whirling sound rang through the cockpit.

Nye yelled from mid-ship. "What's going on? Get this tank up!"

Kingsbery tore off his headset and turned his head. "It still won't feather down!"

The ship jolted and smoke billowed from the engine toward the cockpit as the other ships moved ahead of Satan's Sister, up and away to a place Clark knew they would not go today. His stomach lurched. They were being left behind. Communication protocol came to mind.

"Everyone better have their headsets on."

Before he could say anything else, something pelted the side of the plane, rocking Kingsbery halfway out of his seat.

"What was that?" Clark leaned to look out the window.

Kingsbery jerked his head. "The engine is breaking apart. What now?"

Clark gripped the wheel with all his strength. The entire ship convulsed, dislodging anything not nailed down. He studied the gauge again. Still only about 300 feet. *Oh, God, I'll have to bring her down.*

"Salvo those bombs over this marsh and we'll ditch her when we reach a clearing ahead." He looked square into Kingsbery's eyes—eyes sparkling with fear. "We have to dump the whole load. This is the safest place. On my signal."

He unstrapped himself to be in position. He hollered into the headset. "Preparing to jettison!"

Clark's churning stomach calmed as the noise of the engine seemed to disappear. All noise seemed far away instead of raging close enough and loud enough to change his heart rhythm.

Kingsbery slid off his chair and reached below to grab the salvo handle, sweat dripping down his temples. His knuckles whitened as he braced himself, then jerked the handle toward his torso. The top of the handle snapped in his hand. He held it up and turned, white-faced, to glare up at Clark.

Clark spoke through gritted teeth. "We're out of time. Kick it!" He pushed the nose up a little more as he tried to steady the rocking plane.

Kingsbery used the heel of his boot to slam against the remnants of the handle. The first kick yielded no results. Clark gritted his teeth and blinked salty sweat from his eyes. He tried to keep his focus on the field in the distance and listen for the sound of the bomb bay doors opening. He heard a growl and then a hard thump followed by the clang. Watson had hoisted up from his position and thrown his leg over, kicking the handle loose.

"Done! Good job, Willy." Kingsbery moved back to his seat.

Clark could barely hear them yelling over the roar of the engine running up again. Then a deafening explosion slammed the plane hard to the starboard.

"One of them just blew! The tail is half gone!" Nye screamed from where he had been thrown against the turret.

Crewmembers scrambled to a safer position. Clark hit the wheel with his fist.

"Take a look back there. Hurry."

Kingsbery leaned over his chair and craned his neck just far enough to see down and to the back. "There's a gaping hole where half the tail used to be."

Wind blew through the ship, sweeping the acid smell of hot metal and fuel into the cockpit. The nose pitched down and Clark tried to pull the wheel up with his arms, but it wasn't enough. He leaned in with his chest, wrapping his arms around the sides of the wheel. The plane's violent shaking pounded it against his ribs. The only thing in his control was to ease the plane down without breaking apart. The crew knew how to do the rest.

"Clark, we're going to hit that church steeple." Kingsbery pointed to the sharp tower. "I see houses beyond it. Can we stay up long enough to clear them?"

"Yep. Hold on." Adrenalin raced through Clark's blood. He pulled harder.

Pain shot up both arms to his shoulders and neck, until he thought he would break in two. He locked his jaw, praying to miss the steeple. It looked close enough to scratch the bottom of the plane, but in seconds they passed it and all the other buildings, heading straight for farmland.

God, keep my crew safe.

"Crash positions!" It was the instruction he had always swore he would never have to give. He gripped the wheel again, grunting loud. He turned to make sure Kingsbery was following the crash procedure. Kingsbery squinted at him.

"Your lip's bleeding."

Clark licked his bottom lip, tasting the salty blood dripping down his chin. He had bitten through it in the fever pitch of alarm.

Clark pulled back the throttles, as his co-pilot did the same with the turbochargers. A strange chuckle rolled out of Clark's mouth as he saw sheep in the field where he planned to land. The poor things didn't know what was about to hit them. Nothing about what was happening seemed real, floating by like a dream, but it was time to do the unthinkable and land safely.

As he braced for touch-down, another piece of the engine ripped loose, breaking through Kingsbery's window. He fell forward, blood dripping off his forehead. The rest of the engine blew apart like firecrackers, away from the plane.

Every muscle in Clark's upper body seized as all motion slowed in his mind. The ship had to come down before she broke apart even more.

"Everyone! Hang on!"

Clark took one last look at the best co-pilot around. *Live, my friend.*

A thunderous rumbling pealed as the earth grabbed what was left of the belly of the plane. Sliding along the soft ground, the plane squealed. The tall dirt berm directly in Clark's view devoured the nose. Clark closed his eyes to brace against the force. He heard a thunderous crash, then a chilling wind sucking the air from him. Suddenly, he felt as if he were floating in the center of a violent storm.

Then darkness.

Chapter Fifteen

The lullaby of the train rattling on the tracks made Martha drift in and out of a sleepy haze. She had risen early today to catch the first train of the day out of Pasco. The train made so many stops, she lost count of all the towns. Now at almost midnight she had several hours to go before reaching Wyoming. Her fuzzy thinking gave way to a dream state. She was back at the vineyard with Clarissa. The breeze blowing off the hills sent chills up her arms. A storm rolled up over the tallest ridge, then a flash of light.

A loud noise jarred her awake. Eyes wide, she sat up straight and grabbed the edge of the seat. The dark train car was illuminated only by a dim light coming from behind her. Her heart thumped against her chest. Looking around, she saw nothing that could have made that terrible sound. Crunching metal? Or could it have been her tote falling from above?

The few other passengers didn't seem alarmed. The mother across the aisle shifted in her seat, trying not to wake the baby in her arms. Surely she heard the sound. Everyone else was asleep. She looked up to the rack above her seat to see her suitcase secure where she left it.

"Clark." Her heartbeat skipped. "No. I was dreaming. He's fine." Whispering comforting words to herself didn't ease the shaking in her hands. The shivers up her arms extended to her neck. She pulled her coat onto her shoulders and slipped her arms through the sleeves, tucking her cold hands into the pockets. The window was cold on her forehead as she pressed her head against it.

Shake it off. Clark's fine. Everyone's fine.

The rumble of the tracks beneath her reached up like a soothing massage. She forced her eyes to shut and begged the night to let her sleep again. "No more loud noises, please."

Recite something boring. Sister Clatilda had made all her students memorize the Florence Nightingale nurse's oath. That would do the trick.

I solemnly pledge myself before God and in the presence of this assembly, to pass my life in purity and to practice my profession faithfully. I will abstain from whatever is deleterious and mischievous, and will not take or knowingly administer any harmful drug. I will do all in my power to maintain and elevate the standard of… my profession…

The motion of the train changed and Martha opened one eye. Darkness still shrouded the car and the vast outdoors. In the distance lights twinkled from a building. Martha checked her watch. 4:00 a.m. Had she slept all this time? She reached in her pocket to pull out Hana's instructions. Still a ways to go, but this would be a layover stop for about an hour before catching a bus to her destination.

The train slid into the station in lazy rhythm. By the light of the station building, she could see the ground was free of snow. None since she noticed a few drifts coming through Montana. Perhaps Wyoming would have experienced an early spring, and she wouldn't regret leaving her hat and gloves at home. Martha pulled the comb from her purse and ran it through her hair. Too dark to apply lipstick, she would wait until she found a place to get some breakfast, if there was anything open at this hour.

As the train lurched to a halt, the smell of coffee wafted. *There must be some at the station. Coffee would be a start.*

The conductor reached out to assist her down the steps to the ground. "Careful," he said, never meeting her gaze. Her growling stomach gurgled up courage to ask about a restaurant.

"Excuse me, is there anywhere nearby to get breakfast at this hour?"

He held out his hand to the next passenger, the mother with her baby. "Yep."

The mother wobbled to the ground, juggling the baby and a satchel. Martha took a step forward and grabbed the bag from the mother's hand. The petite girl's smile couldn't disguise her tired red eyes. "Thank you."

The thought of this young mother maneuvering very far with her bundles took attention away from the crackling in Martha's stomach. "Can you manage all this? Where are you headed?"

"I'll be all right." She moved away from the distracted conductor and shifted the baby to her other arm. "I heard you ask about a restaurant." She pointed to her right. "There's a small café over there that's open all night. They have good coffee."

Martha glanced over her shoulder to see the neon sign flashing. The coffee smell had to be coming from there.

"Great, thank you."

The mother nodded and held out her hand for the satchel. Martha's heart ached for her. Alone with a baby and looking quite sad, and thin.

"Would you care to join me for some coffee in that café? And maybe some breakfast?"

The mother's chin quivered. "I-I don't have much money, but it would be nice to get some warm milk to fill my baby's bottle."

Martha tucked her purse under her arm and grabbed her suitcase with one hand and the mother's satchel in the other. "Let's go then. I'm cold and need some of that coffee."

A drop of moisture hit her nose, then another on her cheek. The mother looked up.

"It's starting to rain. Oh no." Her chin quivered again. "Why does it have to rain today?"

Martha tipped her head toward the building. "It's all right, we won't get too wet if we hurry."

The mother shook her head as a tear fell down her cheek. She pulled her baby close and put her head down, then hurried alongside Martha to reach the café. Once inside, Martha headed for a table and set the baggage down on a chair. She pulled out another chair for the mother.

"What's your name? And your baby's name?"

The mother stood shivering, her thin coat covering the baby. "Jean." She pulled back her coat. "And this is Robert. He's named after his daddy." Another tear escaped. She sat opposite Martha.

"I'm Martha Jensen. Nice to meet you." The urge to inquire about Jean's sadness broke through the silence in the café. "Is there anything I can do?"

Jean shook her head slowly. "No. I'm sorry to be so emotional. You see, my husband is in a sort of prison right now and we are on our way to see him. It's just very hard."

"*Sort of* prison?"

Jean's eyes darted around the room. She leaned in to whisper to Martha.

"It's an internment camp not far from here. Well, they call them relocation centers, but it's like a prison. They have guards with guns and everything. Anyone from our home in Seattle who is even a little Japanese has been sent there or to one of the other camps."

Martha studied Jean's face. As Caucasian as could be, so it seemed.

"You... you're married to a Japanese man?"

"Yes, but he's American. He was born in Seattle and doesn't even speak Japanese. This is our son." She uncovered the baby's face to reveal a beautiful child with olive skin and black hair. The shape of his big eyes made an unmistakable statement.

Martha leaned in. "He's cute as can be."

Jean covered his face again, looking around the room. She held him close as a waitress came to the table. "Coffee?"

"Yes, for two," Martha jumped in. "And I'd like some toast and eggs as well." She tipped her head at Jean who rested her spare hand on the purse around her shoulder. She shook her head.

Martha held up two fingers. "Make that toast and eggs for two." She smiled at Jean. "My treat."

"You shouldn't bother. But thank you."

Before the waitress reached the counter, Martha called after her. "And a glass of warm milk, please."

The waitress frowned but nodded. "Sure."

Jean's eyes teared up. "I can't repay you."

Martha leaned back and slid her jacket off her shoulders. "Yes, you can."

"How? I don't have any money."

All at once the troubles of an army wife seemed small. Her worry and anxiety over Clark's well-being had softened into pity for a young mother and her child. She might have had a child of her own to care for, but it wouldn't have been in these conditions. A father behind barbed wire, imprisoned for nothing more than looking Japanese.

Martha revealed her solution to the poor woman's debt.

"You can help me find my way to the relocation center you're going to. I've never been there and I need to visit a friend. Will you let me go with you? I'm pretty nervous about it."

And she was. Since the startling imaginary noise on the train, her insides had been jiggling. At least now there was someone to finish this journey with.

"Yes, I can do that. It's not hard to get there—just a short bus ride, and then going through the process. We might have to wait a bit. Who are you visiting?"

"A dear friend."

She considered asking Jean exactly what she was in for, but decided she didn't need the extra apprehension. Hana had described just enough in her letters to let Martha know it wasn't the best of places. Armed guards and barbed-wire fences—an incomprehensible image. This she would never understand. How many other sweet Hanas were incarcerated in these terrible cities of shame?

The baby stirred and whimpered. Jean pulled an empty baby bottle from her overstuffed purse. "I'm glad to have you along. It's been a long few days traveling this far alone."

The waitress appeared and set the glass of warm milk on the table, then scurried off toward the kitchen.

Martha reached for the bottle. "Let me fill it for you."

She poured the warm liquid into the bottle, wondering if she would have made a good mother like Jean. Would she have made this monumental effort to visit her baby's father for only a few short hours? Yes, she would. Sister was right. *Struggles serve to make us stronger.*

Two plates of toast and eggs waved in front of Martha, balanced on the arm of the waitress. The girl pulled back a bit.

"You did say scrambled, right, honey?"

Martha smiled. "I didn't say. But that's perfect. Thanks."

Jean stared at the plate, then up at Martha. More tears flowed.

Martha had to cut the sadness. "Eggs are nothing to cry about, my new friend. Eat up."

Jean propped the bottle so the baby could drink.

Martha choked down her first bite of eggs through her own tear-clogged throat. Was Hana going to eat eggs this morning? Martha shuddered at the images of terrible conditions her Hana must live in.

The scene across the table would have been sweet except for the very reason this mother and child were here in the first place. The world had to get back to normal soon. For everyone. Too many husbands and wives—families had been separated long enough. Like this young mother, Martha wanted so much to be with her husband again.

Stay safe, Clark.

Clark pried his eyes open at the sound of Wagner screaming for him to wake up. The wheel pressed into his chest, sending searing pain at his throat. He tried to move his arm to touch the tickle of fluid dripping down his face, but the limb seemed to be stuck to his torso. His vision blurred by some kind of fog, he blinked hard. The air reeked of fuel fumes and hot metal. People were shouting and the air echoed with popping sounds.

"Wagner? Is that you?"

"Yes, sir." Wagner coughed out the words. "Where are you hurt? Help is coming, but we have to get out of here. The plane is on fire."

Clark could see Wagner out of the corner of his eye. He too had blood on him. He struggled to bring his ball gunner's face into focus. It was then he saw the source of Wagner's blood covered face and jacket.

"Albert. Your head is bleeding. A gash…" He closed his eyes, wanting to move more.

Wagner touched a long raw spot spreading back over his head from his right brow. A small trickle of red liquid dripped onto the cockpit floor.

"It can't be too bad. I feel fine."

A loud repetitive sound came from the back. Clark tried to crane his neck to see. "What's that popping noise?"

"Ammunition going off." Wagner wiped his face with his

sleeve. "I pinched the fuel line so there's no more gas running out, but we could still go up. Can you move?"

He'd been trying to move during the conversation, but his arms and legs weren't working with him. Taking deep breaths sent stabbing pains into his chest. The thought of burning up in this ship shot his adrenalin into high gear. At last his hands tingled and he could tap his right foot. He couldn't feel his left one.

"What about the rest of the men?" Clark turned his neck to test its limits. No pain there. Blood eeked into one eye and he blinked it clear. If only his arms were free, he could wipe his face.

"Watson, Hanna, and Keegan are pinned under wreckage. We tried to free them, but we need help."

The crackling of bullets had stopped, and now the sound of voices. The fog of smoke cleared a bit, and he could hear women hollering.

"Are there rescue crews out there?"

Wagner replied through intermittent coughs. "Some women working in the field nearby, I suppose. When I looked out they were throwing dirt on the flames." He blinked hard, as if trying to see better, then pulled debris from around Clark's chair.

Nye stumbled into the cockpit and reached over Clark to clear glass near his face, moving in strange silence, his eyes wild. A siren blared in the distance.

Clark filled his lungs with as much air as he could. "Hurry up!"

"We are, sir," Nye shot back, his voice shaking. He wiped tears from his face and kept working.

"No, I meant the siren. Go help the others. I can wait."

Wagner and Nye stood their ground. Wagner held his arm tight against his side and winced.

"That's an order. Go."

The men kicked pieces of metal away to crawl to what was

left of the waist. Clark could turn his head enough to see behind him. Satan's Sister was destroyed. How many crew had she taken with her? The realization suddenly hit him. Kingsbery and his chair were gone. He squinted through the jagged gaping hole in the windshield glass where the chair should have been. Dirt and rocks covered the entire front of the nose. Barely any sky showed through.

"I hit the dirt berm. Blast it!" He felt his fingers fold into a fist. At least they could move. He wanted to laugh, but breath wheezed out of him faster than he could suck it in. Something was very wrong. He closed his eyes to concentrate. *Slow, breathe slow.*

A large hand pulled his chin up. "Sir? Can you hear me? "

He nodded slightly at the young man with an English accent.

"We're going to check you over quickly before we try to move you. Right?"

A wheezy *yes* was all he could muster. While two men in white uniforms checked his arms and legs, he cried out each time they touched his left shoulder or left foot. His vision still blurred from blood and whatever else had invaded his eye. After what seemed like hours of clearing debris, the workers carefully loaded him on a cot. The fire in his limbs and head threatened to take his consciousness, but he fought back by thinking of Martha and how he wished she were here to nurse him.

One of the men patted his cheek. "Take it easy, sir. You're looking pretty shocky. We've got to get you over this mangled mess."

Holding his breath so he wouldn't scream, he prayed for relief. The steely fumes gave way to some fresh air once they lowered him onto the ground. The area buzzed with commotion. Through one good eye Clark could see the devastation. Far from the wreckage he could see the plowed line where the belly had scraped the ground—a straight crater about two hundred yards long. On either side of it lay dozens of dead sheep. An older man stood over one, then looked over the field, once green pasture and now a mess of metal and heaved dirt. A curious chuckle erupted from Clark's belly. So many dead animals—an ironic carnage. He was supposed to drop bombs on buildings, not massacre sheep.

His heart slammed against his aching chest. Had one of his crew died? He grabbed the collar of the white coat sticking his arm with an IV needle.

"Was anyone killed?"

Wagner snuck up and knelt beside him. "We lost Watson, sir. Some of the others are badly hurt. Nye and I faired the best." He placed his hand on Clark's shoulder. "But you did a great job landing this girl. No one on the ground was hurt."

Clark struggled to hear the words. The spinning in his vision made him want to vomit. "Watson? Oh Lord. I'm sorry." Clark looked around the area again. "Where's Hank? He was hit with shrapnel and now his seat is missing." He heard himself talking, but nothing made sense.

Wagner stood, but his balance seemed to waver. "He was thrown clear, seat and all. He's alive but not sure how bad he's hurt. They just took him and some of the others in the ambulance."

Another white-coated attendant appeared and squatted next to Clark. "And you're next."

As the medics lifted Clark's cot, Wagner saluted, his face as pale as a china plate. Clark tried to return the gesture, but the pain shooting up to his neck made sparks dash before his eyes.

"Well done, Sgt. Wagner. Tell the others I'm sorry."

"No need, sir. But I'll tell them."

In Clark's last look at Wagner, an attendant came up beside him and grabbed his arm just as his ball-gunner's knees buckled.

Men and some young women still scurried around the wreckage, some splashing flame retardant from a long hose connected to a yellow truck. The noise of panic and destruction buzzed in his ears. If only he could have been flying Old Faithful, they would never have gone down.

Martha. She would be hearing about the crash soon. He had to talk to her himself. Who was going to tell her? His commanding officer… no, The Red Cross… no. The bouncing of the cot as the men jogged to the ambulance flipped his stomach upside down again. Darkness fell over him—he had to sleep.

Someone patted his face. "Sir, you must stay awake."

The motion had stopped, but his stomach still twisted. "Why?"

"Sir, we don't know the extent of your injuries. You probably have a concussion. You must stay with us. Talk about something. You have a girl back home?"

The darkness gave way to a dull blur of dim light. "Girl? Yes. Wife."

The man speaking reached over and patted his cheek hard. "What's her name? Is she pretty?"

Clark lifted his head and glared at the kaleidoscope of features on the man's face. "Of course she's pretty. Her name's… Mar…Martha, and she's a nurse."

He let his head fall back on the flat cot. There was so much he could say about Martha, but what would they care? If he died, she would be heartbroken. *I can't die.*

"Martha. That's a nice name. And a nurse to boot. You're a lucky man. Stay with us. Don't sleep. You don't want to make Martha a widow, do you?"

He would punch the guy if he could use his arms. He concentrated hard on images of Old Faithful, the auto garage, the vineyard… and Martha. Who would take care of her if he died? A $10,000 military life insurance policy wouldn't heal the wound in her heart.

Clark managed to lift his right arm at the elbow, and held up a fist to both of the young men about to lift him into the ambulance. "She won't be a widow. You better see to it, mister. And take care of my crew."

One of them wrapped his palm around Clark's fist. "We'll do the best we can, soldier. You just relax."

Clark closed his eyes and let out a long groan.

"But don't go to sleep, right?"

"Right," both men echoed.

All he wanted to do was sleep—to stop his head from spinning and voices to stop mumbling. He closed his eyes and could hear jumbled words, then a whispered phrase he clearly understood.

"Pity. Don't think he'll make it."

It didn't occur to her to bring an umbrella. It wouldn't have done any good against the strong winds anyway. Cold air and rain had blasted her and Jean as soon as they stepped off the bus, pelting their faces with flecks of frozen sand. Jean had taken off her coat to wrap around baby Robert. The two of them leaned into the gusts and quickened their steps from the bus to the administration building.

The drab exterior of the long narrow building set the tone for the dreary interior of unpainted walls and tiny windows. Small offices on one side of the room opened up for each visitor. One by one, families and single persons were called up to inspect contents of purses, satchels, bags, and coat pockets.

The cold air drafted in each time the door opened. Jean huddled on a bench jiggling the baby who cried softly.

"Where are you from? Who are you here to see and why?" The same questions confronted Martha when her turn came.

"I'm here to see Miss Hana Kato. She's a nurse at the hospital and she's expecting me." Martha turned her head to a window overlooking the end row of barracks. "I thought she would be here to meet me."

The uniformed guard at the desk in front of her finished searching her bag and purse and handed them to her, not once looking at her face. "Is she Japanese?"

"Yes, of course."

He tipped his head to the side and smirked. "Many of the nurses here are Caucasians from town. That's why I asked. Anyway, no meetings until you're screened. You'll see her outside. She can take you around the camp."

He made it sound as if Hana would be a guide at a tourist attraction. Martha didn't care about the Caucasian nurses or the camp, she only wanted to hug her friend. It had been so long and so much had happened to both of them. Life had gone terribly wrong for Hana, while Martha had experienced her own brand of heartache. No one could comfort like Hana, but she was the one to be comforted this time.

Martha picked up her belongings. Jean stood in the next office, baby in her arms, watching the guard search her satchel. Jean caught Martha's eye and nodded. Her eyes pleaded for Martha to wait. The clock on the wall marked 7:30 a.m. The breakfast from the diner had long since worn off. Martha set her satchel on a bench and pressed her hand onto her stomach to stop the growling.

Jean appeared at her side, groaning. "I hate this every time. I should be used to it by now. How did it go for you? Will you get to see your friend?"

Martha pointed to the door marked Camp Entrance. "She should be on the other side of that door somewhere. I can't wait to see her. I just wanted to make sure you were all right. How's little Robert?"

Jean peeked under the blanket. "Sleeping. Finally."

Loud voices filled the other end of the room. Jean jumped and backed closer to Martha.

"What do you mean? Why can't I see them?" A balding

Caucasian man stood just inside one of the offices, his tattered winter coat covered with blotches of dirt. His face was unshaven and he looked as though he had walked a long way in the rain.

"Sir, please calm down. You cannot see them because they have been moved from this camp."

The man continued to shout. "Why? What have you done with them?" He stepped close to the guard. The other guards in the room tuned in to the disturbance.

"Your sons were troublemakers. They were sent to Tule Lake Camp yesterday." The guard motioned for another couple to come forward from the line. "Next."

The man shoved the desk. "How am I supposed to see them now? I walk all the way from town once a week. I can't walk to Tule Lake. When are they coming back?" The increased volume of his voice echoed through the now silenced building. Two other guards rushed him, each grabbing an arm, gently at first, then forceful as the man resisted. Martha stood to put herself between a possible violent scuffle and Jean.

"Perhaps you shouldn't have adopted two Jap kids, mister," one of the guards needled.

Martha's frozen stance weakened. Jean slid off the bench and moved to the corner of the room. Martha couldn't stop staring at the man, the sorrow in his eyes shining through tears. She glanced back at Jean, who shook her head at Martha. It was clear that Jean and this man had much in common. Loving a perceived enemy of their own country had to be the heartbreak of all heartbreaks. The two guards tugged on him. "Sir, you have to leave."

A small child toddled toward the scuffle. Martha dropped her purse and sprinted across the room to scoop her up. The little girl giggled as her mother pulled her from Martha's arms. Martha lost her balance and stumbled away from the commotion, catching herself on the doorjamb.

"Let go of me!" The man screamed and thrashed, forcing the guards to manhandle him toward the door. As he bolted from them, his arm slammed against the glass window. The guards let him drop to his knees when he clutched his left hand, wincing in pain. Blood dripped from his wrist onto the floor.

"Mr. Kirkland, are you all right?" The guard that had questioned Martha ran to kneel close to him. Everyone moved to the edge of the room. All eyes were fixed on the broken man who had lost his sons. A minute ticked by as the guard helped him remove his coat.

One guard whispered to another. "We need to get him out of here."

Mr. Kirkland wept and rocked. Martha knelt next to the guard. "I'm a nurse. Can I help?"

"So am I." A familiar voice echoed behind Martha.

Hana.

Hana touched Martha's shoulder and set a box down on the floor. The senior guard frowned at her. She looked straight at him, meeting his determination blink for blink.

"I was outside waiting for my friend and heard the glass breaking, sir. I thought I might be needed. The other guard let me in."

She held up the white box. "I grabbed this off the wall over there. Limited first aid supplies, but it might help."

He scooted back and waved Hana forward. "See what you can do for him."

Martha returned to Jean. "That's my friend Hana."

Memories flooded her mind—Hana and her working side by side at Our Lady of Lourdes hospital, having lunch with Clark on the lawn, her wedding day with Hana by her side. The overwhelming feelings choked her. Had it really been so long?

"How wonderful that you can be together, even for one day."

"Jean Hito?" Someone called out from the door to the camp.

Jean grabbed her bags. "Yes, here." She turned to Martha. "Thank you so much. I hope to see you again someday."

Martha gave her a one-armed squeeze. "Take care."

At least someone would see her husband today. As she watched Hana wrap Mr. Kirkland's hand, Martha wondered what it must be like for Hana to work with Caucasian nurses in this place. Hana had never said a word about it being a problem. There must be Caucasian doctors at the hospital too. At least that would be familiar for her.

The guards lifted Mr. Kirkland by the armpits. Hana wiped the floor with small packaged disinfectant wipe, then collected the bloody gauze and box and turned to Martha. Her wide smile sparked laughter. She wanted so much to hug her dear one, but knew better than to contaminate herself with the blood on Hana's hands.

Hana stepped closer. "Hello at last. I'm sorry you had such a terrible welcome."

"Oh, it's okay. I'm just happy to be here. Can we get you cleaned up?"

Hana looked at her hands. "Better do that right away. Follow me."

Martha scrambled to load her arms with her things and slung her coat over her arm.

"You'll want your coat on. It's still cold out. Are you hungry?"

Martha nodded as she slid her arms through the sleeves.

"I'll take you to the mess in our block and then to our place." She leaned in to whisper over the chatter in the room. "Keep your expectations low."

The chill hit Martha's cheeks the minute they stepped out into the compound. The muddy rut-filled yard spanned for miles, it seemed. Martha stopped short at the sight of endless rows of plain black buildings lined up like houses on a monopoly board. Except this was no game. Hana stopped and spun around, her black hair blowing in her face.

"Oh. I forget how shocking this can be to visitors. It's too bad you had to get here after a rain. You'll ruin your shoes."

Martha took her eyes off the barracks to look down. Her black and white oxfords were now brown with smears of mud, but she didn't care. It was such a small thing compared to what Hana lived every day of her life.

"Come on, I'm cold." Hana waved Martha forward.

After trudging through muck and mud puddles, they entered the mess. It was almost empty, but a few internees lingered at the food line. The clanging of pots and pans and chatter from the kitchen echoed in the table-lined room, like a summer camp for poor kids.

Hana held up her hands. "I'll be right back." She jogged to the kitchen while Martha set down her belongings on the table. The cold air blew in through cracks in the walls, and the faint smell of garbage made Martha take shallow breaths. She had expected to hear the Japanese language in the conversations coming from the kitchen, but all spoke English.

"Okay, where's my hug?" Hana jumped in front of Martha holding out her arms.

Martha couldn't hold back the tears as she embraced Hana. Her small frame felt even thinner than she remembered. The tears wouldn't stop—some for missing her friend, and some of shame for having it so well compared to her.

Hana pulled away and half-laughed, half-cried. "Don't be sad. I'm okay."

"How can you be? I saw the guards, the guns, the barbed wire. You shouldn't be here. No one should be here."

Hana wiped her own tears.

"Well, I admit I have my moments. Mama-san says God will help us. I have to believe her."

Martha sighed. She swallowed down the rest of her grief and smiled for Hana's sake.

"Martha, there are all kinds of prisons. Many of our own making. It's hard here, but I must learn to stay free in my heart. It's a challenge though, keeping my brother and sister going. It's easy for them to get into trouble here. Not like at home."

Free in her heart. The words hit a target deep in Martha that she had protected for so long. It stunned her to hear them, but a certain release filled in to sooth the wound. Leave it to Hana to speak the truth when it was most needed.

"When Sister found out where you were, she told me the priest who visited you in the hospital in Hawaii was concerned about your state of mind. He thought you were very angry about something. I can imagine it was a horrible thing to go through."

Hana stared straight ahead. "It wasn't just the bombing. Something else happened to me that day that I'm still working through—an encounter with some Caucasian men. Someday, when I'm out of here I'll tell you about it."

"They didn't…"

"No, not that."

Martha took Hana's hand. "I won't press you. As long as you know that whatever you're working through, I'm here. We can console each other."

The tour of the camp was a surprise in some ways and a shock in others. Amazed at how Hana's people had made the best of a deplorable situation reinforced Martha's admiration for Hana. Her heart ached to see little children playing in the space between the tar-papered housing and barbed wire fences—guards watching them every minute. The only bathrooms were in with the laundry facility, toilets with makeshift partitions where there obviously were none before.

The time with Hana passed quickly. As they walked to the

gate at the end of the day, Martha wondered how Hana's family would ever be able to overcome this period in their lives.

Martha stared up at the guard, then back to lock eyes with Hana. "Write me as much as you can. I want to know you're safe."

Hana hugged her tight. "Keep me up to date about you and Clark. I hope he'll be done with his missions and home soon."

Martha turned and waved before stepping on the bus taking her to her hotel. Hana stood back a ways, bundled in her coat, blowing a kiss. She looked so very small with the backdrop of the landmark Wyoming mountains behind her. Martha wanted to etch in her mind the things she saw here.

She didn't see how she could ever forget, and knew Hana never would.

Chapter Sixteen

Martha trudged through the doors of the hospital and nodded to Nadine sitting at the front desk. Nadine stared at her, wide-eyed and white-faced. What in the world was the matter with the girl? Martha made her way down the hall to the locker room, barely able to keep her eyes open. The two-day trip home from the internment camp had taken all her energy. She would write to Clark and tell him about it tonight. Now she had to muster some strength to get through a shift.

Inside the locker room, a small group of nurses whispered in a circle, then turned as Martha entered. Becky moved toward her, tentatively, hands behind her back. Her eyes avoided Martha eyes.

What did I do now?

Becky held out her hand. A small yellow envelope fluttered between her trembling thumb and fingers.

"Nadine said this came a few minutes ago. I was just heading to Sister's office to give it to her. It's for you."

Martha's composure threatened to flee. Her knees wobbled as she stared at the notorious Western Union telegram envelope. This wasn't happening. Not to her... not to Clark. She closed her eyes, calling up his face, his tall frame, his wide smile. Wouldn't she know if he were dead?

She stumbled back and to the bench in front of the lockers. Becky glanced back at the other girls. Martha stuck out her hand.

"Give it to me."

Becky inched toward her and remained when Martha snatched the envelope. The front said Mrs. Clark H. Jensen, and in the corner the words War Department. Martha wanted so much for the name on the telegram to be someone else's, the moment she lived right now to be anyone's moment but hers. Her hands shook so much, she could barely lift the flap or unfold the paper.

DEAR MRS. JENSEN,
REGRET TO INFORM YOU THAT YOU HUSBAND, LT. CLARK H. JENSEN, HAS BEEN SERIOUSLY WOUNDED AFTER CRASH LANDING HIS PLANE OFF BASE IN ENGLAND. MORE INFORMATION COMING SOON ABOUT HIS CONDITION AND WHEN YOU MAY CONTACT.
SINCERELY,
COL. JACOB J. BROGGER, C.O. 446TH

She crumpled the paper in her hand. Becky sat next to her and the others moved in like protective tribe members. She looked up at them.

"He's not dead, badly wounded. Crashed his stupid plane."

Becky put her arm around Martha's shoulders. Martha looked at her, wanting Becky to say it was all a cruel joke. Instead, she saw a tear dribble down Becky's cheek. At least *she* felt something. Martha was numb. No tears would come, her shaking stilled.

The other girls walked away. Martha hardly knew Becky, but it seemed she was the only true friend in this unreal bubble of time.

"Martha, why don't you go down to the chapel? I'll go tell Sister to join you there. Would that be all right?"

The chapel. Is that where God was? She would rather He be right by Clark's side. She would rather *she* be by Clark's side. Silly of her to think God was only one place at a time. Sister would scold her for that kind of reasoning. She couldn't seem to find any reason in her thoughts now. The news she had been certain she would never get was crumpled in her closed fist.

She stood with Betsy and walked the noisy hall to the tall wood chapel doors. Staff went about their duties and visitors roamed around corners looking for their loved ones' rooms. How she envied them. To touch and speak to Clark while he lay in some hospital in a foreign country wasn't possible for her. Or for so many other wives who got a telegram today.

She stepped into the dimly lit room. Only one other person shared the space with her. She slipped into the back pew, trying to remember when she had been in here last. The votive candles flickering on the altar reminded her of the last night she and Clark spent together. A candlelight dinner in their apartment in Denver might have been a foreshadow of this day—candles glowing for Clark.

The woman sitting up front stood and tiptoed out of the room. While she waited for Sister, she filled her mind with positive thoughts. Clark would be okay. He would come home to her whole and fit. For all she knew the telegram could be a mistake. She had heard of misinformation reaching loved ones at home before.

No. This wasn't the time to feed herself false hopes. Only real hope would do. She just had to find it.

Sister Clatilda slipped in the pew next to her without speaking, behind her, Sister Mary Margaret, Sister Josephine. Soon the entire front four pews were filled with nurses, students, and a janitor or two. Were they all here for Clark?

The nod and smile from Sister Clatilda was her answer.

She could barely put one foot in front of the other. Each night since the telegram had been a wrestling match with nightmares and insomnia, with fatigue being the only winner. She had to go to work to keep from going insane. She had received only the basic information on Clark's condition and whereabouts. Until he returned to the states, she couldn't go to him.

"He's alive, Martha. You should be thankful," Mama had said over the phone.

Alive, yes. But for how long? Not until she saw him face to face, felt his pulse, kissed his stubbly cheek would she be free from the worry. Then she would be able to give more than superficial thanks to God for sparing him. How soon that would happen was up to the army and Clark's recovery.

She left the children's ward, and turned down the hallway that led to the chapel. A curious summons to meet Sister there had fed her a little-welcomed adrenalin. Martha had confided in her about her anxiety over Clark's injuries, her frustration at not knowing what kind of husband she would soon see. She had heard all the stories, and even seen cases first hand of men coming home so broken physically and emotionally, their wives couldn't recognize the husbands they fell in love with.

An older woman pushed through the doors from the chapel as Martha approached. Her red eyes and stooping posture a common sight for those who spend time in there. She imagined a mother praying for her son, a wife mourning the loss of her husband. Or she could have simply been there to find peace and quiet for a while.

Martha found Sister on the far side of the chapel on her knees. The altar was full of lit candles today—not a good sign perhaps. She followed the aisle to Sister's pew and stood to wait to be noticed. So many times over the years in nursing school and working here she had seen Sister Clatilda praying for… well, everything and everyone. It was a wonder the woman could walk from being on her knees so much. Martha's religious upbringing was much less formal, but she respected Sister's way of worship.

Sister lifted her head. She pushed herself up to sit and patted the wood pew, beckoning Martha to come. Martha joined her, relieved at the chance to get off her aching feet. She expected a suggestion to take time off, and prepared herself for a battle of wills once again. It seemed their relationship had been a sort of loving war from the start.

"Good morning, Sister."

"How are you doing, Martha? I haven't talked to you since you received word of Clark. I know these are hard days of waiting for you." She turned and smiled. "You aren't exactly a patient person."

"I know. I wish I had more patience now. I don't know when I'll hear more about his injuries or when he's coming home. The army's channels of communication are hazy at best. All I know is that he will be at a hospital in a place called Norfolk, England for some time."

Sister stared straight ahead at the altar. "Are you afraid he'll die?"

Martha had been examining her feelings for days, wondering if her worry was based on the same old fears she battled with for so long.

"I don't think so, but I'm worried for sure. It's not knowing the details that drives me crazy. I don't sleep very well and I don't have much of an appetite. If that's what fear does, then I guess I'm fearful."

"Or you're just concerned like any wife would be. It sounds like you are facing it. I was just wondering if there were deeper struggles for you. It could be that you'll hear something soon. I wish I had some connections in Europe. You'll just have to lean on your faith."

"And pray for patience?" Martha smiled.

"Oh no. Don't do that. You have enough trials to handle for now."

Martha knew Sister never made a joke, so she was serious. As she used the pew in front of her to stand up, it was plain to see the aging nun had seen her fair share of trials, many of them the burdens of others. The lines around her eyes and mouth had deepened, even in the last few months. Her once perfect posture wavered slightly to one side, and her steps had a hesitancy about them. She had given her all to the dozens of silly young nurses in her charge. Patience had not eluded her.

Martha moved into the aisle to let her pass. "Thank you, Sister."

"For what?"

"Everything. For being there for me, teaching me, putting up with me. I'm sorry I've been a stinker at times."

Sister started to walk away, then turned. "Martha. You aren't the only stinker I've had to deal with. And you turned out pretty well."

In a moment she pushed through the chapel doors. Martha stood in the aisle, shocked at such a revelation from Sister, who never used a word like stinker. She had waited a long time to hear a morsel of approval from her mentor. *Pretty well* was high praise indeed.

She checked her watch. Not much time left on her shift, but even a minute seemed an eternity as her legs turned to jelly. Just outside the doors, down the hallway, a young man stood with his back to her, leaning on the front desk counter, talking to Jill, the charge nurse. Her heart jumped to see someone who looked so much like James.

She shook her head and took a few steps in the opposite direction, but then a familiar voice stopped her. She spun around. It *was* James, yet it couldn't be. He wouldn't come here after all this time. The closer she got to him, the more she knew.

"James?"

He turned his head, then moved from the counter. A crutch

dropped to the tile floor with a bang. He flinched, then bent to pick it up and tuck it under his arm.

"Hi, Martha. I didn't know you were still in town." His face flushed as he snatched an envelope from the counter. He looked at Jill. "This can wait."

Jill looked at Martha and shrugged.

Martha's heart lurched to realize it was really the boy she was so fond of, but he had changed so much. His bright eyes dimmed now—his face covered with a man's stubble, and his frame thin and taller. No longer a boy at all. His expression showed a burden all his own.

She hurried to embrace him, and he reached around her with one arm to hug her. She could feel him shaking and stayed still until he released her. His eyes filled and she wanted to cry seeing him so sad.

"What are you doing here, young man? Where have you been?" She gave him a soft sock in the arm and smiled.

He juggled his crutch to steady himself and cleared his throat. "Long story. Can we sit somewhere?"

She felt her stomach tighten. He was in pain.

"Tell you what. You sit in the front waiting room. I'll be done with my shift in 20 minutes. We'll get caught up."

He nodded, then maneuvered himself around. She watched him hobble away and blinked back tears. Something was very wrong. At least he was here—but why?

The café was nearly empty this time of day. One of Martha's favorite singing groups, The Mills Brothers, played on a radio perched on the counter near the kitchen. The door let in a cold breeze each time a customer came through. Martha motioned for James to follow her to a booth in the back. She slid in, still shivering from the cold, early spring that felt more like winter. For a moment she flashed back to her visit with Hana just weeks ago. She hoped spring would come soon for her friend.

James sat opposite her and rested his crutch close to him on the table's edge. He shifted in his seat, looking all around the café. Martha guessed she'd have to start a conversation, as he hadn't said more than five words in the car.

"So, how are you? Why the crutch? Don't tell me you broke your leg playing football, because I know you hate sports." She finally felt warm enough to pull off her coat.

His temples twitched before he spoke. "I might as well tell you. I've been overseas with the Army Air Corps. Plane mechanic, pilot hopeful. Got injured. Lost most of my right foot, so they sent me home to get fixed up."

Martha winced inside, but gave a cool reaction. His flat affect and monotone voice broke her. She swallowed down tears to answer his devastating explanation.

"James. I had no idea. Sorry for the crack about football. I… I don't know what to say. I'm so sorry. Do your folks know?"

His eyes scanned the tabletop. A young waitress slipped alongside him, glancing back and forth between them. "Would you like a menu?"

"I'd just like coffee, black. James? Do you want something to eat?"

"Just a Coca-Cola, please."

His eyes followed the waitress, but he answered Martha's question.

"My folks don't know where I've been or what's happened to me. I did call them to let them know I was okay and going to make it on my own. Mom would worry and Dad would tell me to come home if they knew about the injury. I have an errand to run here before I decide where I want to be. Right now I'm not sure where I'll go."

"Do you have a place to stay? I have a nice comfy couch. That is until my wounded husband comes home. I'd gladly put you up until your errand is done."

His eyes lit up for a moment. "Well…"

"Really, it's no trouble. Your mom would be happy to know you're with friends."

He rubbed his chin. The waitress brought their drinks and set them on the table, her eye on James. She hesitated before backing up two steps.

"Don't I know you from somewhere? Did you go to high school here?" She kept her gaze on James, smiling and fidgeting with her apron. Her long brown hair was tied up with a bow and dangling down her back.

Martha pursed her lips to hold back a grin. James blushed, barely looking at the girl.

"Yeah. Graduated a few years back." He looked over at his crutch and straightened his posture.

"I thought I recognized you. I was in the class behind you. Nice to see you again." She waltzed away and flitted through the kitchen doors.

James shrugged to Martha.

"Cute girl. Know her?"

"Nope."

"So, will you stay at my place?"

"Sure. Just don't bug me about my folks."

"Deal. Do you have a suitcase or something?"

The strain left his face. He had always held a special place in her heart. Now he was grown. A troubled man, but still seemed like a boy to her. Hopefully she could help him with whatever was eating at him

"I left it at the bus station. If you want to drop me off there— oh, I still have to do that errand at the hospital. Do you have time to wait?" He took a long gulp of his drink.

"Sure. I'll finish my coffee and then we'll make the rounds. What errand do you have at the hospital?"

He glanced at the kitchen doors. The waitress still had not emerged.

"Have a letter from a friend to his wife. He gave it to me when I left England to get shipped home." He pulled out the envelope he had been holding when she first saw him at the desk. "I didn't have a chance to ask the nurse if she could give this to the right person." He looked at the name on the envelope.

Martha leaned over. "I might know her. I work there, you know."

"I don't know her first name. It's Mrs. Clark Jensen."

Martha shook as if a lightning bolt had struck her. The mug in her hand tilted, spilling coffee on the table. James jerked his head to look at her. She lost her breath for a moment, questions flying through her mind.

"What's wrong? You know her?"

She grabbed a napkin to sop up the dark liquid as her insides danced. She held out her hand. "I'm Mrs. Clark Jensen."

His eyes opened wide—the envelope remained tight in his grip. "What? You're married to Clark Jensen? How could I not know? He never said—"

She took the envelope. "You talked to Clark? How do you know him?"

James rubbed his temples. "I don't believe this. Lt. Jensen is your husband—the one mom talked about, but never met. I don't remember her saying his name, though."

Martha stared at the letter, delivered by someone who was now a mutual friend of Clark's. Her name in his handwriting sent tingles up her back. Why did he not just mail the letter? She felt a lump in the envelope and looked over at James.

"Is there something in here?"

He leaned back. She couldn't tell if he was happy at the

coincidence or annoyed. She wanted to probe him about the whole story, like she had pulled a string on a sweater thread and couldn't help but to keep pulling.

James nodded slowly. "Yes. He doesn't know when he'll be home so he wanted to send you something. Since I was coming back to the Northwest…" He placed his fists on the table. "Wait. You said your wounded husband. Has Lt. Jensen been hurt?"

Martha grasped the letter, wanting to open it, but now had to tell her young friend of Clark's misfortune, and all the uncertainties of his well-being. James's fears needed a sounding board, and she was the only one who could do the job. She understood more than James could know.

"Yes. All I know is that his plane crash-landed and he was badly injured. Head injuries plus other issues. I have been waiting for more word for days now. I don't even know where he is or when they will send him home. I do know that most of the crew survived." She blinked away tears as James did the same.

"I didn't know. When did it happen? Was he up in Old Faithful?"

Martha shrugged. Her insides churned to try and imagine the crash. Her nightmares had been replays of a movie she never saw—one where Clark crashes in a plane with metal strewn over the ground. Her mind fought a battle with wanting to see the real scenario and wishing she couldn't envision it at all.

"I might be able to find out some information. I'll telephone one of the guys in maintenance. Do you have a phone at your apartment?"

"Yes. You really think you can just pick up the phone and call someone there?"

"If you know the right people and have the time change straight in your head." At last he smiled. Martha could only guess the phone call had given him a cause, a mission to make his own. She needed the information, so they would both benefit. It seemed there could be a special reason why Clark gave James a letter to deliver. How else would they have connected the dots? Maybe they could help each other heal.

James pulled out his wallet. "I wrote down some numbers. Let me look through them."

Martha took the moment of distraction to open Clark's letter. As she unfolded the small sheet of paper, a medal of some sort fell onto the table. She and James exchanged glances, but he offered no explanation. She picked up the object to inspect it. Wings on a pin. She read the words.

Take care of my wings until I come home. I love you.

She closed her eyes and clutched the pin. He had given this to James before the accident. She didn't know if he would ever fly again. He had given her his wings to save for him. It didn't matter why or what it meant. Now, just knowing his condition would be a relief.

James put his wallet back in his pocket but held onto a slip of paper. He looked into her eyes. "You okay?"

"I will be."

His eyes still locked on hers, he folded his hands on the table. "I want you to know what a fine man Lt. Jensen is. His crew liked him a lot. He was a great pilot. I looked up to him. He was nice to this dumb kid who wanted to be a pilot. He always had time for me. I just hope he gets home soon so I can thank him."

Even though she hated hearing him talk about Clark in past tense, she understood what James had tried to tell her. There were still so many questions she wanted to ask him—one in particular.

"James, why didn't Clark know who you were and the other way around? I told him about the Wilding family."

"He never knew my last name, I guess, or was probably too distracted to put two and two together. Plus, I went by Jimmy while I was there. We just didn't exchange enough personal information to make the connection."

Martha shook her head as she slid out of the booth. "How odd."

The waitress was headed their way when James got to his feet. Martha put the note in her purse, then handed the girl a five-dollar bill. "Keep the rest." She felt like tipping big today. The possibility of hearing more details about Clark had jolted her adrenalin and eased her pain.

James turned toward the door but called over his shoulder, "See ya, Jenny."

The girl smiled. Martha winked at her and followed James out the door. He stood by the passenger door twirling his crutch.

"So you knew her after all."

"Who forgets the head cheerleader of your high school?"

He slid into the seat and pulled his crutch in after him. Martha grabbed the door before he could shut it.

"Obviously *you* don't."

Chapter Seventeen

April 1, 1944

Clark gripped the sides of his mattress. He felt as if he would explode from the inside out. His head already pounded, but now it worsened with the Chaplain's pronouncement.

"I'm sorry, Clark. I know you were hoping the news would be better. It's tough to lose family under such circumstances. There are thousands of people getting the same news about loved ones every day now. We may never know the exact toll this war has taken on the world."

Clark opened his eyes. "How did they die?"

The only information I have is from one witness who reported that a small group of people from their village attempted to cross the border into Holland. A German plane dove down and shot at them. Only a few survived, and the witness was one of them. Your grandparents died instantly. They didn't suffer if that's any comfort to you."

Clark shook his head. "I'm sorry, Reverend Thomas. I disagree. They suffered for years under a cloud of fear and uncertainty. They lived every day wondering if they would be taken to one of those camps, lose their home, or be bombed by Americans like me. If that's not suffering, what is?"

The reverend pulled a chair to Clark's bed. "You've done what you had to do. It wasn't your bombs that killed your grandparents. Even if it had been, they would never have blamed you. Many had to die to stop this terrible régime from taking over Europe. God help us all to deal with our sense of guilt and helplessness."

Clark knew in his head the man was right, but his guts still panged with shame. He had wanted to fly planes and kill Germans—just not innocent ones. How was he supposed to kill and protect at the same time?

"Reverend, I don't know if I'll ever understand what has happened. To me or to Oma and Opa."

A doctor marched up behind the reverend's chair. "I'm sorry, Reverend. I need to take a look at Lt. Jensen."

The reverend stood. "Of course."

Clark reached out to him with his one good hand. "Thank you for coming to tell me. And thanks for working so hard to find out what happened to them. I never dreamed when I asked you a few weeks ago that you would have information so quickly."

"I'm glad to help. Since it happened a year ago, the information was recorded. Just had to find the right person to dig for it. I'll see you again before you go home."

He backed away and waved before walking out the ward's double doors. The doctor busied himself taking a pulse then peeking under Clark's bandages. A nurse had edged her way passed the doctor to take his blood pressure. When she was finished she scowled and reported out loud.

"184 over 100."

The doctor didn't flinch. "Not surprising, considering the news you just had. I'm very sorry by the way. I've lost family myself."

"I'm trying not to be angry, but it's so tragic that a couple of old Germans had to be shot down only for wanting what we all want—freedom."

The doctor motioned for the nurse to leave. He pulled up

Clark's eyelids to shine a small light in his eyes. Clark could feel the muscles behind them tense. His double vision still appeared now and again, but he kept that to himself.

"I need the straight scoop, doctor. I'm still pretty fuzzy about what happened and about my injuries."

The doctor sat in the vacated chair. "It will take time to heal from your head injury. I'm afraid the arm was broken so badly we had to pin it. The rest will also heal eventually with proper medical attention. We'd like to keep you here for at least another two weeks until we can clear you for travel."

"Travel? Can't I go back to duty? I've already been here two weeks."

"Your injuries are extensive enough to send you home, Lieutenant. You can't possibly fly in this condition and I can't say when you will ever be able to return to flying. You'd better start accepting the prognosis now." He stood. "You're one of the lucky ones."

Clark swallowed hard. "I know. I don't mean to sound ungrateful. I just wish I had another stab at the enemy. Especially after what I know about my grandparents. I guess I've had my fill of flying anyway."

It wasn't the whole truth. He would never be over wanting to be up in the clouds. It had been his dream for so long he couldn't imagine life on the ground, and he hadn't even considered the possibility he would be grounded. He had seen the world from up there. It was so much more than he knew existed.

"What about the crash? Is there someone who can fill me in on the parts I can't remember?"

The doctor glanced at the door. "I think there are a couple guys here who can answer your questions.

Clark lifted his aching head to look at the object of the doctor's attention. Two familiar faces approached his bed. Albert Wagner and Johnny Keegan both grinned as they caught sight of their pilot. The doctor backed out of the way, then walked down the ward aisle, greeting some of the patients.

Johnny was on crutches, dressed in a hospital robe. Clark couldn't see all of him to tell what his injury was. Albert seemed fine, in uniform.

"Hey, guys. Good to see you." Clark tried to sit up as Albert plumped his pillow behind him.

They all shook hands while Clark breathed deep to still the dizziness.

"Good to see you, sir. We thought we might have lost you for a while." Johnny tapped the bottom of the bed with his crutch as he plopped into the chair.

"I'm missing bits and pieces of my memory about the crash and after, so I want to know about everyone. Starting with you and those crutches."

Johnny's expression turned somber. "They had to put my leg back together with pins and such. My back is still healing, but the rest of me isn't too bad. I'll be going home soon."

Clark cringed, remembering Jimmy's injury and trip home.

Albert pulled up another chair. "You remember that Hank was thrown clear from the wreck. They transferred him to another hospital. Willis Hause has a broken leg and burns, but he'll be okay. Walter Nye is in a bad way with mental trauma. Not sure where he is. Wayne Back has two broken legs. They sent him home, I think. Melvin Howard has a fractured skull. He's still in this hospital, but we haven't seen him. Ed Hanna will be okay too. He went stateside the other day."

Clark pointed at Albert. "You look well, at least."

"That gash on my head has some hair on it now, but the concussion took some time to heal. I'm about to catch a transport back to base. I'm just glad I wasn't down in that ball when we hit."

Clark mentally counted up the names he had mentioned.

"Okay, that leaves Willy Watkins. Where is he?"

The men exchanged looks. Clark's heartbeat ramped.

Albert spoke low. "Sir, he didn't make it. Don't you remember? I told you at the scene."

Clark closed his eyes. "Oh. No. I don't remember any of that."

The silence stretched on until Albert finally moved closer. "Sir, as I told you on the scene, you did all you could to keep that plane up. You missed hitting a bunch of houses and a church before you landed that beast. We just had a pile of difficult circumstances to overcome. We're all grateful for what you did."

Clark couldn't speak. No words of comfort could ease the burden of responsibility crushing his chest at the moment. Willy was a good engineer—all of his crew were the best at their jobs. Had he really done all he could? He would never know.

The nurse's shoes squeaked across the cement floor. His obvious exhaustion would show her the guys had to leave. He hated to see them go, but it was time to move on and each go their own ways. Time to let go of them, Old Faithful, and the sky.

With Albert's help, Johnny stood. "Goodbye, sir. Take care."

"Bye, Johnny… Albert. Thanks for everything. You guys are the best. I mean it."

Watching them walk out the door was like a death. Besides losing Willy, he had lost his crew. They would all scatter and maybe never see each other again. After all they had been through, they would never again hoist themselves up the belly of Old Faithful. Someone else would get her now, at least she had been spared.

The nurse held a pill in one delicate hand and a glass of water with a straw in the other. He took it from her and swallowed his medicine. She had been a nice nurse, but he wished with all the wishing he had left that it was Martha instead. She must know everything by now. The doctor had promised a phone call home tomorrow, so he would explain why he couldn't talk to her before, now that his lingering confusion had to clear a bit.

The thought of hearing her voice made him smile. He was going home to her. Some of her fears had come true. Just not the worst of them.

For that they could both be grateful.

The long wait was about to end. Since that day in the café when James told her he would find out more about Clark's condition, Martha's world had been spun in a fog of hopefulness, restlessness, and impatience. But not fear. To her surprise, she had taken one day at a time, calming her anxiety and staying positive, especially once she heard his crackling voice on the phone. With James around to prod her moods, she found a new refreshing outlook.

Questions had remained, but standing here at Felts Field in Spokane, they seemed unimportant now. She would soon know if Clark's injuries had somehow changed him from the man she married. The letters they exchanged had become her lifeline, and even though full of words of hope, there were some things that could not be said in a letter. She suspected he felt the same. There would be time now to dig deep and unpack the emotions of the last few months.

"Are you nervous?" James stood a few yards away, the wind blowing his brown hair.

He still used a crutch to walk long distances. The tedious road back to balancing without half of one foot had been more difficult than either James or Martha had anticipated. She had helped him with exercises and massages, but left it up to him to adjust mentally. The fact that he might never fly a plane of his own was still a burden to be faced. She wondered if Clark had put down the same burden.

She shrugged at James's question. "Not really. Just wanting very much for that plane to hurry up. It's a little late."

"Planes are always late. Something I learned while in the army."

"I really can't wait to see his face when he sees you, *Jimmy*. I'm glad we kept it a surprise. And don't think that once he arrives, I'm going to call you anything but James."

"That's okay. I'm giving up that nick-name. The Lieutenant will just have to get used to the new me." He looked to the sky. "He'll see me out the window and wonder what in the world I'm doing here. I sure am glad he's okay. I talked to one of the mechanics on the recovery crew who went to the crash site. He was shocked to see the wreckage. Dead sheep everywhere and what a mess. He said he couldn't believe anyone could survive."

"Did you ever work on that plane... Satan something?"

James took a few steps toward her. "I did. Never liked her. Old Faithful was my favorite." He winked. "But I was partial to the pilot."

Martha smiled. "Funny. So am I."

A speck in the sky caught her attention, headed for the airport. She remembered the day at the Pasco airfield when Clark's flying lesson almost came to a dreadful end. Her fears in those days had been like daggers in her heart—a disease eating away at her life. She had witnessed too much since then to hold onto something so debilitating. Her childhood trauma had given way to seeing the world as a grown woman with enough faith to know who was in control.

The roar of the engine set her heart fluttering as the plane came close enough to see faces peering through tiny windows. The tires screeched once, twice, then hummed along the pavement to circle the plane in front of them. Martha moved forward to clutch the chain link fence separating her from Clark. James stayed back, but nodded from his perch on a bench, his crutch on the ground beside him. His grin brought back his boyish look—the face she knew from their first meeting.

The engine turned off but the blades continued to spin. A crew moved in what Martha felt was slow motion to push a staircase up to the now opened door. She tapped her foot to keep from running to the plane. An older lady, a mother with two children, a young man, a couple holding hands. They all emerged through the door. Then a gap in passengers.

She glanced at James. He didn't move his head, but she knew he saw her concern. Another gentleman and his wife appeared. Martha wanted to sneak around the fence. Where was Clark? Had he missed his plane? A stewardess stood in the doorway, looking out over the small crowd of passengers who walked off the tarmac.

James stood shielding his eyes, searching. She inched toward the gate, squinting to see inside the plane. The stewardess moved aside as Clark hobbled to the doorway. He stopped and pulled on his uniform cap. He too searched the tarmac, then beyond to where Martha stood. Her knees wobbled. She grabbed the fence post near the gate, tears bursting from their dam.

Clark gave a wide wave—a broad grin covering his face. She froze the image in her mind. A homecoming wasn't supposed to be so bittersweet, but it was the best one she had ever seen. She waved back and took uncertain steps in his direction. His limp was aided by a cane, his face bruised under one eye and his right arm in a sling. As he neared her, she could see how thin he was. How time had etched its pain on his face.

They collided in a hard embrace. He held her so tight with one arm she thought her heart might stop beating. He still had his strength—that was evident. She kissed him over and over as he mumbled how much he had missed her. She choked down tears, nuzzling her face in his neck like she used to. They stood still in each other's arms for a few moments.

264

"Hello, sir."

Martha pulled away so Clark could see James.

"Jimmy!"

A hand shake and bear hug ensued. Martha laughed. Would he guess?

"What are you doing here?" Clark patted his shoulder and looked James up and down.

"I found your wife and gave her your note. But you see, if you had just told me her first name, I might have known it was my friend."

Clark frowned and looked first at Martha, then back to James. Martha put her hand to her mouth.

"Sir, I've known Martha Watkins for a long time. We lived on the same vineyard together. I'm James Wilding."

"James Wilding? The Wildings' son? No. I don't believe it." He pulled Martha in close under his arm and squeezed her. "So you saw her first."

James blushed. "Well, to be honest, if I had just been several years older…"

Martha interrupted. "Oh stop, both of you. Let's get you gimpy guys home. We have a two and a half hour drive to talk."

"Home," Clark echoed. "Sounds like heaven." He turned to Martha. "We have so much to talk about."

She nodded. James looked back at his crutch and then grinned at Martha. His eyes opened wide. She noted the surprise.

"You don't need it, James. Leave it for someone who does."

"Yes, ma'am."

They worked their way to the parking lot. Betsy had been brightly polished for the occasion. James opened the back door for Clark. "I'm driving so you two can snuggle in the back seat all the way to Pasco."

Martha hesitated. "James, your foot might get tired."

"I'll let you know if I can't take it."

She shrugged and slid into the back seat with Clark. "Just for that, James, you're staying for dinner before you leave."

Clark raised his brows. "Leave?"

"He's been staying on our couch, but has somewhere to go tonight."

Clark looked disappointed. "Do you have to go so soon? I wanted to catch up."

James stared out the side window. "I'll be back to find work, but first, I need to go to Kansas to see my folks. Haven't seen them for a few years. They deserve to know what's happened to me. Martha told me I better do it now before I lost my nerve."

Clark reached his hand to pinch Martha's ear. "I suppose she has been bossing you around."

Martha tingled at the tease. It had been far too long since they had a good banter. She glanced at James. "He's a good kid."

Clark turned back to settle in his seat.

"That I do know for sure."

The ride back to the apartment sped by with stories of the 706th and Old Faithful. Martha let them ramble on. She would have Clark to herself tonight.

And for many nights to come.

He had fallen asleep on Martha's lap on the ride home. It would take time to adjust to the time change. He awakened in time for James to pull the car up to the curb in front of the apartment. Martha kissed him before they got out of the car.

"Welcome home."

The smell of home soothed the pain of regrets and grief. The daffodil blooms had just popped. The hint of spring permeated the air with the promise of new life. Clark knew that soon he would stop beating himself up with thoughts about the crash and losing Willy. Through dinner he listened to Martha and James joking, teasing like family. This is what all the guys back on base wanted more than anything—to be home with a stomach full of home cooking.

Outside, the evening closed its light, sharing a dim glow through the front window. He wondered if Albert had found a new crew to fly with. They would get a darn good ball gunner. The rest of the Old Faithful crew would scatter and she would have a new pilot in the big chair. He never thought it would all end this way. The memories of that day had returned, aching like his broken arm and healing head.

He would miss those guys. Their months together went so fast, yet at times seemed to drag into eternity. He had been blessed to know them, but finding complete peace about the crash would test his faith. How does God decide who lives or who dies?

"Clark?" Martha knelt next to the sofa where he had been resting. "Coffee?"

She had been so attentive since they arrived from the airport. His favorite foods had been served and pillows were arranged on the sofa to tuck under his arm.

"No thanks. It was a perfect meal. It's so good to be home."

She kissed his forehead and stood. "James—uh, Jimmy—is ready to go. His bus leaves in an hour and I thought you two could have a few minutes before I take him to the station. I know he wants to talk to you."

"You were right. He's a good kid. Your friend would be proud of what he did over there. Maybe I'll write to tell her someday. And it's *James* from now on."

Martha kicked off her shoes. "I'll go change and let you two have some time, okay?"

James came down the hallway and dropped his duffel bag by the front door. Martha stopped at the bedroom door. "I won't be long, so get caught up fast."

James's grin made Clark smile. He guessed he had an admirer for life. He swung his legs off the sofa and patted the chair across from him.

"Come sit."

James grabbed a small book from his duffel bag, handed it to Clark, and leaned in to show him the contents.

"It's a little photo album I made. Took pictures sometimes when none of you were looking. Had to be careful 'cause they don't like photos of certain areas. Got chewed out one day. They took my camera, but let me have the film. Ruined my fun."

Clark flipped through the book, his gut stinging at the memories. He realized that James had always been in the background, fixing and helping. How hard it must have been for him considering how much he wanted to be a pilot. He must have felt left out—without a crew of his own to pal around with or be sad with.

He handed the book back to James. "It's great." He glanced down at James's foot. "How are you doing anyway? What do the doctors say?"

"No flying for now. Maybe in the future there will be a prosthesis that will allow me to move around a plane better. I'll be fine. Just need to find a way to support myself."

Clark wondered if now was the time to mention his scheme. It could give James something to look forward to. He had to know the kid's state of mind first.

"You have a girlfriend?" Clark nudged him with his good elbow.

James leaned back in the chair, smile gone. "Who's gonna want someone with a deformed foot? I'd be embarrassed. I don't even take my socks off in the warm weather. I might always have a bad limp. I don't think girls will be lining up for a chance at me."

An honest answer, but not the truth, and Clark knew James

couldn't believe the words coming from his mouth. His pride would be what stood in the way of love, not his foot.

"You underestimate the female capacity, my friend. Give it a chance. You'll have them flocking to you once you show some confidence." He reached out and swiped his knuckle over James's face. "Shaving would help."

James laughed and Clark wondered if he had done much of that since his accident. James had his serious side, but he was too young to avoid fun altogether. Now would be a good time to spring the great plan on him. Clark shot a quick look at the bedroom door.

"I want to let you in on something and see if you'd be willing to help me."

James leaned forward. "Sure. What?"

"I have a plan in the works for a business investment. I'll need someone who can come in on it with me. It would be hard work and a learning process, but if you're willing, I'll fill you in. I won't know for sure for a while. I'm mustering out of the army after my leave. Martha doesn't know. What do you think?"

James looked down at his foot, then back at Clark. "If you think I can handle the job... well, then I'm in."

"James, I think you can handle just about anything. I want you to believe that for yourself—the sooner the better. I think God has a plan for us. You go see your folks while I finalize things on my end. I'll keep you posted. Deal?"

James reached out his hand and Clark squeezed it hard. If all went as he hoped, he and James would be in the perfect place to finish healing and find a new purpose in life. Flying was out for both of them indefinitely, but there were other kinds of flight. Clark was determined to experience them.

All he had to do now was surprise Martha with the plan and convince her it was the right thing. He would tell her in time, and time was all he had for now.

"Ready?" Martha had emerged from the bedroom wearing wide-legged pleated slacks and a short-sleeved plaid shirt. A sprig of hair rested on her forehead. He'd been waiting so long to be with her again, he had almost forgotten what a fine figure she had.

Clark hobbled beside James to the door where they shook hands again. Martha kissed Clark's cheek. "Be right back."

James turned and waved at Clark as he stood in the window, hoping he had done the right thing. The kid had a ways to go before he was free of doubt and a bit of anger. Clark knew how he felt. They both needed a place to feed their souls.

Chapter Eighteen

May 1944

"I don't see why we couldn't stay at Mama and Pop's a while longer. California weather is so nice, and you have another two weeks of leave before reporting to your new army job, whatever that is. Your mother would probably have liked us to stay with her longer too."

Clark stifled a grin. An army job wasn't on his permanent agenda.

"Martha, we're hundreds of miles from there. I wish you would stop bringing it up. We're going home. We'll be there in two hours." He just wouldn't tell her where home was. His plan had been set in motion and he wasn't about to let her ruin the surprise. "I have unfinished business that needs to be taken care of. Just go along with me on this please."

He had been successful in the last week to put her off about discussing their future. Martha had thrown out several suggestions about what he should do. He hadn't told he had been medically discharged. He glanced at her, staring out the window. His stomach fluttered to think they would soon be home, really home. That was *if* she liked his idea.

"You're awfully quiet, Mrs. Jensen. Are you mad at me?"

She bit her lower lip as she slid closer to him. "No."

"Then what gives?"

She sighed and pulled her knees up to her chest. He rolled up the window to cut the road noise. The warm afternoon sun would heat the inside of old Betsy, but he would rather not miss a word of what was bothering her.

"Well, you keep talking about me going along with whatever it is we're doing or wherever it is we're going, so I'll do that if you go along with something I want."

Here is was, a bargain to throw him off track. He had seen her mental wheels turning for days, but was afraid to ask. It seemed he would soon have his curiosity quenched.

"Okay, what is it you want? Not something expensive or elaborate, I hope."

She hugged her knees tighter, then abruptly faced him. The thought occurred to him he should pull over in case her obvious enthusiasm meant something he must say no to. She grinned and he couldn't imagine why she was being so coy.

"I want to try for another baby." She blurted it out and then settled back in the seat, her smile gone as if she expected a negative reaction.

Clark let off the gas pedal and turned off to the side of the road. The car came to a stop in some gravel next to a grove of walnut trees. Their shade looked inviting, but he had to address the announcement.

He rolled down the window again and leaned against the door to see her fully.

"I don't think that's something to joke about, Martha."

She sat up straight. "What makes you think I'm joking? I'm very serious. I know I said I didn't want any children, but that was a long time ago. Since the miscarriage, I've thought of nothing else."

Tears brimmed in her eyes. He reached for her hand, and wondered if she could feel it trembling. It was his turn to be fearful…of bringing up a child in this crazy world. He never dreamed she would want to try again this soon.

He swallowed hard to speak without wavering. "Would you be upset if I wanted to think about it for a while?"

Her expression went from wide-eyed anticipation to blank. She played with the radio—pushing buttons until he had to grab her hand. He squeezed it tight.

"I just want to be sure. Okay?"

Martha looked in his eyes. "It's okay. At least you're considering it. I understand how you must feel. A recent brush with death isn't the ideal timing for this kind of thing. We'll talk about it more when we're settled and you're done with the army. Better yet, when this stupid war is over."

Everything in him wanted to dismiss the idea. He could see in her demeanor how important this was to her. Both their worlds had been shaken over the last few years, and time would tell who could return to normal first.

The next two hours drifted by in silence, except for the whizzing traffic going in the opposite direction, and the soft music Martha found to play on the radio. He was delighted to see her flipping through a magazine rather than paying attention to which streets he took as they headed into the rolling hills of Kennewick, away from her apartment in Pasco. With any luck she wouldn't notice.

He hummed along to the Tommy Dorsey song she had tuned in. In just a few miles they would be there. The next time he looked at her, she had leaned her head back and closed her eyes. His poor wife would remain clueless, a perfect climax to his surprise.

Old Betsy turned onto the rutted driveway hitting a few potholes. Martha was tossed to one side. Her eyes opened and she pushed herself up to lean forward.

"What? Why are we here?"

He stopped the car and pulled the brake lever. The afternoon shadows turned the vineyard into a masterpiece painting—the perfect mood for his announcement.

"We're home."

She jerked her head in his direction. "What are you talking about? We need to get out of here before the owners find us here. This isn't funny, Clark."

He refrained from answering, but opened the car door and stepped out onto the yard next to the cottage. He had only seen the place once or twice, but it was everything he remembered and more. Any minute he expected Mr. and Mrs. Watkins to come out onto the cottage porch. The breeze coming off the river felt warm, and the air heavy with the sweetness of blossoms.

Martha slammed the car door and marched up to his side.

"Clark Jensen, what is going on?"

He watched her consternation dissolve as she too caught a glimpse of the flowering orchard and green vines. Her shoulders relaxed as she took a few steps toward the Hawthorne tree. She sniffed in the fragrance of the place and turned to him with the question still written on her face.

"I told you. We're home."

She returned to his side. "I don't understand. This can't be our home."

Clark chuckled and her face reddened.

"Clark." She pressed her hands to her hips.

"Okay, okay. I had the idea as I recovered after the crash and after I found out about Oma and Opa. They were farmers. My dad wanted to be a farmer. Your folks farm. Why not us? So I wrote to your dad to ask if anyone was working the place. He sent me George's information. It so happened that the fellow leasing the vineyard wanted to move on and George needed a new man to take over. So here we are."

"Just like that?"

"Yep. Just like that. Except I think God moved things along. You know."

She shook her head as she scanned the yard. "I can't believe it."

"I told George we'd be fine in the cottage for now until we get ahead." He might as well say it. It had been on the tip of his tongue the last two hours. "Or until our baby comes."

Martha threw her arms around his neck. Her whole body shook as he held her with is good arm. She pulled away, wiping her wet cheeks.

Clark pushed back her tousled hair. He saw the look he had been waiting for since he got home. The look of hope. "Like my surprise?"

Martha turned to face the nearly setting sun.

"I thought I had said goodbye to this place, but I'm tired of goodbyes. I only want hellos for a long time to come."

He knew what she meant. Now more than ever before.

September 25, 1945

Martha repressed the urge to rescue Clarissa from Mama's fussing. It wouldn't do any good to remind Mama she wasn't the mother of the groom. Besides, Clarissa had been quite willing to let her take charge. Everything was arranged except for setting out the food, which would wait until the reception. The mother of the bride had agreed to switch some of the traditional wedding responsibilities around to suit the vineyard venue. After all, James and Jenny would be living in the cottage after the honeymoon.

Each time she saw the young couple together, Martha thought back to the day in the café when James had pretended not to know the girl batting her eyes at him. It hadn't taken long after his return from Kansas to get in touch with her. It was clear that James had left *Jimmy* behind in another time and place.

Hope, now a long-legged, starry-eyed girl of eight, followed

Clark around, but he had his hands full with his own baby girl. He took seven-month old Bonnie in his arms and held her out to chase Hope across the lawn.

"How do I look?" James moved in front of Martha, fidgeting with his tie. His fingernails were crusted with dirt and he hadn't changed out of his boots yet.

"Are you kidding? Terrible. First, go put on your good shoes, then scrub your fingernails, then come back here and I'll straighten your tie. Jenny will be mortified to see you like this." She brushed off his suit coat shoulders as he side-stepped away. At least he wasn't in uniform like Clark had been on their wedding day here in this spot. Now that the war was over, neither Clark nor James would ever have to worry about uniforms again. Her dear Hana would soon be free from the camp, and able to come for a visit.

She found a chair in the last row. Pop had done his usual measuring to make sure all the chairs were lined up straight. The white picket arbor made a perfect portal to view the vineyard. The vines had been harvested and trembled in the cool breeze of the day, waiting for winter's pruning.

A shiny white car rolled past the cottage and up to the gravel by the big house. Jenny emerged from the back seat as her father held the door open for her. James had picked a beauty. No hot wedding suit for this young lady. Instead she wore a long white satin dress with a sweetheart neckline and long, lacy sleeves gathered at the shoulder. A single strand of pearls lay around her neck.

Her mother slid out of the driver's side door and handed Jenny a small bouquet of pink, baby roses. Martha sighed, thinking if she had it to do all over again, she would choose the same dress. Or would she?

"Isn't she lovely?" Clarissa looped her arm through Martha's and rested her head on her shoulder.

"Yes. She is. And James will look just as lovely as soon as he finishes cleaning up. He and Clark stayed too long in the orchard this morning."

Clarissa startled. "Oh, I'd better tell him not to come out yet. You go show Jenny to the big house so she can freshen up and wait for the music." She turned and took three steps toward the cottage. "Oh, and tell Frank to get his boutonnière on and help James with his."

Martha laughed. She loved seeing Clarissa marry off her oldest. Having them here from Kansas was not only a gift for James, but a special treat for the Watkins family. Everyone together again. All except one, but she dare not mention him to Clarissa. She had enough to cry about today.

Before Martha could whisk Jenny away, Clark, carrying little Bonnie, had already escorted her and her mother into the big house. The minister stepped up to the vine covered arbor and cleared his throat.

"If everyone will take their seats, we will begin in just a few moments."

Clark nudged Martha forward. "Everything is set. I'll tell the quartet to start playing if you'll take Bonnie."

Frank and James crossed the yard and took their place next to the minister as Martha took her seat, Bonnie on her lap. The music floated over those gathered. Martha was sure it could be heard all the way to the river. Her eyes tickled with tears to see Clarissa escorted to the front row. Mom and Pop stood in the back, guarding the cake.

Just as Jenny approached James, Martha saw a shadow next to the willow tree to her left. For a scant second, she thought she saw the dark face of a man in overalls. When she blinked, the image was gone.

Clark slid into the chair next to her. She leaned in to whisper what she saw, then decided against sounding foolish. She turned to enjoy the short ceremony and stood with the rest of the crowd to clap for the newlyweds. A new beginning for so many—not just for the world at peace, but for all those here she loved so much.

Clark left with Bonnie on his hip, and everyone rushed toward the new couple. She would make her congratulations when there was a break in the line of well-wishers.

Her eyes traveled again to the willow tree. She meandered toward the spot where the shadowed face had been, but stopped herself.

"Don't be silly. If it were Elijah, he would have shown himself."

She reached down to fix her sandal strap. There on the ground next to the tree lay a red bandana, like the ones Elijah used to wear. She picked it up and turned her head to see if anyone saw her. Mama waved the couple over to cut the cake and the crowd moved in rhythm behind them.

The sun hovered over the horizon as if hesitant to disappear. Martha thought about all the days to come, here with Clark and little Bonnie. Her world was so different now. Everyone's was. The war had changed people on many continents, but fear no longer shrouded the future for her small world.

She walked along the side of the house to the cottage porch. Rolling the red bandana in her hands, she tied it on the porch post, as James and Jenny's first blessing. They'd never know where it came from. It didn't matter.

Clark peeked around the corner. "Are you coming? They already cut the cake."

She took his hand. By the time they reached the food table, the sun had set and the strings of lights around the yard illuminated the festivities. Guests donned their sweaters and coats as the evening chill floated in. Clarissa and Frank came to stand next to Clark and her.

Frank turned a misty eye to Clark. "Thanks for taking care of our boy over there. He thinks the world of you."

Clark suddenly seemed a continent away. "He did his job well there. You can be proud."

Clarissa sniffled into a tissue. Martha put her arm around her, but kept her eye on Clark as he gazed at the stars. She tugged on his sleeve. "Wishing you were up there?"

He shook his head and grabbed her chin.

"Everything I need is here."

It was true for her, too.

The Real Story...

you won't want to miss.

$\mathcal{D}$ear Readers,

I hope you enjoyed reading *All My Goodbyes*. It is a story very personal to me, and I would like to now reveal to you why and how I came to write this book.

This book is inspired by the life of my mother and her bomber-pilot husband in WW2. Martha Watkins Jensen is the real name of my mom, and Ruth and Ed Watkins were my grandparents. Clark Jensen was my mother's husband, although not my father. My sister and I had known that Mom was married before Dad (who died when I was 12), but never knew much about her previous husband, actually only his name.

But let me start at the beginning—at least where I came into the story. Several years after my mother passed away in 1998, I wanted to write a story about her life as an army nurse in the Corps. I asked my sister, Leah, to look through my mother's foot locker to see if there was anything I could use as research for the story I intended to write. She called sometime later saying she hadn't found what I wanted, but did indeed find something interesting. In her words, "You won't believe what I found."

She brought me a box, and as I opened it and pulled out its contents, I was astonished to see Clark Jensen's personal and military effects. Also in the box were a photo album of their life together, letters, documents, and Clark's medals. My sister and I filed slowly through each item, treasuring them as my mother must have done many years ago. A new world opened up that day—a world I knew nothing about, and with people I didn't know existed, people who had sacrificed so much. It was as if the story begged to be told.

Among the items was a handwritten letter from one of Clark's B24 crewmembers. You see, my mother had written his wife wanting to know what happened the day Clark died. Yes, the real Clark Jensen did not survive the crash of Satan's Sister. Instead of going home to the vineyard in Washington State that day in 1944, he was actually taking his last breaths in a field in the English countryside. He and one other crew member, the character I named Willy Watson, were killed when the plane hit a dirt and rock berm in the field where Clark so masterfully landed. (I renamed the deceased crew member Willy Watson because by coincidence, his real last name was Watkins and I didn't want there to be any confusion) The rest of the crew survived, but my mother lost the love of her life. In an instant she was one of the thousands of war widows we always heard so much about.

The letter revealed how the crew had not been flying their usual ship, Old Faithful. It also described the crash in moment-by-moment detail, and after reading it and poring over all the other things in the box, I knew I had to write this story. Since Mom had never spoken to me or my sister about her life with Clark, I was missing the information I needed to put their story together, so I began a journey of research that spanned over a year. This became a life-changing experience for me, for my sister, and some other dear people.

In the process of searching the internet for more information about the crash and Clark's military experience, I left my email address on any crash related photo or other document that would allow comments. Because of this, I was contacted by some folks who were directly involved in the incident that took Clark's life. The first was a woman from England, whose grandfather owned the field where Clark crash-landed Satan's Sister. She explained to me that he was one of the first on the crash site, pulling crewmembers from the plane while ammunition exploded through the air. Here was a hero whose granddaughter was curious enough about my comment on a picture of Satan's Sister to email me. Amazing.

Another person who contacted me was a young lady from the mid-west named Jamie Wagner. Her father had been researching his deceased father's military experience, and had come across the picture of Satan's Sister I had posted on my Pinterest page. She asked me if I knew anything about the plane—that her grandfather had been a crew member. My insides melted to hear her words. This lovely young lady and I started a conversation and I discovered that her grandfather was in fact Albert Wagner, the ball gunner you read about in this story. The best part was that Albert's wife, Evelyn, was still living—the only living spouse of the crew, who had all since passed. Can I say I was thrilled? I stayed in touch with Jamie, and she and her family have been a great source of encouragement to me while writing this book. I actually had the deep pleasure of meeting Evelyn Wagner. When my husband and I made a cross country trip in the fall of 2019, we made a special detour to see her. We had a great time talking about Albert and spending time with her and her granddaughters Jamie and Hope. It was a visit I shall never forget, a connection most people never get to make. I am proud to have had the privilege of putting Albert Wagner's intersection with Clark Jensen's life in this book.

During one of my research gathering sessions I ran across an article about the crew and crash in a magazine. At the bottom was the email address of a man whose last name I recognized. The article said he was the son of the co-pilot Henry (Hank) Kingsbery. Did I write him? Of course I did! I asked him if he happened to remember his dad talking about Clark at all. I needed some insight to Clark's personality. Joe Kingsbery answered my emails. He and his brothers got together and recalled several of their father's comments about Clark, which I used to fashion his temperament and style in the book.

Many other amazing things happened to me while I researched. In the box was the little wedding guest book signed by the folks who attended the wedding of Martha and Clark. As in *All My Goodbyes*, it was a small wedding at the vineyard, attended by only some friends and family. Clark's sister and her baby daughter were there from Portland, Oregon, and the sister's signature and address were in the guest book. I decided to try and find any family of Clark's, and I knew the only person from the guest list who might still be living would be Clark's baby niece, Carol. I set out to find her, but after months of searching I ran into too many dead ends to keep going.

I finished writing the book, but had grown too close to the story to polish it for publication. I worried I had not portrayed those real-life characters properly, and found myself torn over whether to tell the truth about Clark's death or give my mom a happy ending with him. I set the book aside for almost 2 years. When I decided to include the story in my *American Dreams* series, I started the re-write process and tried again to find Clark's niece. I joined Ancestry.com, and lo and behold—I found her. I was so nervous to contact her, but got up the nerve to call her.

We met and had a wonderful chat about the future of the story, and I shared with her what I had learned about Clark— the uncle she never really knew. Although I hated to part with them, I also gave her Clark's medals Mom had kept, knowing they should go to his family. It was a delight to meet her and share this special common ground from the past.

Another point of fascination came to the forefront as my sister and I re-examined the photos in the album from the box. Clark sent home to Martha many pictures of his time in training and also after he was deployed to England to fly his B24, Old Faithful. Those photos were always signed "Martha, love, Clark." We took special notice of two photos in which the signature changed. Those two pictures of Clark, one signed "To Mom, with love, "Pop", and the other "I love you, "Pop". My sister and I looked at each other with the same incredulous question in our mind. Was our mother pregnant when Clark deployed? The timing would have been perfect, and there was no other obvious explanation to the signature. Later, the signatures went back to normal. We had to surmise that Mom may have had a miscarriage. So I added that to the story as fact.

The chapter depicting the crash of Satan's Sister is adapted from the letter my mom received from Ed Hanna while he was in the hospital recovering from the crash. What a thrilling but difficult scene to write, knowing it was leaving the tragedy of Clark's death untold.

I had no one else to get information from about my mother's life at that time, except for my aunt. She and my mother went to nursing school together at Our Lady of Lourdes with the real Sister Clatilda and became good friends. So good in fact, that after Clark was killed, my mother was introduced to her friend's brother-in-law, Paul Cherry. After a while Martha and Paul were married and had my sister and me, and now the friends were sisters-in-law. I called my aunt when I started the book to ask her what Mom was doing while Clark was in flight school and then deployed. She told me she had lost track of Mom during those years and had thought that Mom followed Clark from base to base during training. The next time she saw Mom was after Clark's death. I had so hoped I would have a living testament to help me string the pearls of this story together, but again, I had to rely on research and fiction.

I want you all to know how difficult it was for me as an author to write the true story of my mother and Clark, and still fictionalize in between to make a novel people would want to read. The other consideration to deal with was the historical timeline of the war I had to follow. The dates of Clark's actual involvement in the war and bombing raids over Europe was adjusted a little in order to fit the other timelines going on in the story. The big picture you just finished reading was once a large disassembled puzzle I had to put together with my researcher's mind, and a daughter's heart.

Of course, what I have just told you is only part of the story that involves me. As I said, many interesting things happened. So if you would like to know more and see actual photos of the characters and others, I have dedicated a page of my website—jancline.net/amgstory—with pictures and more of the whole, true story just for my readers. While you are there, please sign up for my newsletter. You'll receive a free short story, and you'll get interesting emails from me once a month or so, and information about any future book releases.

Also, if you would like to know what happened to Martha's friend Hana Kato, you may want to pick up my first novel, *Emancipated Heart*. It's Hana's story. I brought her back for this novel to tie in the Japanese American internment story that is dear to me.

I hope you will forgive me if I spoiled anything for you, but I felt in my heart it was important for my readers to know the real life story and to know how much I wanted to give my mom something she deserved... a happy ending.

Finally (and this is a big request), if you liked this story, would you consider leaving a review wherever you bought this book, or on your favorite social media platform? I love this story and want as many readers as possible to discover it, and your voice can help do that. Leave a review and tell a friend! Word-of-mouth is the best way to introduce this story to other readers.

Thank you, dear reader, for giving your time to read this book. Stories need an audience. It means a lot that you trusted me to entertain, and hopefully excite, you with this story.

May you all have many happy endings,

Jan

Special Thanks

To all the men and women who served in WW2, and the families who shared their stories with me.

To Gail Kittleson for her generous help.

To all my writer/author friends, and my sister who encouraged me to fight for this story. To the Albert Wagner family for their kind support.

To the Albert Wagner family for their kind support.

About the Author

$\mathcal{J}$an Cline is a firm believer in late bloomers. She began her writing journey at a young age, but didn't venture into fiction writing until 2009 when a friend dared her to write a novel. Her love for relics and history pointed her to America's untold stories of the 1930s and 40s, and her first published novel, *Emancipated Heart*, tells the story of a Japanese American family living in an internment camp during WW2.

To Jan, researching is just as fun as putting pen to paper, especially when it requires travel to places she's never been. Her current women's fiction series, *American Dreams*, takes readers from the dust bowl years of America's heartlands through WW2.

Her writing credits include magazine articles, devotionals, anthologies, and a women's self-help book. She is a former writers conference director and enjoys teaching at conferences and writers groups.

Jan lives in northern Idaho with her husband and spoiled dog, and enjoys golf, crafting, painting, and spending time with her nine grandchildren at the family lake cabin.

Visit her online at:

JanCline.net

Facebook: https://www.facebook.com/JanClineAuthor/

Twitter: https://twitter.com/Jan_Cline

Pinterest: https://www.pinterest.com/JanClineAuthor/

Also available from

WordCrafts Press

Grace Extended - Sisters of Lazarus, Book 3
  by Paula K. Parker

Angela's Treasures
  by Marian Rizzo

Until Then
  by Gail Kittleson

The Mirror Lies
  by Sandy Brownlee

You've Got It, Baby!
  By Mike Carmichael

www.WordCrafts.net

Made in the USA
Lexington, KY
20 December 2019